93-50

PUZZLE FOR PLAYERS

PUZZLE FOR PLAYERS

by

PATRICK QUENTIN

LONDON
VICTOR GOLLANCZ LTD
1973

First published February 1939
Reissued 1973

ISBN 0 575 01638 8

MADE AND PRINTED IN GREAT BRITAIN BY
THE GARDEN CITY PRESS LIMITED
LETCHWORTH, HERTFORDSHIRE
SG6 1JS

Chapter One

W E WALKED TO the Dagonet Theater up Broadway, heading west at Forty-fourth where the Wrigley goldfish loomed, lurid and popeyed, above the International Casino. I was feeling dangerously pleased with myself. I'd been that way for exactly three months and two days, ever since the morning when Henry Prince's *Troubled Waters* had drifted into my office, and I knew I'd stumbled on the surest fire script the theater had struck since *Rain*.

We passed the Shubert, the Broadhurst, the St. James, all putting on a brave show of lights. There had been a time when the sight of a lighted theater had sent me off into an envious decline. That was over now. For all I cared every house in Manhattan could be plastered with Standing-Room-Only signs. Peter Duluth, Inc. was in production again with a swell play and a knock-out cast. I was headed for a big come-back in the show business which had tabbed me as the youngest has-been producer on record. I was going to town.

I was certain of it. I wasn't even crossing my fingers.

Iris's gloved hand rested on my sleeve. She was looking indecently beautiful with Asiatic furs and a trick hair cut. As usual, passers-by stared with a sort of inquisitive awe, trying to make up their minds whether or not she was Someone with an Autograph.

She said for the thirteenth time: "Peter, do I really have to make my sensational debut in the worst theater in Manhattan?"

I said for the fourteenth time: "You're very lucky to be making your allegedly sensational debut in any theater at all. No other producer in the world would have given a fat part to..."

"...to an unbridled ex-debutante with no experience and nothing to recommend her except a certain amount of low

5

cunning," completed Iris serenely. "You've said that before, darling. I don't think it's at all a nice thing to say to the girl you hope one day to make your lawful wedded wife."

She paused to brood over a domestic picture of the Lunts outside the St. James and then started forward again. "It isn't only me, darling. Gerald Gwynne says the Dagonet Theater's jinxed. And Mirabelle doesn't like it either. When she heard we'd been switched from the Vandolan, she hit the ceiling."

"What did she say?" I asked uneasily. It really mattered what Mirabelle Rue said.

Iris looked dreamy-eyed. "She said 'Hell.' "

"Very characteristic."

"And Theo Ffoulkes was the same."

"Did she say 'Hell,' too?"

"She said: 'Typical of that damnable syndicate to switch us at the last minute into a blood mausoleum like the Dagonet.' "

I said: "What charming ladies I seem to have in my cast." Iris ignored that and began a cautious navigation of Eighth Avenue. The reassuring atmosphere of Shubert Alley didn't reach this far. We were moving into a region of dark stores and grudgingly lit restaurants where the Theater had no real foothold.

Although I wouldn't have admitted it to Iris, a little bug of uneasiness stirred in my mind. I didn't give one solitary damn for any old wives' tale about the Dagonet's jinx. I didn't give a damn that it had a bad location and an even worse reputation. But my whole personal history was staked on the success of *Troubled Waters*. If we went to town with it, I'd be solvent, I'd get back my lost self-respect, I'd be a person again with enough of myself to offer to make a fairly adequate husband for Iris. But, if anything, any little thing materialized to jimmy up the show, I'd probably be back at my recently and tentatively cured habit of putting away two quarts of rye a day; I'd be back again on the straight and very narrow path down hill. And I wouldn't have Iris. I'd made her swear she'd walk out on me if I ever started drinking again.

Now, as we threaded through the other pedestrians toward the Dagonet, that two-way future was frighteningly clear in my mind.

Iris was still looking like Cassandra about to prophesy the destruction of Troy. She said: "Darling, I don't want to be difficult, but isn't there anything we can do about the Dagonet?"

"Nothing," I said patiently. "The syndicate has the right to switch me into any of their houses. It's in the contract. So for pity's sake stop whining. Besides," I added with an attempt at brightness, "the Dagonet isn't so bad. It's large and it has a pedigree a yard long. Bernhardt played there."

"It's probably where she lost her leg," said Iris.

And, as she spoke, the Dagonet reared ahead of us, throwing an ornate portico over the sidewalk. Plump caryatids supported plump stone pillars. Torn posters on the billboards advertised some long-forgotten flop. The electric sign, shorn of bulbs, stared from a hundred empty eye-sockets.

It wasn't exactly a stimulating setting for the most vital and hazardous venture of my life.

I stared through the iron grille down the dreary alley which led to the stage door, feeling oddly nervous and wishing to hell I'd fought a bit more desperately to keep my lien on the stream-lined Vandolan, where we'd been rehearsing for three weeks.

We had just moved into the alley when an anxious voice behind me called: "Mr. Duluth."

I turned to see Lionel Comstock, an old-timer down on his luck, whom I'd hired for the one small part in the play. He was hovering outside the grille, his actor's face, beneath a black fedora, showing white and uneasy in the November darkness.

He asked hesitantly: "Are we really rehearsing here tonight—at the Dagonet?"

I looked at Iris, Iris looked at me. "Yes," I said.

Comstock was still peering through the grille as if he was reluctant to come inside. "I'm sorry, Mr. Duluth. When I was hired, I understood we were opening at the Vandolan. I don't think I could play here—not at the Dagonet."

"What have you got against it?" broke in Iris. "Is it the jinx?"

"No, its not the jinx." The old actor moistened pale lips with a paler tongue. "It's just that I played here once many years ago. Something happened. I swore then I'd never enter this theater again. I—I don't think I care to."

This cryptic statement made me unreasonably angry. Comstock meant nothing to the show and I could easily have replaced him. I almost told him to get the hell out and take his bogies with him. But I remembered he'd been sick and broke when I took him on. I didn't want him to throw away his bread and butter.

I said: "Stop crepe-hanging, Lionel, and come into rehearsal like a sensible human being. And, if you have got any dirt on the Dagonet, for God's sake keep it to yourself. I don't want the rest of the company rattled."

He didn't seem to pay any attention. He just stood there, his eyes remembering something nasty. Then abruptly he squared his sparse shoulders, tilted his chin in an Irving gesture and muttered:

"Perhaps it is best this way, after all. Perhaps if I go back to the Dagonet and am not afraid—I shall be able to lay her ghost."

He didn't say that to us. He was speaking to something inside himself. Pushing past me, he headed down the little alley and swung through the stage door.

Iris made a grimace and squeezed my arm. "Looks as if we're in for a cosy evening," she said.

Neither of us said anything else. There wasn't anything to say.

Most theaters are pretty depressing when they've been dark for some time. But the Dagonet was in even poorer shape than Eddie Troth, my optimistic stage manager, had led me to believe. As soon as we entered the stage door, the smell of dust and last year's make-up slapped us in the face. A few yellowing notices clung forlornly to the call board; there was a jagged coating of rust on the iron banisters which stretched up to stage level; even the doorman, standing on the threshold of his meager alcove, had a graveyard gauntness as if he had been snatched unwillingly from the nearest cemetery. He was clutching an old scrap-book against the front of his faded cardigan and staring curiously up the stairs after the disappearing figure of Lionel Comstock.

He blinked at us and extended a spectral hand. "The name's Mac," he offered. "Watched 'em come and go at the Dagonet forty years, I have." He patted the bulging scrap-book and displayed one or two teeth in what was probably intended for a smile. "Not a play's opened since '99 but I kept the notices."

I had visions of him gloating through the years as each successive flop added another raft of clippings to his grisly hoard. He seemed particularly suited to the Dagonet.

Having made sure that Eddie Troth had gotten him straight on the names of the company and all rehearsal details, I hurried after Iris up the stone steps to stage level where we ran into my stage manager propping a pane of glass against the wall of the star dressing-room and whistling "Home on the Range" cheerfully through his teeth.

Eddie Troth, a one-time Western cowboy, had come East to be a masseur. His first job had landed him in the Thespian Hospital, a specially endowed institution catering only to actors, and, after a few months massaging theatrical muscles, he'd got the Broadway bug. Now, instead of carpentering ligaments, he carpentered productions. And he did a damn good job of it.

That night he seemed the one person who could face the Dagonet with equanimity. He grinned his wide-open-spaces, Montana smile and announced that the set-up wasn't as bad as it looked. There were a lot of rats around and the glass panel in the swing-door leading to the stage was broken. But it wouldn't take him long to fix it up. Eddie loved fixing.

"How's the company taking it?" I asked apprehensively.

He scratched his lean jaw. "Well, you may get a bit of trouble at first. Know how funny actors are. But they've all of 'em been on the road now. They've struck plenty worse than the Dagonet in their time." He grinned. "Don't let them start anything, Mr. Duluth."

Which was presumably intended to reassure me. It didn't. I

felt a growing conviction, fostered by Comstock's cuckoo behavior, that it wasn't going to be easy to stop the company starting anything.

It was in this defeatist mood that I gave my hat an arrogant tilt appropriate to a successful young producer-director and preceded Iris through the swing door with the broken panel onto the stage.

With the exception of my two leads, Mirabelle Rue and Conrad Wessler, the whole company was waiting for me. Old Comstock stood by himself, staring disconsolately out into the house. Theodora Ffoulkes, Gerald Gwynne, my very young juvenile, and Henry Prince, the author of *Troubled Waters,* were grouped in wintry silence under the proscenium arch. The stage was illuminated by a single working light whose beams played across the worn floor boards and the random assortment of property chairs and tables. Behind the dead footlights, the vast body of the house stretched, in tier upon tier of dust-covered seats, back into thick, musty darkness.

It was all very bleak.

I went over to the others and said aggressively: "Good evening, everyone. I know this is a lousy theater, but there's nothing I can do about it. So, for God's sake, don't anyone moan."

Theodora Ffoulkes, looking like a fashionable greyhound in slick English tweeds, turned on me a pair of alert brown eyes. "We aren't moaning darling. We're being bright and brave. I might almost be cheerful if it wasn't for the damnable draft." The English actress glanced at the broken panel in the door and shivered. "Unless you have any strenuous objections, Peter, I think I'll go backstage and find a dressing-room to huddle in until you're ready to start. I'm developing a narsty 'acking corf and I don't want to die on you before the opening night."

"Okay," I said. "I'll send Eddie up when Mirabelle and Wessler get here."

As Theo pushed briskly through the swing-door, Gerald Gwynne said: "Wessler's here already. It's only Mirabelle who hasn't shown up. Wessler's rooting around backstage."

And, as he spoke, the door opened again and my Austrian star loomed on the threshold, his huge shoulders stooped slightly to keep his head from hitting the lintel. One of his great hands was closed around a small clay figurine of a woman, holding it tenderly as if it were alive.

Conrad Wessler had taken to modeling in clay at a time when he was recovering from an airplane accident, when it looked as if his injuries would prevent him from ever acting again. It had been, I suppose, a sort of anodyne to help him forget his facial disfigurement and the fact that his beloved half-brother, Wolfgang von Brandt, had lost his reason as a result of this same accident. The two of them had made a spectacular escape from the tragedy of a Nazi Vienna, only to run into this personal tragedy on their arrival in the States. Now Wessler was well again and the scars on his face had been hidden by plastic surgery and a very Aryan beard. But he still kept up his modeling and was seldom to be seen without one of his little figures in his hands.

Somehow this made him appear even more impressive. With his enormous frame, his beard, his shock of blond hair and the statuette between his fingers, he looked like a pagan god in the act of creating a protoplasmic Eve.

He came across the naked boards of the stage toward me. "Mr. Duluth," he said in his slow, uncertain English, "it ees true that we all the time in this Dagonet stay?"

I was getting rather tired of that question.

Wessler stared down at his little statue, which, intentionally or not, bore a curious resemblance to Mirabelle Rue. "Mr. Troth tells me the second dressing-room from the stage is for me."

"That's the usual custom in America theaters," I explained. "The female lead gets the first star dressing-room. Mirabelle will have it."

"So!" Wessler's lips were oddly stubborn. "Then I must against custom go. If we play in this theater, I take the dressing-room of Miss Rue, please." He paused, his blue eyes flickering. "I cannot be in the second dressing-room from the stage."

Ever since we started rehearsing, there had been an increasing and pointless antagonism between Wessler and Mirabelle Rue. I thought this was just another manifestation of the feud. Then suddenly it dawned on me that Wessler wasn't just being temperamental. I could tell that from his eyes. I had the crazy impression he was scared—scared of something he had seen in the second dressing-room from the stage.

I asked uneasily: "Is anything wrong with your dressing-room?"

"Wrong? No, it is enough convenient. Miss Rue will be there comfortable. But I—I cannot go in that room again."

He added in a queer, subdued kind of voice: "It ees the mirror."

"The mirror!" someone echoed sharply.

I turned to see it was old Comstock who had spoken. He was gazing at Wessler, his mouth half-open. Then the door opened again on Theo Ffoulkes, returned from her excursion backstage.

I don't know why we all swung round to stare at her. There was nothing really out of the ordinary in her entrance. At a first glance she was the normal, matter-of-fact Theo Ffoulkes. And yet there was something about her, something subtly different which we all picked up and reacted to.

We stood there, in awkward silence, as she moved down the path of the working light toward us. She held out her hand to me for a cigarette. As I gave it to her, I saw that her slim, hard fingers were shaking.

"Children," she said very quietly, "be warned by Mother. Never, never go upstairs in the Dagonet Theater at night."

She laughed an unstable laugh that tilted off key. Apart from a mania for brewing tea at odd moments and a confirmed habit of falling in love with the wrong person, Theo was the sanest woman in the theater. I'd never seen her this way before.

"Peter," she said in that same alarmingly flat voice, "the Dagonet doesn't happen to be haunted, by any chance?"

I exchanged glances with Iris. "No ghost was specified on the lease," I said.

For a moment Theo just stood there, twisting the cigarette.

Then she flicked ash onto the floor and stabbed at it with her toe. "Listen to a little story," she said. "I went upstairs to take a look at the dressing-rooms. I got to the first one on the top of the steps. The door was open but the light wasn't on. I went to the door and found a switch."

She looked straight at me, speaking very slowly.

"I snapped on the switch, Peter. It was the switch for the mirror—just the little lights around the dressing-table mirror. The rest of the room was dark. From where I stood by the door, I could tell no one was there. And yet, reflected in the mirror—" she paused—"reflected in the mirror, quite plainly, I saw a face."

Coming on top of what Wessler had hinted about the mirror in his dressing-room, that was pretty nasty. "But, Theo, darling . . ." began Iris.

"I know what you're going to say and it's not true." The English actress's lips made a wry smile. "It wasn't my own face. The mirror's on a side wall. I was standing by the door. It couldn't possibly have been my own reflection. It was somebody else's face looking out at me from the mirror. And there was no one in the room."

Wessler took a quick step forward. I said weakly: "But, Theo, you must be crazy. What kind of a face was it?"

"It wasn't at all a nice face." Theo was still staring me straight in the eyes. "It seemed to be a woman's. I had the impression of a light tan fur around her throat. Her cheeks were white as death, her mouth . . ."

"Miss Ffoulkes!" Lionel Comstock pushed roughly past Wessler. His breath was coming in quick, erratic jerks, his skin a sort of bluish gray. He'd looked that way once before at rehearsal when he'd had some kind of heart attack. "Miss Ffoulkes, you saw a woman's face reflected in a mirror?" The old actor repeated Theo's words haltingly like a little boy learning his lines.

"Exactly." Theo's cigarette hung poised in mid-air. "Do you know anything about it?"

"A woman's face!" The veins in Comstock's temples stood out

13

thick and pulsing. "A girl's face, white, with staring eyes, with her lips twisted in a last struggle for breath. A girl with a rope tight around her neck—hanged."

The cigarette dropped from Theo's fingers. "My God, she *did* look as if she were being hanged. But how do you know? You weren't there. Have—have you seen it too?"

Lionel Comstock gave a little gasp. One hand groped futilely forward for support. As his knees sagged, Gerald Gwynne and Henry Prince jumped toward him, gripping his arms, holding him up.

"I knew it." The old actor's voice broke into a tiny whisper. "She never went away. She's still here. Lillian *is* still here at the Dagonet. . . ."

Chapter Two

T HAT WAS A dandy way to start rehearsal. For the first
few moments I couldn't think much about anything except
Comstock himself. He was crumpled in Gerald Gwynne's arms
like a limp black sack and his breathing sounded harsh and
jarring as if someone was sawing through wood. With Gerald and
Henry Prince I managed to get the old man to a chair, and sent
Eddie Troth for some water.

We must have made a pretty crazy tableau as we stood around
that grimy stage, waiting for Eddie to bring the water. Theo
Ffoulkes held her head high and kept her lips in a set pale line,
silently defying any of us to disbelieve the incredible thing she'd
told us. Wessler, his huge fists limp at his sides, was looking at
her with a sort of blank fascination. It was almost as if he, like
Comstock, had had some previous inkling of what Theo was going
to see in that upstairs dressing-room. The rest of us, Iris, myself,
Gerald and Henry Prince were grouped around like a lot of
badly rehearsed extras.

At last Eddie came with a paper cup of water. Comstock got
it to his lips somehow and slowly, as he sipped it, his breathing
came back to normal. There were hard, shiny drops of sweat on
his forehead.

Theo Ffoulkes was the first to break that queasy silence. She
said bluntly: "This is absolutely balmy, Lionel. You've got to
tell us what you mean. You described that face I saw upstairs and
you've never left the stage since you've been here. How did you
know? And who is Lillian?"

The old actor let the paper cup slip from his fingers. He
forced a sickly smile. "I must apologize. It is just that what
you told us—it reminded me of something which happened very

15

long ago—My—my feelings carried me away. You must please none of you pay any attention to what I said."

I was thinking, of course, of the odd way he'd behaved outside the theater. It was pretty obvious he knew quite a lot more than he intended to tell.

I said uneasily: "If you know anything that can help explain what Theo thinks she saw, Lionel, you better tell us."

"But I don't. Indeed I don't." Comstock's voice had a desperate quality, as if it were less important to convince me than it was to convince himself. "I—I am as astounded as the rest of you. If Miss Ffoulkes really saw a face in the mirror upstairs, it must have been her own reflection or—or some trick of light."

That was the only reasonable explanation. But, in spite of reason, I still felt a darn twittering in the pit of my stomach. I was sure Theo hadn't scared herself with a trick of light. She just wasn't that sort of person.

It was Iris who crashed through with the next unsettling remark. She was staring curiously at Wessler. "You complain of the mirror in your dressing-room, Herr Wessler. You didn't see anything—funny in it too, did you?"

Conrad Wessler's hand moved slowly over his blond beard, and the light blue eyes, turning to Iris, seemed to be gazing straight through her at something beyond. "It is never good too long to look in mirrors," he said haltingly. "In mirrors I have seen things far more horrible than what Miss Ffoulkes describes because the things I have seen were real and I knew they could not by turning away from the glass be banished—or by trying to forget."

I guessed what was behind that queer little speech. I could tell the Austrian was thinking back to the days of horror and disfigurement after his airplane accident. Conrad Wessler must have had every reason to shun mirrors.

But Theo didn't seem to catch the allusion. She said crisply: "If Herr Wessler's suggesting I had a hallucination or something, it's not true." Her eyes, worried but stubborn, met mine. "You know I'm not one of those females who go psychic all over the place, Peter. And you can take my word that I'm not tight. But I

16

did see something damn queer in that dressing-room and I'm not going to be particularly fond of the Dagonet until I've found out what it was."

"That shouldn't be difficult." Gerald Gwynne, looking very young and very handsome and very tough in a high-necked polo sweater, was watching us with a sardonic smile. "Since we seem to have a spook on our hands," he drawled, "the thing to do is to lay it. I'll run upstairs and cope with Lillian."

That was the first sensible thing anyone had said. I offered to go too. But Gerald said quickly: "Don't bother. I can scream for help if I feel ghostly fingers around my throat."

I got the idea that he didn't want me to go with him. But I insisted. After all, I was the boss. I was the sucker who'd leased the Dagonet and its crazy mirrors.

I asked Theo which dressing-room it was.

"The first when you come to the top of the stairs." The English actress added wryly: "You can't miss it. I was so petrified I left the light burning."

Gerald and I went to the door. The others trailed after us, grouping themselves around the threshold of the stage watching with wan anxiety as if they were saying good-bye to us at the foot of the scaffold. We started along the bleak passage toward the even bleaker stone staircase which led up to the dressing-rooms on the higher floor.

I admit I felt a bit jittery. My juvenile, however, seemed to be taking the whole impossible situation very calmly. But then, nothing ever fazed Gerald unless it affected Mirabelle Rue for whom he acted as a kind of passionate body-guard. Whenever Mirabelle was in trouble, which was often enough, Gerald sloughed his six-months-old Broadway veneer and reverted to the tough little Mid-Western he-man he was. But this was only a ghostly face in a mirror. Things like that didn't bother Gerald.

That typically Dagonet odor of damp and disuse invaded our nostrils as we climbed the sheer stone stairs. The corridor light on the upper level was burning ahead of us, dim and wispy with cobwebs.

17

"The first room," said Gerald.

We saw it at once, straight in front of us at the head of the steps. The door was half open, but the room was in darkness.

"Theo said she'd left the lights on," I said.

"Well, they're not on now," remarked Gerald laconically and moved to the door.

The darkness inside was thick and musty. I don't know what I expected we'd find in that room. Rather unsteadily I fumbled for a switch and snapped it down. Instantly the little bulbs around the mirror on the side wall sprang into light. Some of them were dead, leaving blank spots in the gleaming chain, making the mirror look like a gaping mouth with several teeth lost. The glass itself was brightly lit. Nothing unusual was reflected there, of course.

Nor was there anyone in the room.

Gerald found another switch which illuminated the ceiling light and revealed the regular dressing-room props. A table in front of the wall mirror, a few wooden chairs, a long curtained clothes closet. Gerald crossed to the closet, pushed his head between the faded green curtains and brought it out again, brushing dust nonchalantly from his shoulders.

"No Lillian," he said.

"Then what the hell scared Theo?"

Gerald glanced at the mirror. It was only too obvious that Theo couldn't have seen her own reflection from the door. "Probably a rat—or a desire to make herself romantic for Wessler's benefit. I have a hunch she's hatching one of her thwarted passions for him." Gerald seemed suddenly bored by the whole expedition. "Still we might as well make a thorough search while we're about it. I'll take on this floor. You can embark upon the unknown upstairs."

Before I had time to do any more looking around the room, he had hustled me out into the passage toward the stairs which led upward again to the third and last tier of dressing-rooms.

It struck me as odd, Gerald suddenly assuming authority that way. I was also worried about the light being out when Theo had said so definitely that she'd left it on.

But I didn't give either of those points a great deal of thought at the time. There were other things to get intense about as I started alone up the dark stairs to the third set of dressing-rooms.

The corridor light ahead of me was not burning. After I'd taken the bend in the stone steps, I couldn't see a foot in front of me. It was like walking up into nothingness.

The higher one went in the Dagonet, the more unpleasant it became.

I raised a leg and brought it down firmly on a step that wasn't there. I stumbled, throwing a hand against the cold wall for support. Presumably, I had reached the landing.

I stood still an instant, trying to get my bearing, figuring where the electric light switch was most likely to be.

It was at that particularly inconvenient moment that I heard the noise—a soft, rhythmic padding moving toward me out of the pitch darkness ahead.

Probably, if I had been anywhere else in the world except the top floor of the Dagonet Theater, that furtive sound would have done no more than arouse my curiosity. But here, coming on top of what Theo had sprung, it was rather hellish. It connected up with nothing tangible. It was just a sound and a presence in the darkness—a sound which was getting closer, a presence which seemed uncannily to have sensed the fact that I was there. I didn't like it.

I threw out a hand, more or less at random, searching the invisible wall at my side for a light switch. My fingers met up with something small and alive that scurried away, a cockroach probably. I dragged my hand back. Then, as I made another stab for the light switch, the thing that had been making the noise reached me. I felt an unidentifiable body, soft and pliant, pressing against my trouser leg.

I shook my leg wildly, trying to brush away that warm, almost caressing pressure. It went. But, in an instant, it was back again, clinging, persistent.

I found the switch then. As the thin corridor jumped into light, I looked at the thing at my feet. It looked back at me with a bored, aristocratic stare. I felt distinctly foolish. The sinister presence in the darkness had been nothing more supernatural than a cat.

But it wasn't an ordinary cat. The coffee fur was set off by the dapper chocolate of its ears and paws. Its eyes were calm, swooning blue. Tied around its neck was a pink ribbon.

A Siamese cat of obvious pedigree with a pink bow around its neck was hardly the thing one expects to run up against in the dreary heights of a long-uninhabited theatre.

I had picked it up and it was brushing haughty whiskers against my chin before I realized just how unusual a cat it was. Hanging from the pink ribbon, flat against the fur of its throat, was a label. There were little silver trumpets designed around the edges—a sort of Christmas gift label. On it, in large, round handwriting, was the unpromising legend:

HERE'S A MASCOT FOR YOU. MAY IT BRING YOU BAD LUCK.

At first I thought that someone who'd heard we were opening at the jinxed Dagonet had played a fool practical joke. Then, as I stared once again at that unfamiliar handwriting, I wasn't so sure. In the show business, people take good luck and bad luck seriously. If that cat, with that label around its neck, had wandered on stage during rehearsal, it could have started a mild panic. I knew that. Anyone else in the Theater would have known it too.

I guessed then that I was up against genuine malice. Maybe what Theo had seen was part of the same business.

I stood there with the cat in my arms, feeling uneasy. Then I remembered Gerald waiting for me on the floor below. I yanked the label off the ribbon, stuffed it in my pocket and started down the stone staircase.

My juvenile was waiting on the landing below.

"All quiet on this front," he said. Then he saw the cat. "My God, where did you get that from?"

"We've been wrestling upstairs," I said. Then I added, although I didn't believe it: "Probably belongs to the doorman."

"Whoever it belongs to, it clears up our spook." Gerald's astonishment had given way to an almost exaggerated relief. "That cat is obviously Lillian."

He seemed positive the cat was what Theo had seen reflected in the glass. I wasn't so sure.

We took the animal down to the stage where the others were grouped around in wilted silence. Once again Gerald assumed all authority. He explained emphatically how the cat must have been somewhere in the dressing-room and how Theo must have caught its reflection in the mirror. To my surprise, everyone swallowed the story. There was an immediate slackening of tension and some of them even started wisecracking about it.

I was glad as hell. I had my company back to normal. But, even if I hadn't known about that crazy label, I couldn't have sold myself on the theory that Theo Ffoulkes, the most level-headed English importation we'd had for years, had scared herself with a cat.

While Gerald carted the animal away to the doorman, Theo strolled over to me where I was standing apart from the others.

She said: "You know perfectly well, don't you, Peter, that it wasn't any Siamese cat I saw in the mirror?"

I nodded gloomily.

"I'm not insisting, Peter, because I don't see any point in getting the others worked up. But I wanted you to know. What I saw in that glass was the face of a woman I've never seen before. It's loopy, but that's what I saw."

I asked: "Are you sure you left the lights on in that dressing-room?"

"I'm positive," she said, adding curiously: "Why?"

"Because they were turned off when we got there."

I realized suddenly just what that implied. Theo did too. I said: "But for Pete's sake keep it under your hat."

"Of course I will." When Theo gave you her word, she meant it. She looked at me, a rueful smile on her mouth. "Not a very promising start, is it, darling? But don't you worry. We've got a swell show and a swell producer." A slight flush crept into her cheeks. "And Wessler, of course, is a dream. We're giving all we've got to make this a success for you and we're going to set the Thames on fire—spooks or no spooks."

It was sort of swell of her to say that—just then when I needed it badly.

Gerald had come back now with the news that the cat didn't belong to the doorman. The toothless Mac, however, had fallen in love with it and wanted to keep it as the theater mascot. It didn't look like a particularly auspicious mascot, but I gave my okay. After all, someone had to take care of the animal, and I was relieved that no one thought to ask how the hell it had gotten into the theater.

I was just set to start the rehearsal without Mirabelle Rue when the swing-door burst open and I heard the familiar throaty voice behind me caroling:

"Darlings ... darlings ... I'm utterly late ... Peter, angel, what a simply divine theater. I've always loathed the Dagonet. God, isn't it cold?"

Mirabelle had arrived and suddenly nothing else seemed to matter very much. She swept across the stage, dazzling and electric as some major meteorological disturbance. She was hurling herself from one member of the company to another, strewing kisses and random requests in her path. "Eddie, darling, a glass please ... Oh, before you go, unearth the brandy, that's a dear ... I must have a teeny-eeny one ... it's somewhere under my arm ... yes, that's right . . . Iris, honey, how can you look so agonizingly beautiful? God, it must be wonderful to be young . . . Gerald, darling, isn't it gorgeous to be young or is it agonizingly sad? I forget. It's so long ago ... and who's this nice young man? Oh, the author, of course ... a marvelous play, Mr. Prince, marvelous. ... Theo, my poor sweet, your *nose*! It's positively scarlet ... look at it, Peter, isn't it scarlet? ... A cough? My dear, how perfectly ghastly."

Mirabelle had seen us all a few hours before at the Vandolan, but she always greeted the company with breathless fervor as though we had been miraculously restored to her from some frightful catastrophe.

All of us, that is except Conrad Wessler. I had never been able to understand just why Mirabelle had taken such an instant and fanatic dislike to her Austrian co-star. But there it was. And, like all of Mirabelle's other emotional relationships, it was dramatized out of all reasonable proportions.

When everyone else had been greeted, Mirabelle moved very slowly toward Wessler who was standing by the proscenium, his bearded face expressionless, his eyes gazing down at the little female statuette in his hands.

Mirabelle stopped dead in front of him, her head with its fantastic red hair tilted backward, holding out both her hands to him.

"Good evening, Herr Wessler. No, don't bother to shake hands. I see you've got your hands full. Whatever is it—another little doll? Aren't you cute with your little dolls, so simple and unaffected." She peered at the figurine in his hands with mock absorption. "Heavens, she's quite slim for a change, not at all buttocky. Who is she meant to be?"

Wessler had raised his eyes now. He was watching her with a queer kind of intensity. "The statue, Miss Rue, she is of you."

"Me!" Mirabelle gave a shrill little laugh and waved over her shoulder to the rest of us. "Did you hear, darlings? He's made a cunning little statue of me. What do you suppose he's going to do with it—stick pins in it?" There was absolutely no change in the sweet dangerous flow of her words. "And, Mr. Wessler, while we're talking about these darling things, I just peeked into my dressing-room and I see the dressing-table is loaded with odd-looking lumps of clay. You left them there? A mistake, of course, I don't much care for lumps of clay in my dressing-room. You'll remove them, please."

Gerald was at her side now, dutifully holding out a tumbler of neat brandy. Until her recent and harrowing divorce from her ex-leading man, Roland Gates, Mirabelle had never touched liquor. Now she couldn't act without brandy constantly on tap. That was the only visible sign of the nervous ordeal she'd been through. I had been worried about her drinking at first. But I wasn't now. Mirabelle was acting like a dream. She could take care of herself.

She had just turned from Wessler when the Austrian said very firmly: "I am sorry, Miss Rue. The first dressing-room from the stage, she must for me be. I do not like the other. The mirror, me it does not suit."

Mirabelle spun back, staring. I could tell she was fighting mad at this casual contempt for her traditional privileges. But, to my astonishment, she did nothing about it. She merely flourished the brandy in front of Wessler, ignoring his expression of stubborn disapproval. Wessler was fiercely teetotal and I knew Mirabelle was getting rather an unholy kick out of shocking him.

"To you, Herr Wessler!" she exclaimed. "To the play and to the Dagonet." She swallowed the brandy at one gulp and tossed the empty glass back to Gerald. "And let us hope that the mirror in my dressing-room it will you suit."

Even then, when she said it, that remark seemed fairly ill-omened. But it was not until much later that I started realizing just how very ironical it was destined to be.

Mirabelle and Wessler were still staring at each other like a couple of fighting cocks, maneuvring for position. I wasn't going to stand for any more nonsense that night. I called the rehearsal sharply to order.

Mirabelle was instantly a changed person. She forgot Wessler, she threw off her hat, slipped down into the house, found a seat in the front row, ran her hands through her stunning hair and lapsed into sudden and absolute stillness. Mirabelle was always like that in the few moments before she went on stage. It was as if she turned off the unquenchable stream of her vitality at a spigot, letting it bank up inside her.

Eddie had switched on a single spot. He gave Henry Prince and me our copies of the script and took up his prompting position in the wings. Wessler deposited his statuette in the disputed dressing-room and returned.

"Okay," I said. "Mr. Wessler—Iris. Ready for the first act, please."

Theo, Gerald and old Comstock moved onto the side of the stage, waiting for their cues. Henry and I joined Mirabelle in the darkened house.

Our first rehearsal at the Dagonet was under way.

Chapter Three

AFTER THE THEATRE'S ungracious welcome, I had resigned myself to a ragged performance. I was wrong. The various and sundry disturbances of the first half hour seemed to have put the whole company on its mettle. The show got off to a flying start.

From his first line, Wessler picked it up and had it in the palm of his hand. He used a brutal, aggressive type of playing all his own—something I'd never seen in America. It was perfect for his role in *Troubled Waters* as the Pennsylvania Dutch farmer who ruled his family with a fist of steel. In spite of his enormous European reputation, wiseacres had prophesised that the airplane accident would have left scars on his talent as it had left them on his face. They were cockeyed. Conrad Wessler was going to take New York by storm, and I was lucky as hell to have him under contract for his American debut.

It was incredible luck, too, that *Troubled Waters* should have come into my life just when I had rejected over a hundred scripts. I had decided that my old enthusiasm for the stage, the one major passion in my life, had been sozzled away in drinking days and would never flare up again. And then, five minutes after I had turned the last page of young Henry Prince's first play, the blood had begun hissing in my veins like champagne and I was raring to dash headlong into production.

Not that *Troubled Waters* was a work of sublime genius. It wasn't. Like *Rain*, like the *Lady from the Sea,* it threw a world-weary glamour girl up against a group of primitive characters. In *Troubled Waters*, Cleonie, the heroine-menace happened to be a sort of honky-tonk suffragette from a pre-war cabaret; the milieu happened to be the farmhouse of the Kirchners, a typical Pennsylvania Dutch family; the force that marooned her there happened to be a flood. Those were just trimmings to the time-worn pattern of two different worlds clashing—and clashing like hell. *Troubled Waters* was derivative, but it was a grand piece of theater with a swell dramatic punch.

But there were a dozen pitfalls. If any wrong stresses were given, the whole thing could have collapsed into burlesque. With the right direction and the right cast, however, it had an excellent chance at the really big time. And, that night at the Dagonet, as the first act got under way, I realized with a sense of elation just how right my cast was. Wessler *was* Hans Kirchner, the young patriarch, down to the last hair on his beard and the last guttural in his accent. Even Iris, who had never acted until a crazy hunch of Dr. Lenz's and mine had landed her in this show, was turning in a honey of a performance in the tricky role of the frustrated farm girl. It was a joy watching Theo Ffoulkes shedding her brusque English personality and put all her splendid technique into the embittered drudge who was Wessler's wife.

Gerald Gwynne was grand, too. He had made only one previous Broadway appearance and, if it hadn't been for Mirabelle's insistence, I wouldn't have dared entrust to him the part of the patriarch's tough kid brother. But, as usual on all stage matters, Mirabelle had been right. Her young protégé was proving that his smash success in his debut had something real to back it up.

For the first fifteen minutes of that rehearsal, there was virtually nothing for me as director to do. I just sat in my dusty seat, gripping the arms. I didn't give a damn about the Dagonet or its face in the mirror. Let all the spooks in Christendom come and jingle their jinxes—they couldn't stop us from haunting Broadway for at least two seasons to come.

It was in this exhilarated mood that I turned to Henry Prince, who sat, earnest and bespectacled, in the seat next to mine. It still seemed almost unbelievable that good luck could have come to me from so unassuming a person. Although this, his first play, showed all the zip and self-assurance of a born headliner, Henry still seemed to me after three months just an uninteresting small-town boy, bewildered by the prospect of success. Since the

27

evening of the very first reading, he had been too timid even to attend rehearsals and it had taken a good twenty minutes to persuade him to come to the Dagonet that night. He was scared of actors, he said. He was afraid of getting in the way.

I felt very paternal about Henry.

"Going nicely, don't you think?" I said.

"Oh, yes," whispered Henry. "I think it's wonderful."

"And what do you think of Wessler now?"

Henry's only manifestation of stubbornness had been his reluctance to have Wessler play the lead. Wessler was an Austrian and he had wanted a real Pennsylvannia Dutchman in the part. I'd never dreamed of falling in with his ideas, but I made a point of showing interest.

He smiled a little wistfully now and whispered: "I think he's grand. I wish father could see him."

That was Henry's highest form of praise—to give anything his father's vicarious approval.

Mirabelle didn't go on for just over twenty minutes. All this time she had been sitting at my side, her hands crossed in her lap, her eyes staring straight ahead of her. Now, just a few seconds before her cue, she slipped up into the wings, poured herself another jigger of brandy, patted Eddie Troth on the shoulder and waited, looking small, almost mousey—utterly unlike a great actress.

And then her cue came. As soon as she entered, half staggering, half supported by Gerald, you could feel all the coldness and the vastness of the flood waters outside the farmhouse; you could feel the exhaustion, the fear, the instinctive suspicion of the hard-boiled cabaret girl who had been rescued from the raging river only to find herself in a human set-up completely alien to her. In two seconds, Mirabelle had set that dreary theatre on fire; it was Bankhead and bitters, Cornell with a kick.

And to me it was a miracle. A few months back, Mirabelle had been a bundle of shattered nerves, convalescing in the Thespian Hospital. I knew just how shot she'd been for we'd been very close to each other ever since the days when we were two unknowns battering together at the locked door of Broadway. She and her actor-husband, Roland Gates, had for years run the Lunts neck and neck as the biggest box-office marital team in the theater. And, like the Lunts, they had been boosted to a million fans as the most successful love-match in the profession. No one had ever guessed about Roland—not even I who knew him as well as I knew anyone. Mirabelle had never breathed a word of the incredible mental and physical torture she'd been subjected to during those years as the stage's happiest wife.

And then, when their last show closed after a season's smash business, Mirabelle cracked. One night she told the truth to Gerald and me. She told us the unbelievable things Roland did in those odd moments when the suave, drawing-room idol had amused himself by brutalizing her. Mirabelle had taken it all those years, partly because she didn't want the world to know the truth, partly because she was scared that if she split the team she'd be through on Broadway.

Gerald and I virtually railroaded her into a divorce. Gates contested and the details brought out in court made a seven-day holiday for the yellow press. We couldn't keep publicity back. Roland was hounded out of town and, for a while, Mirabelle was through. They told me at the hospital there was a good chance of her going nuts.

But they didn't know Mirabelle. On the night I read her the script of *Troubled Waters,* she left the hospital—just like that. And no power on earth could have stopped her. She admitted it was crazy but she said she'd rather die than pass up a chance of playing Cleonie.

That was the reason she gave me. I knew there was another. Mirabelle was a hell of a good friend. She saw that my one chance of breaking through and making something of myself again rested on that play. She was going to do her damnest to help me up.

That's why I never kicked at her drinking brandy at rehearsal; that's why I gave her her head even in her rather undignified victimization of Wessler. I never forgot just what Mirabelle was doing for me.

Actually her attitude to Wessler was a cinch for the play because the script had the two of them reacting violently to each other from the gun. That night, as they went into their first big scene together, the stage was electric with their pent-up antagonism.

I was watching them, quite carried away, when Mirabelle broke off in the middle of a sentence and swung round toward the door leading from backstage. I looked too and saw a man pushing through the door—a stranger in a camel's-hair coat and a derby hat. Under his arm he carried a large portfolio.

I had made it plain to the doorman that, with the exception of Dr. Lenz who was backing the show, all visitors were vetoed at rehearsal. I was just about to get tough when something about Mirabelle stopped me. I knew she hated interruptions too. But she wasn't registering just ordinary irritation. There was another expression on her face—an expression of surprise and something else that was almost fear.

The stranger strolled toward her. I thought he was going to speak, but at the critical moment she turned her back and said shakily:

"Sorry I blew up, Wessler. Give me the cue again, will you?"

But Wessler didn't give her the cue. He was peering at the man in the derby hat. Wessler had an incredible memory for faces and a queer habit of scrutinizing strangers as if he were trying to check them up against some vast identification file in his mind. I had the odd feeling he was trying to recognize this man while Mirabelle was doing her utmost to pretend she didn't know him.

The rehearsal had stopped completely. This unknown individual seemed suddenly and without the slightest effort on his own part to have become the focal point of that whole cavernous theater. For a split second I tried to figure out what it was all about, then my irritation swamped other, more obscure sensations and I bawled:

"Who let you in?"

The man in the derby hat skirted Wessler and Mirabelle and picked his way down the house toward me. A small mustache stretched in a smile of apology. He was about forty, plump and too pink. I disliked him on sight.

"I just wanted to see if the author . . ." He bent across me calmly and peered at Henry whose mouth had dropped in an astonished O. "So it is you, Henry. I hardly recognized you."

Indifferent to the fact that he was holding up the rehearsal, he pushed his heavy bulk past my knees, sat down next to Henry and started to talk in a confidential whisper. Henry was looking acutely self-conscious. I heard him mutter: "You're disturbing them, Uncle. We mustn't talk here." He rose hastily, almost dragging the man in the derby hat over my knees again out into the aisle. His solemn face stained a deep pink, he said. "Mr. Duluth, this is my Uncle, George Kramer. He didn't realize he was disturbing you. I'm sorry."

While he continued his apologies, Mr. Kramer gazed up at the stage, his beady, impertinent eyes fixed on Mirabelle.

"You are certainly lucky to have Miss Rue in the cast, Mr. Duluth," he said suddenly. "An artiste—a very great artiste."

He didn't say anything else. He didn't even look at me. Accompanied by the agitated Henry, he moved up once more onto the stage and made for the door with the broken panel. I watched him pass Mirabelle. She didn't pay the slightest attention. But she was conscious of every move he made.

Then, just as the uncle-nephew combine had reached the swing-door, Wessler called: "One moment, please excuse."

The two of them turned. Wessler took a step toward them. He said excitedly: "In Vienna, yes, in 1936, you are there at the American Ambassador's reception?"

That odd remark didn't seem odd to me or to anyone else who knew Wessler. His amazing memory was linked up with a passionate desire to place people whose faces struck him as familiar. Already he had pinned Iris down at the Boeuf in Paris, Theo at Nancy Cunard's in London, and me in any one of a thousand bars. The only surprise in this particular instance was the fact that Wessler had met Kramer before.

31

He was staring at the two men, waiting for a reply, Kramer stared back, his plump face completely unconcerned. After a rather too protracted second, he turned to his nephew and said:

"Henry, Mr. Wessler is speaking to you."

Henry started and said: "No-no Herr Wessler, I have never been to Vienna."

It seemed to me that Kramer had deliberately passed the ball to Henry. But the two of them disappeared immediately and I forgot both the incident and Mr. Kramer—at least, I forgot them until later when there was nothing about that first rehearsal at the Dagonet that I didn't remember with most unpleasant vividness.

In spite of Uncle George's interruption and the dramatic appearance of a rat on stage, the first act kept up its breathless pace until old Lionel Comstock's entrance. Comstock played the business magnate who had been taking Cleonie out on a dubious weekend and had been caught with her in the flood. Rescued some time after her, he had little more to do than to die and be put in a coffin which those pre-war Pennslyvania Dutch, with a sort of pessimistic efficiency, kept in the back kitchen in case of emergency. That evening, since the coffin had not yet arrived, Comstock had practically no business and only two lines. But he hammed impossibly.

I didn't call him down. Although he'd denied it, I knew there was something about the Dagonet that had him scared. I knew too that he was sick. Besides, I didn't want to risk another hysterical scene which would have thrown the company right off the rails as it had done earlier in the evening.

When Lionel Comstock was safely dead, the rehearsal progressed without interruption for a while. Then, just after I had launched them into the second act, a rhythmic shuffling sounded from behind me in the dark house. I turned in my seat to see two figures winding their way slowly down the aisle toward me. They were both of them large colored men in overcoats. Between them they were carrying a long black coffin.

This madhouse procession moved past me and up onto the stage, completely disrupting the rehearsal. With great reverence the

32

• •

colored men deposited the coffin on the boards and stared at Eddie. He said "Okay" and they disappeared.

While I was still recovering, my stage manager strolled to the coffin and gazed down at it affectionately. He explained that he felt we needed the coffin at this stage of the rehearsal and he'd been able to pick up the genuine Pennsylvania Dutch article from a pal in Lancaster. To a rather shaken Comstock he pointed out the coffin's various highlights, its heavy old-fashioned upholstery, its solid brass fittings and its general air of respectability. He also assured the old actor that sufficient air-holes had been bored to guarantee enough air during the period when he had to stay in it with the lid down.

Eddie was all for running through the coffin sequence again. But I vetoed it. Comstock had put up with enough harrowing experiences already that evening. While the coffin loomed darkly in the center of the stage, I got the rehearsal going again, finished the second act and went into the third.

It was some time later that I first noticed Dr. Lenz. He had appeared as if by magic and was moving gravely through the seats toward me. Although he had suddenly and generously put up the money to finance the show, Lenz had never before come to rehearsal. One of America's busiest psychiatrists, he spent all his time either at his own santorium or in consultation with other equally prominent and impressive personages.

He dropped into a seat and, when I caught his eye, he raised a large hand to indicate that he did not wish his unexpected arrival to interrupt the rehearsal. Then, settling back against the worn upholstery, he fixed the stage with an alert, critical gaze.

I hoped against hope that he would give the seal of his approval to the way I'd treated the script which he had read with surprising enthusiasm. Dr. Lenz was one of the few men in the world whom I respected to a degree bordering on idolatry. With his little imperial, his benign profile, his imposing front, he always made me feel he had just stepped down from a cloud and dismissed a train of minor prophets. If *Troubled Waters*, in its present shape, got by with him, it would be Something with a very capital S.

During the next few minutes my attention was fixed on his face rather than on the stage. I watched with a mixture of pride and uneasiness. Then all uneasiness slipped away. A slight smile had moved his mouth; his eyes crinkled up at the corners. There was no doubt that the play had gotten him.

In my consequent exhilaration I didn't notice at once that Eddie Troth had quit his chair in the wings. Presumably my stage manager had decided no more prompting would be necessary and had sneaked out for a quick drink.

The last act was drawing to a close. Theo made her final exit—and then Gerald.

"Okay," I called to them. "Don't wait unless you want to. That's all till tomorrow. Eleven-thirty."

Gerald ran a comb through his glossy black hair and moved toward the swing-door. Theo stifled a cough, buttoned her tweed jacket and followed. They disappeared together.

"Unless you need me, I think I'll go, too." Old Lionel Comstock's voice sounded vaguely in my ear, "I would like to take a look around the dressing-rooms. It's been a long time. A very long time."

I was dimly conscious of his gaunt face peering earnestly at me. I muttered, "All right, Lionel," and he shuffled away, leaving Lenz and me alone in the auditorium.

On the stage Wessler and Mirabelle were working up to their final scene, while Iris hovered in the wings.

The varied emotions of *Troubled Waters* had played themselves out, leaving behind them a trail of havoc and frustration. The two Kirchner women, Theo and Iris, have insisted that Cleonie be turned from the house even though the flood has not yet abated. Surprisingly, Kirchner has taken the part of the woman whom he ought to hate for menacing the security of his home. He must choose between the known and the unknown. Left alone with the girl, he tells her how he has hoped to save her immortal soul; how he is ready to sacrifice even his domestic happiness for her salvation. In a magnificent finale Cleonie opens his eyes to the fact that it is her body, not her soul, that he has wanted. And she has really wanted him despite the dreary narrowness of his outlook. They are man and woman. Will he have the courage to face the flood with her? As the curtain falls, they are moving together toward the door—toward the impassable waters and their problematical future.

I'd always been a bit bothered by the actual ending. To me, Kirchner's willingness to succumb to the lure of sex seemed to ditch honest psychology in favor of derivative cynicism. No one but Wessler and Mirabelle could have carried it off. But they did that night—through the sheer force of their playing.

Lenz and I watched in silence as the two of them, the heroic, bearded man and the slim, red-haired woman, walked hand in hand away from the footlights toward an imaginary door. In spite of the naked stage with its few odd props and Eddie's bleak coffin, there was a real illusion. You could feel exactly how the characters in the play were feeling—Cleonie's triumphant excitement at the success of her toughest piece of man-baiting, Kirchner's dread of leaving the known and his blinding desire for the unknown. Wessler was working up to the curtain. He was timing superbly. His great hand moved forward, clutched the handle on the door that wasn't there and threw it open.

Almost he made you feel the cold blast of wind sweeping into the farmhouse; made you see the vast stretches of water which buried the land that had been his past, and which still set up an almost insuperable barrier between him and his future.

The two of them stood there with their backs turned to the house, holding the tension. They had that whole, empty theater in their spell.

And then it happened.

Suddenly, without the slightest warning, the swing-door burst open and a man staggered onto the stage. I scarcely recognized Lionel Comstock. His face was contorted with panic. One hand half covered his eyes as if to shut out the memory of some frightful, invisible thing.

He groped his way forward like a man in a dream.

35

"The mirror!" he gasped. "I saw it. It came out at me—out of the mirror! Lillian! ... Lillian ... !"

As his words faded into the silence, there was a faint sound offstage, a throbbing musical sound like the tinkle of falling glass.

Comstock uttered a single groan. For the fraction of a second he stood erect and theatrical in the wide path of the spotlight. Then his shoulders crumpled; he swayed; he threw out a helpless hand and collapsed onto the boards, one arm sprawling grotesquely over the coffin.

It had all happened too quickly for me. Vaguely I was aware of Iris hurrying from the wings and dropping to her knees at his side. I was conscious that Dr. Lenz had risen and was making his purposeful way toward the stage.

But for some reason, it was Mirabelle who attracted my particular attention. She was standing exactly where she had been, her hand still in Wessler's, her face gray as the dust sheets in the auditorium.

"He's dead," she said in a flat, funny voice, "I know it. He's dead."

Chapter Four

Dr. LENZ WAS up on the stage, bending over Lionel Comstock, his capable fingers on the old man's pulse. I joined him, feeling as helpless as I looked. Comstock's lips were blue-gray; one leg was doubled back under him; his face, with its blind, staring eyes, showed stark terror. There was something horrible about that arm of his straddled across the coffin. There was something fantastically horrible about the whole set-up.

"Quick, Mirabelle," I said. "Your brandy."

Mirabelle seemed only half there. Vaguely she moved across the stage toward the table where the bottle stood. She was back again.

"There's none left, Peter. The bottle's empty."

"It is too late for brandy." Lenz looked up, his bearded face very grave. "Miss Rue was right. This man is dead."

"Dead!" Conrad Wessler's huge shoulders were stooped as if in resignation to the inevitable. "*It came out at me—out of the mirror.*" He repeated Comstock's amazing words in a blurred whisper. "Once again, it is the mirror."

"Yes." Mirabelle's hand fluttered to her cheek. "What did he mean about the mirror, Peter? What did he see?"

It was a relief that Mirabelle, at least, hadn't heard about Theo's crazy experience upstairs. I looked at Iris. Neither of us spoke. For a long moment we all stood around ineffectually. Then Lenz said:

"You had better telephone for an ambulance, Mr. Duluth."

Glad of a chance to get away, I ran offstage, down the stairs to the doorman's room.

"Mac!" I called.

I put my head around the door. No one was there. As I hurried toward the telephone, Mac came shuffling from the direction of

37

the stage door, carrying a Siamese cat and wiping furtively at his lips.

"Just run out for a glass of beer . . ." he began.

"To hell with your beer," I said. "Call an ambulance right away. It's Mr. Comstock. A heart attack."

"Comstock?" The old man stared at me, open mouthed.

"Yes. And for God's sake, get that ambulance." I was starting back up the stairs, then I called: "Are all the others out of the theater?"

"Lot of 'em just went."

"Then don't let any of them back in again. Tell them rehearsal's over, tell them anything, but don't let them in."

As I hurried back to the stage, I was still pretty stunned. All I could think was that something incredible was happening at the Dagonet, something that was endangering the very existence of my play. I had to get Mirabelle and Wessler out of the theater as quickly as possible. They were both of them strung up to snapping point. If either of them cracked, the show wouldn't be worth two red cents.

I found them standing side by side, close to the huddled body their hands linked, instinctively posed as they had been for the last act curtain. In the shock of death they seemed to have forgotten their mutual antagonism.

"Wessler," I said, "you'd better take Mirabelle home. There's nothing you can do."

The Austrian actor glanced at me vacantly as if English were a language that meant nothing to him. Then he did something with his feet that gave the impression of clicked heels.

"*So gut,* Herr Duluth."

Mirabelle whispered: "All right, Peter." She went across the stage, picked up her brandy bottle, slipped it under her arm and moved back to Wessler.

I wondered vaguely why she had bothered to take an empty brandy bottle with her. But I didn't really worry about it. I was too glad to see them go.

Dr. Lenz, Iris and I were alone on the stage now. Lenz stood

38

there, tall and imposing, his hands clasped across an ample vest.

"Comstock had a weak heart," I ventured lamely. "There'd been an attack before. It—it must have been the strain of acting."

Lenz nodded but he did not speak. In fact, he didn't open his mouth until the men from the ambulance came and carried Comstock away on a stretcher. Then he said quietly:

"I shall go to the hospital with them, Mr. Duluth, but I shall come to your apartment later." He paused and added: "Meanwhile, try not to worry unduly."

I tried not to worry unduly, but it didn't get me very far. The Dagonet had done enough to my nerves already; this latest and worst episode had started them running around in circles. I looked at Iris who was making an effort to light a cigarette as if everything were under control. Just to see her did something to me.

"Darling," I said, "before you say what you're going to say, you must let me tell you one thing. You're very beautiful and I love you very much."

"That's two things." She smiled fleetingly. Then she looked serious executive. "Peter, we've got to do something."

"About Comstock?"

She nodded.

"Poor old fellow," I began. "He had a bum heart, the strain . . ."

"Don't talk like an infant. You know there's more to it than that." She paused, watching me curiously: "Didn't you and Gerald really find anything upstairs in that dressing-room?"

"Yes," I said. "We found a Siamese cat with a pink ribbon around its neck."

"I don't mean the cat. It wasn't the cat that scared Theo. You know that as well as I do. And it wasn't the cat that scared Comstock, either. Both of them saw something in a mirror, something bad enough to frighten Comstock to death. You saw how he looked when he rushed on stage Peter. It's crazy to say he died of an ordinary heart attack. He was frightened to death. And he'd expected to be frightened before he ever came to the theater."

I'd been thinking the same thing, of course. There was no point in pretending I hadn't.

"So what?" I asked bleakly. "Do we believe there's a disembodied reflection running amok in the Dagonet?"

"I don't know what we believe, Peter. But Comstock was scared of someone or something called Lillian. And there's only one sensible thing to do. We've got to look for Lillian."

She took my arm firmly and started for the swing-door. There was nothing for it but to follow her lead, although it seemed pretty wild—searching a theater for a performing mirror and a ghost called Lillian.

We moved out into the corridor. It had been eerie before. It was even more so now. The frugal light from the ceiling bulb came blurred through a coating of dust; the silence was stifling. Since Iris was on top of the situation, I made a point of playing the two-fisted, what-the-hell male. But I was very frayed.

Ahead of us was the closed door of the first star dressing-room, the *casus belli* in the most recent battle between Mirabelle and Wessler. We paused in front of it. Iris slipped her hand into mine. I turned the knob, opened the door and switched on the light.

I hadn't seen this room before. It was more or less like the one upstairs that I had visited with Gerald, only larger, boasting a regular stand-up wardrobe with a full-length mirror instead of the smaller curtained closet. Iris's fingers closed more tightly on mine as we looked at the dressing-table.

The mirror immediately above it was splintered and cracked from side to side.

I don't know why that came as such a shock. After all that had happened already, I should have been able to take a broken mirror in my stride. But there is something in show-people, quite independent of reason, that reacts violently to this hoariest ill-omen in the Theater.

Iris was taking it calmly. She moved to the shattered glass.

"This must be the room where Comstock was frightened." She turned to me, her pupils widening. "He said whatever it was came *out* from the mirror. With the mirror broken and everything, it's almost as if something really had been coming out, stepping through from the other side. Peter, how beastly!"

For the first time she looked rather shaken. Unexpectedly, that made me steadier.

"Nuts," I said without conviction. "Wessler probably broke the mirror himself before rehearsal."

Iris let go my hand and walked across to the wardrobe. She swung open the door, revealing Wessler's black hat and the brocade opera cloak. There was something spectral about them hanging there where he must have forgotten them in his hurried departure with Mirabelle. I was going to make some flip remark when Iris gave a little cry and said: "Look!"

She had bent and was picking something from the floor just at the foot of the wardrobe. She moved back to me, holding it out.

"Look, Peter."

I looked. In a way, that was the most unnerving of all our discoveries. In Iris's hand was Wessler's clay statuette—the little figure of Mirabelle Rue. That evening, before rehearsal, it had been perfect down to the last exquisite detail. It was different now. Although the body had not been touched, the neck had been brutally crushed, as by the pressure of rough fingers. The tiny head lolled limply, lending the figure a horribly realistic resemblance to a woman whose neck had been broken by strangulation—or hanging.

"You remember what Theo said?" Iris dropped the figurine onto the dressing-table with fingers that shook. "She said the face she saw in the mirror was white, contorted like the face of a woman being hanged. Hanged! Let's get out of here, Peter. I've—I've had enough."

So had I. Plenty. That wretched experience of Theo's was getting out of hand; it was growing into a Juggernaut that had already crushed Comstock to death and seemed all set to go berserk through the entire theater.

We hurried out into the passage. We had just started toward the stairs leading to street level when my toe knocked against something that tinkled. I looked down. Lying on the floor, gleaming in the drab light, was a fragment of glass. I glanced around and saw another—and then another. I bent and picked a piece up. It was ordinary plain glass.

"What is it?" Iris asked nervously.

I remembered then. "It must be the new glass panel Eddie got for the swing-door." I looked up at her quickly. "Iris, just after Comstock dashed on stage, did you hear a sound—like breaking glass?"

Iris nodded. She too had heard that curious, musical tinkle which had echoed through the silence backstage.

"Then it must have been broken after Comstock came on stage," she said. "He couldn't have done it himself."

"And it couldn't have slipped and fallen of its own accord. If it had, it would just have been cracked—not smashed into fragments like this. Someone must have kicked against it after Comstock had been frightened."

Iris's eyes were incredulous. "But no one was in the theater except all of us on stage. The others had gone—all of them, that is, except the doorman."

"He'd gone too," I said. "He'd gone out for a glass of beer."

As we started down the stairs to the stage door, I was still too confused to do any thinking. There was only one thing I wanted to do—and that was to get out of the Dagonet Theater as quickly as possible.

I walked faster as we drew abreast of the doorman's room. Mac was the last person I felt like talking to and I would have scuttled past if he hadn't called my name:

"Mr. Duluth."

He was standing at the door of the alcove with his scrap-book clasped in one horny hand. The Siamese cat, looking very smug and sentimental, was perched on his old shoulders pressing her pink bow against his ear.

"Mr. Duluth, I'm sorry I stepped out for a glass of beer. I didn't figure you'd be needing me." The doorman bent toward me and whispered: "I saw them take him out on a stretcher; just the way they did with her. Is he dead?"

"Yes," I said shortly. "Mr. Comstock's dead."

Mac peered over his spectacles, a queer gleam in his eyes. "Strange things happen in the theater. Mr. Duluth. Yes, sir, strange things. It's almost like it was a judgment."

While I was struggling with this superfluous remark, he opened the scrap-book and exposed the fly leaf. On it was inscribed:

"Mackintyre Reed—a Press Record of the Dagonet Theater, 1900-19."

"I got everything here," he muttered. "I put everything in. Everything." He shuffled the pages until he came to a certain place. He handed me the book, pointing at a yellowing newspaper clipping. The Siamese cat on his shoulder blinked and gave a low, unnecessary miaow.

"Read that, Mr. Duluth." Mac shook his head somberly. "Maybe you'd find it sort of interesting."

I stared at the clipping. Iris stood close at my elbow, reading too. The extract was from some New York paper, dated November, 1902. It read:

GIRL FOUND DEAD IN HUMPHREY FREMONT'S DRESSING-ROOM

Police are investigating the tragic and mysterious death of a nineteen-year-old girl which took place last night at the Dagonet Theater during the first performance of the play *Without Honour*. The body was discovered in a dramatic manner by Mr. Humphrey Fremont, well-known young actor, who played one of the leading parts in the piece. After receiving the applause of the first night audience at the final curtain, Mr. Fremont returned to his dressing-room. He turned on the lights and crossed to the mirror, preparatory to removing his make-up. To his horror, he witnessed a ghastly sight. There, reflected from the mirror, he saw the white, distorted face of a girl. Mr. Fremont turned to find the young woman hanging dead in his wardrobe.

Humphrey Fremont admitted to the police later that he had been intimate with the girl but that he had stopped seeing her. It is believed that she committed suicide.

43

The girl was identified as Mrs. Lillian Reed by her husband, Mackintyre Reed, an attendant at the theater.

I shut the book very slowly, trying to keep calm. I didn't dare look at Iris. Then I heard her voice She was whispering almost inaudibly:

"Lillian!"

I stared at the doorman. "She was your wife?"

"Yes, sir. She was my wife." The old man retrieved the book and slipped it under his arm. There had been no emotion, hardly any interest in his voice. "They arrested Humphrey Fremont for a while. Guess they thought he might have killed her. But it didn't come to nothing. He was let go free."

He looked up, his old face dark with some unfathomable memory. I had a dim idea of what he was going to say next—but it was all so fantastic that I wouldn't let myself believe it.

"Maybe you're wondering what became of Humphrey Fremont. I been wondering too—for a long while. He went to England on account of the scandal and I lost sight of him. That is, I did till tonight."

Mac had found a grubby handkerchief and was polishing his spectacles. He seemed to have forgotten we were there.

"Maybe Humphrey Fremont did change his name, but he couldn't change his face. No, sir. I recognized him right away tonight even though it's so long since I saw him last."

Iris's hand clutched my arm.

"Yes," said the doorman, "he might have called himself Lionel Comstock. But he was still Humphrey Fremont to me . . ."

Chapter Five

I R I S A N D I looked at the doorman—owlishly. Then Iris said in an odd, piping voice:

"Come on, Peter. We'd better get going."

That seemed like a very good idea. With a pinched smile at Mac and the Siamese cat, I navigated Iris out into the cold November night of the alley.

We knew all the crazy truth about Lillian now. Lillian had been the doorman's wife; Lionel Comstock had been Humphrey Fremont, the man who had done Lililan wrong and caused her suicide at the Dagonet over thirty years ago.

But where did that get us? It explained why Comstock had kicked at having to play at the Dagonet; it explained why the old man had reacted so violently to Theo's story of what she'd seen upstairs. But apart from that we were still at a dead end—an even deader end. What had come out at Comstock from that broken mirror? What had Theo Ffoulkes seen upstairs? How had Wessler's statue of Mirabelle become so bizarrely crushed and how had the pane of glass in the passage been smashed at a time when there had been no one there to smash it?

My mind was a mixed salad of speculations as I pushed open the prison-like iron grille which separated us from the street and clanged it behind us.

We were just looking around for a taxi when a long-legged figure neatly avoided a speeding automobile and landed on the sidewalk in front of us. With his hat tilted on the back of his curly head and a hand on his hip as if to cover a concealed forty-four Eddie Troth looked more than ever like a Gary Cooper-cum-Goldwyn cowboy. He also looked worried.

"Seen Gerald?" he asked.

Iris and I said no we hadn't seen Gerald.

45

My stage-manager started to tell us how Gerald had been eating a sandwich with him at Sardot's and had suddenly jumped up and dashed out of the place.

"Just as if he'd seen a ghost," mused Eddie. "I wondered. . . ." He broke off, his eyes moving from my face to Iris's. "Talking about seeing ghosts, what the hell's happened to you two? You look terrible."

Eddie had been my stage-manager ever since he quit his masseur career at the Thespian Hospital. He was close to me as my right hand. I told him just what had happened. I also got him to establish the fact that both the mirror in Wessler's dressing-room and the pane of glass in the passage had been intact when he had left the theater. He stared at me blankly for a second, then he gave a low whistle.

"Tie that," he said.

"On the contrary," I said bitterly. "Untie that."

I waved at a taxi, pushed Iris into it and left Eddie gawping on the sidewalk.

In the taxi, Iris said:

"Peter, I've just been thinking. If Lillian Reed was the doorman's wife and Comstock had been responsible for her death, isn't it possible that the doorman . . .?"

"Listen," I said, "will you do me one little favor?"

"Yes," said Iris.

"Leave Lillian in her grave for a while," I said. "Don't make the night any more hideous than it is."

I leaned over and kissed her, letting my mouth stay against the warmth of hers.

"I love you," I said. "And isn't everything awful?"

I guessed I was taking it all more tragically than I need have done. At that stage of the game, there was no real reason to visualize the whole show dropping to pieces. But I was still a convalescent drunk. And there's nothing in the world more liable to fits of suicidal gloom than a convalescent drunk.

For two solid years after the appalling night at the Ashbrook Theater when my wife had been trapped and killed in a backstage fire, I had spent twenty-four hours a day pickled in alcohol. When finally I hit Dr. Lenz's sanitorium, I had been close to the border-line between curable and incurable. Dr. Lenz had performed a minor miracle in getting me back into some sort of shape. But the major miracle had been worked by Iris, whom a peculiarly benign providence had sent to the sanitorium too.

By the time Lenz let us loose again on the world, I had been cured of my alcoholism and heavily infected with two other passions: one to marry Iris, the other to make an actress out of her.

I was making an actress out of her. That was going swell, but Lenz had put his professional ban on the marriage idea. He had told me I wasn't straightened out enough yet to make a reasonable husband for anyone. There was to be a six months' trial of good behaviour before he was prepared to bestow his bearded blessing on the bride and groom.

It was pretty cockeyed, leaving the date of my wedding up to my psychiatrist. But I knew what a mess I'd been in before Lenz played God with my life. I was humble and ready to take whatever he felt like giving.

Not that it wasn't tough at times. Now, as I looked at the soft shadows under Iris's eyes, the exciting curve of her mouth, was one of those times. But I'd learnt to control myself.

"What are you thinking about?" said Iris.

"Never you mind," I said.

The taxi dropped us outside the Belmont where we were both living, chaperoned by the five hundred and eighty-six other inhabitants of the apartment house. Iris had a modest bed-sitting room on the fifth floor. I, as producer putting on a brave show to the world, rented an entire suite in solitary splendor ten floors above.

We took the elevator to my suite. I felt a smashing desire for a drink. But I wasn't going to admit it to Iris. She threw her hat and coat onto a couch and crossed to the window, gazing out at the blue-gray night of the East River.

"Your view's much nicer than mine, darling," she said medi-tatively. Then she turned so that she faced me. "Peter," she said,

47

"why don't we say hell with Dr. Lenz and get married now—right away?"

I stared at her. Iris had never shown signs of insubordination before. She'd never been so stunning to look at either, with her hair blue-black against the cream drapes and her skin so soft, so exciting.

"We know how we feel, Peter. We know what's right for us better than Lenz does. Tonight there was Comstock. If anything else happened to the play—Peter, I'd go nuts if anything else happened to the play and I didn't have you all the time."

I knew then how her mind was working. She wasn't thinking about herself; she was thinking of me. She knew I was getting jittery again; she knew there was a good chance of my making a fool of myself if we had any more trouble at the Dagonet. I had hold of her arm and took her to the couch. She dropped down on it, drawing up her legs like a little girl. I was at her side, my hands on her knees.

"Listen darling," I said. "It's very sweet of you. But it wouldn't work out yet. Lenz said no funny business until we were both normal citizens again."

"But marriage isn't funny business and I feel exactly like a normal citizen."

"But I don't. I feel very lawless and unbridled."

I kissed her twice. That made me feel better. She crinkled up her nose. "Darling, I can do the most spectacular things with scrambled eggs and in my negligee I have often been admired for my old-world charm. I . . ."

"No," I said.

"But I can't wait three more damn months. I can't Peter." I saw her lips were trembling. She looked down at a cushion and started to twist its corner as if she hated it. "And I'm not just an impatient virgin chasing the one sucker who's given me a rush. I'm having other bids, you know. Very attractive ones."

I looked at her. I didn't know what she meant, I didn't have a chance to ask her, either, because the phone by the couch rang. I leaned over her and took up the receiver.

"Hello," I said.

"Where's Mirabelle?" It was Gerald Gwynne's voice, taut, more worried than I'd ever heard it. "They wouldn't let me into the theater. They said she'd gone. She isn't at her apartment. Where is she?"

"She went home with Wessler," I said.

"Wessler? You let her go home with that damn German shepherd?" My juvenile sounded angry now, too. He hated Wessler just because Mirabelle reacted against him. "Why didn't you let her wait for me? You might have known I was coming back."

I told him then what had happened. I didn't see why not. Even if he did look like Robert Taylor's kid-brother, he had the temperament of a heavy-weight prize fighter. Nothing was going to rattle him.

He didn't say anything while I talked. He didn't seem to give a damn about old Comstock, either. All his anxiety was for Mirabelle.

"Was she on stage when it happened?" he asked faintly.

"Yes."

"My God, and she saw it, heard what he said about the mirror. Is—is she all right?"

"She seemed all right when Wessler took her home."

"Did she take her brandy with her?"

"No. That is, yes, she did, but the bottle was empty."

Gerald didn't say anything for a moment. Then he said: "Peter, this is bad. We've got to do something about it."

"About the brandy?"

"Don't be a dope. Listen, I wasn't going to tell anyone: I was scared it would get back to Mirabelle. But you better know. And you've got to do something about it. I was having a sandwich with Eddie in Sardot's tonight and I saw him. He's back in town. Mirabelle's delightful ex—that stinker Roland Gates."

That was a sock between the eyes. "But he can't be," I said. "After what came out at the divorce, he's through on Broadway. No management would touch him. He can't . . ."

"Yes, he can," cut in Gerald furiously. "Gates is so crazy about himself he'd never realize he was through. He'd never even realize Mirabelle was through with him. That's what I'm scared of. She put up with him all those years; he still thinks he just has to whistle and she'll come back. That's why he's here. He's going to try and get Mirabelle again."

With any other man, that would have been incredible, but not with Gates. I knew him.

"I saw him just as he was leaving Sardot's," Gerald was saying. "I quit Eddie and chased after him. He went straight across the street. He was hanging around the stage door of the Dagonet, that damn black hat of his pulled down over his eyes. Waiting for Mirabelle. I went up to him, told him to get the hell away."

I could imagine that scene vividly. Gerald, stubborn, protective young Gerald who guarded Mirabelle like a bulldog and who loathed Gates's guts.

"What happened?" I asked.

"He had the nerve to talk to me. He said: 'I hear Peter's got a hit and there's a swell part for Mirabelle.' I said what of it. Then he said: 'I also hear there's a heavy male lead, quite in my line. Peter's crazy to count on Wessler; he was through after that accident. I'm going to suggest my own services as understudy!' He said that, Peter. He wasn't being funny, either. He meant it."

"He's nuts," I said.

"I know it. But he's dynamite. We've got to keep Mirabelle from seeing him. Thank God I managed to scare him away tonight."

"How did you do that?" I said.

Gerald laughed; it wasn't at all the liquid laugh of Broadway's youngest and most swooned-over juvenile. "I said if he didn't get the hell away and stay the hell away from Mirabelle—I'd murder him."

There was a long pause. Then Gerald said.

"I guess that's all."

It was quite enough. I was going to ring off when he spoke again in a funny, difficult voice.

"By the way," he said, "how's Iris? Is she all right?"

"She's all right," I said. "Goodnight."

Iris was still sitting on the couch, twisting the cushion.

"What did he say?" she asked.

"He wanted to know if you were all right."

She gave me an odd look. Then she said: "What else?"

I told her about Gates, then grunted dejectedly. "If all the goddamndest things aren't happening tonight," I said. "But I guess I may keep out of the gibbering stage so long as I have you."

I shouldn't have given her that opening. I was asking for it. She slid forward again and kissed me.

"You'd have me with you all the time," she said softly, "if you'd up and marry me."

She almost won out then. But I was saved by divine intervention. A shrill, familiar sound cut into my thoughts.

Iris took her lips away from mine.

"Damn," she said, "there's the buzzer."

Chapter Six

I WENT TO THE DOOR. There, like the voice of conscience, stood Dr. Lenz. I straightened my tie, hoped there wasn't lipstick on my ear and tried not to look as guilty as I felt.

Lenz moved into the hall—a magnificently bearded one-man procession. Without speaking, he took off his hat and coat, folded the coat, put them both on a chair and then deposited on top an imposing leather briefcase. His hands clasped behind his back, he walked into the living-room, bowed at Iris and sat down in a steel chair which was both too small and too frivolous for him.

It was an unnerving entrance. I broke the silence: "Any news from the hospital?"

Lenz nodded. "We have examined Mr. Comstock. It is virtually certain that he died from heart failure. Fortunately we were able to get in touch with his regular physician who established the fact that there had been a leaky valve—that any shock or over-exertion might have been sufficient to bring on an attack. I suggested that the strain of acting could easily have been the cause of death." He paused, adding with a solemnity which made each word as imposing as a Delphic utterance: "The other doctors agreed."

I felt absurdly relieved. Ever since that incredible thing had happened at the Dagonet, I had been waiting with lugubrious pessimism for someone to mention the police.

"Then there'll be no inquest?" I asked hopefully. "We won't have hordes of dumb detectives scrambling over the production?"

"An inquest?" Lenz's imperial tilted upward, registering mild surprise. "My dear Mr. Duluth, why should there be an inquest? An elderly actor dies of myocardial failure in the presence of a reputable physician. Why should that require police investigation?"

I glanced at Iris. She was still twisting the edge of the cushion and looking intense. "You don't know the half of what happened," I said.

I told him the whole story then. Lenz wasn't only backing the show; he was backing my return to life. Telling him all was the most comforting thing that had happened to me that loathsome night.

"Now you know what led up to it, don't you think Comstock's death is a matter for the police?" I concluded, hoping to hell he'd say no. Because I knew that if we got the show mixed up with the police, we were through.

There was the faintest twinkle in Lenz's placid grey eyes. "What you have told me, grotesque though it may be, only makes the situation that much more reasonable. Mr. Comstock was an actor, an impressionable, probably a superstitious person. He arrived at the Dagonet in an extremely wrought-up condition, his mind full of memories of this girl, this Lillian Reed. Memory and a conscience can do strange things. After the rehearsal, he went to Mr. Wessler's dressing-room, perhaps following an impulse to revisit the scene of the tragedy. He found the broken mirror. That, in itself, would heighten his superstitious mood. He looks in the mirror, he sees perhaps his own face distorted by the broken glass. How logical to transfer to the mirror the image that was in his mind; how logical to imagine he saw the face of the dead girl." Lenz produced a large pair of horn-rimmed spectacles which he always used to emphasize significant points. "All that, or any of that, Mr. Duluth, would have been more than sufficient to precipitate a fatal attack."

The spectacles were returned to the pocket. Presumably Dr. Lenz considered the situation adequately explained.

I didn't.

I said: "But what about everything else? The broken mirror, the broken pane of glass, the crushed statuette and ... ?"

"And what Theo saw upstairs?" put in Iris suddenly. "She saw a woman's face reflected in a mirror, too. She saw it before Comstock ..."

Dr. Lenz lifted an impressive hand for silence. He got it. "Mr. Duluth, Miss Pattison." He eyed us both with paternal tolerance. "It is easy to make mysteries where there are none—particularly when one is not in an absolutely normal state of health. I am vitally interested in the welfare of your play. So are you, I strongly advise you not to jeopardize your success by worrying—*until* there is real cause to worry."

I didn't like that *until*. It gave the whole show away. It proved what I had already suspected, that Lenz was humoring us both as if we were a couple of nuts in his sanitorium. He knew things were wrong as hell at the Dagonet but he wasn't going to admit it to us because he still didn't trust our nerves.

"But . . ." I began.

It wasn't any use butting Dr. Lenz. Patients didn't pay him enormous fees to tell them everything was going to be all right—for nothing.

I found myself wanting a drink. I was wanting it horribly when the buzzer shrilled again. I went out into the hall and opened to Theo Ffoulkes.

The English actress looked tired, but defiantly matter-of-fact.

"Hellish late, Peter," she said. "But I had to come."

She walked briskly into the living-room, blew on gloveless hands and said: "Iris, be a cherub and make me a cup of tea. I'm frozen." She grinned at Lenz. "Why on earth don't those two get married? Save an awful lot on rent. You're backing the show, aren't you? Saw you at rehearsal tonight. Lucky man, you're going to make a mint of money."

"Don't make bright conversation, Theo," I said gloomily. "If you've got anything to say, out with it." I screwed up my mouth and jerked a thumb at Lenz: "Don't mind him, see? He's okay . . . one of the mob."

Theo sat down on the arm of the couch and tugged off her felt hat, revealing graying, closely cropped hair.

"I went back to the theater for my gloves, Peter. The doorman told me about Lionel. What did he die of?"

Iris moved into the kitchen and started clattering kettles.

"Bum heart," I said.

"That's what I was afraid of." Theo lit a Goldflake, coughing and making a grimace. "It's my fault, isn't it, Peter? I frightened him to death by dashing onto the stage and acting like a chump. In a way, I'm responsible for killing him."

She looked really worried.

"Don't be silly," I said. "Whatever frightened him happened a long time after that."

"But I did see that face in the mirror." Theo's lips mangled the Goldflake. "That's what I came to tell you. I wasn't playing the fool or telling bedtime stories."

I glanced at Lenz slyly. "Dr. Lenz says we mustn't talk about those things," I said. "It's naughty."

Lenz remained imperturbable. He was leaning forward in his small steel chair, eying Theo intently. "You'll pardon my asking, Miss Ffoulkes, but does the name Lillian Reed mean anything to you?"

I saw what he was driving at. He was trying to prove that Theo had already heard the Dagonet legend and had been subconsciously influenced by it.

"Lillian Reed," said Theo. "Lillian! You mean the woman Comstock talked about? Have you found out who she is?"

"Yes," I said. "We have. She's a very charming person. She's a ghost."

I told her the Lillian story. As one of my oldest and sanest friends in the theater and as one of the people who had met up with Lillian's reflection at the Dagonet, I figured she would be better off knowing the truth than having to guess.

She looked very white and queer. "Peter, how weird! That's exactly what I saw." Then she added quickly: "Was Wessler on stage when it happened? Did he see it all? Is he all right?"

I said yes, he was all right.

Lenz was still gazing at the Englishwoman. "You are sure, Miss Ffoulkes, that it was a woman's face you saw in the glass?"

"Why, yes. The face was contorted, well, you know, sort of twisted with pain and I couldn't see the hair because the head

55

was tilted backward. But I'm sure it was a woman from the way she was dressed. There was something brown around her throat. It looked like a fur—a light tan fur."

Theo got up and started marching about the room. "I want to have this out, Peter, before I go home. I don't believe in ghostly reflections and all that bosh. But I've been thinking. There's that curtained clothes closet immediately opposite the mirror. If someone had been hiding in there and the curtains weren't properly drawn, her face could have shown in the mirror although the rest of her was invisible. I'm sure that's what happened."

That was a thoroughly sensible remark. If someone had been hiding there, she could easily have slipped out before Gerald and I arrived. It would also explain how the lights got turned out after Theo left them on.

Theo continued: "But, even if that's what happened, why on earth should anyone want to scare me?"

"You were just thrown in as an extra, darling." Iris emerged from the kitchen with tea on a tray. "If Dr. Lenz is wrong and if someone really was acting up, it was obviously Comstock she was trying to scare. As I told Peter, I'm sure that depressing doorman was responsible for it all, trying to avenge his girl-wife or something. How many lumps of sugar?"

"Three," said Theo. She took the cup, swallowed the tea at one gulp and put the saucer down on a table with a bang. "I thought she might have been trying to scare Comstock, too. But I don't see how it's possible. It all happened in Wessler's dressing-room, didn't it? If the doorman or someone had been arranging some gruesome sort of tableau for Comstock, how could they possibly know he would go into that particular room?" There was an odd flush on her cheeks. "Strikes me there's only one person it could have been intended for—and that's Wessler."

I was beginning to wish we'd taken Lenz's advice and stopped trying to make brilliant deductions. The idea of a diabolical scheme to sabotage Wessler, the bulwark of the play, was too dreary to contemplate.

"Be reasonable," I said. "Who would want to upset Wessler?"

"I could tell you someone." Theo stopped in front of me, her hands jammed in the pockets of her tweed jacket, looking like a handsome wardress in a Reform School for Delinquent Girls. "Mirabelle. She's been foul to Wessler ever since she joined the company. She doesn't give a twopenny hoot that he was in that ghastly accident and ought to have every consideration. She was perfectly furious when he snaffled the first stage dressing-room. I bet she did some dirty trick in the hopes of scaring him out of it, and Comstock just got tangled up by mistake."

I was amazed at the pent-up malice in her voice. Theo was the friendliest soul in the world. I'd never dreamed she felt that way about Mirabelle.

"Theo, darling." I said patiently, "you're cuckoo. Mirabelle wasn't in the theater when you were scared. And when Comstock was scared she was on stage with us. How could she conceivably have done anything screwy like that?"

"I don't know. I don't know anything. That's just what I feel. And if anyone *is* trying to frighten Wessler, I'm bloody well going to see they don't get any further." Suddenly the flush that had been in Theo's cheeks flooded her whole face. She picked up her handbag. "Well," she said gruffly, "having made a prize ass of myself, I think I'll toddle along."

With a rather embarrassed smile at Lenz and a nod to Iris she moved toward the door. Before she got there, a sudden fit of coughing overtook her. She stood quite still, a hand to her throat. She said: "Damn! Any suggestions for this blasted cough of mine, Dr. Lenz? Or aren't you that kind of a doctor?"

During her unexpected outburst against Mirabelle, Dr. Lenz had been gazing up at the ceiling, politely oblivious to what was going on. Now he switched on his personality again and became a dominating force. He produced a fountain pen and a prescription blank and scribbled a note which he handed her.

"I always recommend codeine as a palliative for coughs, Miss Ffoulkes. It is obtainable only on a physician's prescription." He wagged the imperial impressively. "Take care you do not overdose for it is potentially a dangerous drug."

57

"Poison, eh?" Theo stuffed the prescription in her bag. "Thanks a lot. Next time I feel the urge, I can try codeine on my friends. Goodnight, children. Sleep well."

I followed her out into the hall and opened the front door.

"Don't bother yourself too much about this business," I said. "I guess we'll get things in their proper proportions tomorrow."

She didn't say anything. Her long, rather beautiful fingers played with the door handle. Then she looked up, staring me straight in the face with those clear, steady eyes of hers. "I'm sorry. It was filthy of me to spit out like that about Mirabelle."

"Don't give it a thought."

She smiled a funny, twisted smile. "God I'm a mess, aren't I, Peter? And I swore I'd never do it again."

I didn't get what she was driving at. I didn't say anything.

"It's not that I hate Mirabelle really, Peter, I think she's a marvelous actress. A grand person. And she's got more guts in her little finger than I have in my entire system. But I want to slay her whenever she's with him. I know he's not in love with her. He probably loathes her. But he's fascinated. She's made him conscious of her every second." She shrugged tweedy shoulders. "He doesn't even notice whether I'm there or not."

I understood then. Gerald had been right. Poor Theo, with her genius for falling in love with the wrong person, was stuck on Conrad Wessler. "I shouldn't get too tragic about it, my dear," I said. "You never know."

"Never know? I know nothing on earth could make Wessler aware of my existence. Sometimes I wish something would happen to him, that he would crack up and couldn't act any more, couldn't be the Great Wessler. Then perhaps, if no one else wanted him—" She threw out a hand in a gesture of self-mockery. Her lips were smiling but there were two large tears moving slowly down her cheeks. They were round. gleaming like glycerine. I'd never seen tears like that—outside the theater. "It's nice of you to listen, Peter. You're really an awfully nice person."

"I'm just an ex-drunk," I said. "And I'm sentimental."

"I won't be difficult, darling, I swear I won't let this interfere

58

with the show." Theo squeezed my hand and kissed me impulsively. "I'm used to frustrated passions, Peter. I'm one of those women that men forget on stage and off."

She hurried away toward the elevator. I shut the door.

When I got back to the living-room, Iris and Lenz were being amiably banal.

Iris said: "It was funny the way Theo lit into Mirabelle. And I think it was mean of her to go off and leave everything up in the air."

Lenz looked up gravely. "The air, Miss Pattison, is the very best place for the matter to be left tonight." He produced a large gold watch from the end of his large gold chain and stared at it significantly. "Two o'clock. I suggest it is time for us all to get some sleep."

When Lenz suggested anything, neither Iris nor I dreamed of gainsaying him. Iris rose and kissed me demurely while Lenz stood watching—a kind of Olympian duenna. Then I went with her to the door. In the hall she kissed me again, a little less respectably.

"Darling," she said, "promise you won't worry."

I said I wouldn't worry. She looked at me and said: "Why were you out here such a long time with Theo? Was she making love to you?"

"Yes," I said. "Every woman makes love to me. Passionate love."

Iris watched me thoughtfully for a moment. Then she said: "I don't think they do, Peter. I don't think you're at all the type that attracts the normal woman. Your ears are too big."

She kissed me again, told me again not to worry and went.

I returned to the living-room, taking with me Dr. Lenz's formidable black briefcase which contained, I felt sure, documents of the most vital and international importance to psychiatry. Dr. Lenz had crossed to the window and was gazing out at the East River with the self-satisfaction of a deity surveying one of his more successful enterprises.

"Miss Pattison has gone?" he asked in a slightly suspicious tone as if he thought I would clap my hands and materialize her out of his vest pocket.

I said yes. His finger and thumb settled like two substantial moths on the extreme tip of his imperial. His eyes were fixed solemnly on my face.

"Mr. Duluth," he said, "I do trust that you will not let tonight's experience worry you unduly."

We all seemed to be telling each other not to worry. It was a singularly useless thing to do.

I said: "That was just a stall of yours before Theo came, wasn't it? You do think there was something phony back of Comstock's death?" I added uneasily: "And you do think we may be having some more trouble?"

Dr. Lenz regarded his thumb nail. "I do not wish to alarm you, Mr. Duluth, but, at the risk of sounding trite, I must confess that certain things happened tonight for which there seems to be no immediate explanation. I do not subscribe to the supernatural. I do feel, however, that some malicious force may have been directed against some member of your company. Whether that person was Mr. Comstock himself or someone else, I have no means of telling at the present time. But I think that we should be very unwise not to keep ourselves—prepared."

That sounded ominous, but he took some of the sting out of it by adding: "During the next few days I shall have some time free from my duties at the sanitorium and I am willing to offer my services to make a more thorough investigation. You agree with me, of course, that it would be disastrous to introduce the police at this stage. Disastrous for you because your own future is tied up so closely with the play. Disastrous for me—" there was a slow twinkle in his eyes—"because I have invested in it not only a considerable sum of money but the health of my two most interesting patients."

I agreed fervently about the police. And in spite of what his admissions implied I felt a bit happier. Dr. Lenz had tackled mysteries before and I felt there was no problem on earth that could withstand his bearded concentration.

"Meanwhile," he added gravely, "I must insist that you . . ."

"Do not worry unduly," I finished. "Yes, I know."

Dr. Lenz was consulting his watch again.

"Listen," I said. "Since it's so late, why not spend the night here. There's plenty of room."

He inclined his imperial. "That is kind, Mr. Duluth. In fact, when I left the sanitorium this evening, I had that very thought in mind."

His large fingers slid open the zipper of his briefcase. They produced a neatly folded object which he shook out to its full magnificent length. It was a gray flannel nightshirt.

So much for the documents of vital and international importance to psychiatry.

Chapter Seven

B Y S O M E N E F A R I O U S means, Iris suborned Louise, my daily help, into admitting her to the apartment next morning. She appeared at the breakfast table, bearing scrambled eggs on a tray, looking very domestic and hark-hark-the-lark in a tweed coat and skirt. It was all shameless propaganda for her recently launched matrimonial campaign, and I was certain Dr. Lenz would show disapproval. But he didn't. He congratulated Iris on her scrambled eggs and—although I had suspected him of dieting exclusively on manna—he showed flattering and ample appreciation. In fact, he was navigating a third helping across the hazard of his beard when the house telephone announced Henry Prince.

Henry said he was downstairs in the lobby with his Uncle George. I remembered his Uncle George, didn't I—the man who had come into rehearsal the night before? I said rather grudgingly that I did remember Uncle George and asked them up.

When they arrived, Henry was apologetic about disturbing breakfast, but Uncle George Kramer was plump and pleased with himself. He was still wearing the derby hat and still carried the large portfolio under his arm. When I introduced them to Lenz, Mr. Kramer looked ingratiating and said, in what sounded like extremely efficient German:

"*Sehr geehrt, Herr Doktor.*"

I liked him even less than I had the night before.

Neither of them mentioned Comstock and, presumably, they hadn't heard the news. I saw no reason to pass it on to them and depress myself so early in the morning by having to talk about it. There was a rather strained pause which Dr. Lenz broke by launching into a long and congratulatory speech to young Henry about his play. Henry turned a modest pink and squirmed. I knew how much he hated the limelight, so I changed the subject by asking if they were visiting us for any particular reason.

Mr. Kramer glanced significantly at Henry and said: "We have come on a little matter of business, Mr. Duluth. I think my nephew would prefer to explain the situation to you."

Henry obviously didn't prefer to do anything. But in a hasty speech which gave the impression of rehearsal, he explained that his uncle had a photographic studio in New York and had been freelancing for one of the big weekly picture magazines. Mr. Kramer, it seemed, was eager to give his nephew's play a free boost by taking candid camera shots of the show in rehearsal and getting them printed in this magazine which had an enormous circulation. Would I object?

Mr. Kramer had opened the portfolio to show me samples of his Art. They were unexpectedly good. In spite of my distrust of him as a man, I saw no reason to object to something which would give us such obviously useful publicity. I said it would be okay by me.

Mr. Kramer beamed. "That is very kind of you, Mr. Duluth. Believe it or not, I hadn't the slightest idea my nephew was in New York until I happened to run him to earth yesterday. Guess he's too high and mighty these days to bother with his old uncle." He laughed heartily. "But I read the play in bed last night and I'm amazed Henry could have turned out something so slick. There are fine photographic possibilities there, too. I'm particularly keen to shoot the scene in the first act where they put old Comstock in the coffin."

That seemed rather to force the issue. I looked at Iris; I looked at Lenz; finally I looked at Henry and said: "Then you haven't heard about Comstock? He died last night—a heart attack."

Henry's mouth opened; he pushed anxiously at his drooping black hair. "A heart attack, Mr. Duluth!" He paused. "How—I mean after what happened last night, what Miss Ffoulkes told us, there wasn't anything back of it, anything that scared him, was there?"

The new theatrical life was bewildering enough for poor Henry without his having to hear about the malicious influence that seemed to be attacking his play. I thought I'd better produce something non-committal and reassuring to tell him.

"Comstock just went back stage and found a broken mirror," I said. "He was superstitious and it upset him. His heart went on the blink. That's all."

It wasn't a convincing story but it seemed to satisfy Henry. The young playwright gave a sigh of relief and patted at his forehead with a handkerchief.

Uncle George, however, seemed unnecessarily curious. He said: "Who broke the mirror?"

I made some vague remark about not actually knowing. Then, to my complete surprise, Kramer announced: "If a mirror was broken in that theater last night, I'd have a pretty good hunch who broke it." He turned to his nephew. "Wouldn't you, Henry?"

I hadn't expected deduction from Uncle George. Neither, apparently, had Henry.

"I don't understand," he said. "Who do you mean?"

"Wessler, of course." George Kramer's punched beady eyes settled on me. "Didn't you know about how Wessler's always breaking mirrors?"

I said I didn't. But he'd gotten me curious.

"I heard about it all through a friend of mine, a fellow who worked as nurse to Wessler at the Thespian Hospital when he and his half-brother were recovering from that airplane accident." Uncle George waved an arm with the airy gesture of a born raconteur. "Of course, they kept it pretty secret but I'm in well with that place. I've done some photographic work for their laboratories. Even got my nephew a job there once." He gave an avuncular laugh. "That's how I was let in on the story."

Henry shuffled his feet as if he was afraid his uncle was boring us. But Lenz showed sudden interest. He leaned across the remains of the scrambled eggs and said: "Perhaps you'd be good enough to tell us what you know, Mr. Kramer."

"Surely." Kramer crossed pudgy hands over a neatly vested paunch. "You know that airplane accident smashed up Wessler's half-brother. He got hit on the head and he's more or less permanently nuts, they tell me. Well, it seems it did something to Wessler's eyesight, too. When they got them both to the hospital at first, he couldn't see at all and they figured he'd be blind for some time. But his vision came back before they expected—one day when he was alone in his private room. This friend of mine told me Wessler had always been stuck on his looks; he'd been called the most handsome man in Austria and everything. Well, when he found he could see again, the first thing he thought about was his face. He was scared to hell something might have happened to disfigure him. They hadn't told him, you see, just how bad the damage was."

Mr. Kramer obviously sensed that he had aroused our interest. Obviously, too, he enjoyed being the center of attention. "Yes, Wessler got out of bed, took all the bandages off and went to the mirror. This happened, of course, before the plastic surgery operations. You can imagine how he felt when he saw himself in the glass—all burnt and lacerated. When he was still blind, I'd been called in to take some photographs of the injuries for the plastic surgery people and I can tell you just what a terrible sight he was. No wonder he went crazy for a while. This pal of mine who was nursing him at the time went in and found him hitting at the mirror with his bare fists. He smashed it and he smashed every other glass he could lay his hands on while he stayed at the hospital."

Kramer smiled knowingly. "He was hard to handle after that. He found out about the photographs I'd taken and he made me destroy every darn copy and negatives, too. For days afterwards he lay there in his room with the shades drawn—in the dark. He couldn't even stand the idea of his face being seen. And he wouldn't ever let my friend nurse him again—in spite of the fact that he was the only person in the hospital who could speak German. He was switched to taking care of Von Brandt. He never saw Wessler again. That's why I said it was pretty obvious who broke that mirror at the Dagonet."

In spite of Kramer's unpleasantly gloating narrative style there was something tragic about that story. I'd never realized Wessler

65

had been submitted to that cruel shock. It explained so much. It explained why he had refused the second star dressing-room at the Dagonet because the mirror didn't suit him. It explained that touching little speech about mirrors he had delivered on the stage last night.

And it brought out something far more alarming. It showed how utterly defenseless my Austrian star would be if anyone got it into his head to frighten him—through mirrors.

George Kramer was still holding the floor. "My nephew tells me there were some pretty funny things going on at the Dagonet last night," he was saying. "Of course, it's none of my business, but if I was Mr. Duluth, I'd keep my eye very closely on Wessler."

"You are not suggesting," put in Lenz curiously, "that Mr. Wessler is liable to do anything—abnormal?"

"I'm not suggesting anything." Kramer threw out plump hands in a gesture that vulgarly caricatured one of Lenz's favorite mannerisms. "I've done a lot of stage photography, true. I've even acted in my time, but I'm not a producer like Mr. Duluth. Even so, I can tell you this If I was running a show, I wouldn't touch Wessler. He may be a fine actor, but he's just about ready to go off the deep end any minute, the way his half-brother did, believe you me." The beady eyes turned back to me. "Are you running an understudy for him, Mr. Duluth?"

I was beginning to resent Mr. Kramer. "No," I said shortly. "He refuses to have anyone understudy him except Von Brandt, his half-brother, and he's completely out of the running. I'm depending entirely on Wessler."

"Do you think you're wise?" Kramer's pink face loomed at me above the coffee percolator. "Of course, I know suggestions aren't well taken from outsiders. But I am Henry's uncle and I'm interested to see the boy gets a fair break with his first play. Why don't you line up someone else for that part—just in case? It's too late now I guess to make a real change. But I can tell you someone who'd play that part swell. He's free at the moment and I happen to know he'd jump at being a sort of unofficial under-study."

66

"Whom do you mean?" I asked.

George Kramer tapped a cigarette against a fat thumb. "Roland Gates," he said.

Until then I hadn't really thought of Uncle George as sinister. He'd just seemed an over-fed, inquisitive busybody. But now that round face with its little mustache seemed charged with sudden malignance. Perhaps it was the shock of discovering him as an associate of Roland Gates, Mirabelle's ex-husband; perhaps it was a stray recollection of the way both Mirabelle and Wessler had stared at him last night on the stage—as if they had been afraid. But for some reason I had the crazy sensation that he knew much more than he had a right to know and that he was making some obscure threat.

I had to say something. "I'm perfectly satisfied with Wessler. And it's absolutely preposterous to consider Gates."

"You mean because of Miss Rue just having divorced him?" Kramer wagged his head sagely. "Oh, I don't think Miss Rue would object. When she and Mr. Gates were playing together I did a lot of work for them and I flatter myself that I knew Miss Rue quite well. She's an artiste—an artiste to the bone. If we could get her to see that Gates would be right in that part, she'd never let anything personal stand in the way."

My only impulse at that moment was to kick Mr. Kramer out of the apartment on the point of my toe. He seemed to get the vague impression that he wasn't going over so well for he changed the subject abruptly. He said, with an odd glance at Henry: "While we're on the subject of changes in your cast, Mr. Duluth, I guess you'll have to be looking around for another actor to fill Comstock's place. I don't want to push myself but, as I said, I've done a bit of acting in my time. I'd be highly honored if you could give me a chance to take over—just to be in my nephew's play."

I thought that was about the goddamndest nerve I'd ever run up against. But once again I was stalled from speaking my mind. While Henry and I were staring at Kramer with a sort of apoplectic awe, Dr. Lenz took command of the situation.

Very firmly, in a tone of voice I had learned to respect, he said: "I'm sure Mr. Duluth would be more than glad to give you a trial in the part, Mr. Kramer. He was just telling me, the moment before you arrived, that he would very much like to get a man of your type to play that particular role."

That, of course, was the most arrant of lies, and if anyone in the whole length of Manhattan but Lenz had said it, I would have sprung into battle. But I knew Lenz; I knew he had a very good reason for whatever he was doing; I suspected also that his reason was somehow connected with the miserable affair of the Dagonet. Therefore, although the words blistered my tongue, I said I would be extremely pleased to have Kramer take over Comstock's role. I told him to come around to rehearsal that morning at eleven-thirty.

I did add, however: "I suppose you know you'll have to spend quite a few minutes shut up in a coffin?"

George Kramer was grinning as if his very best dreams had come true. "That doesn't bother me, Mr. Duluth. We'll all have to put in a long stretch in a coffin sooner or later. Might as well get used to it now."

That was a joke. None of us were polite enough to smile—not even Henry who seemed as distraught by this sudden turn of events as I was myself.

To my extreme relief, they left then. I went with them to the door. While Kramer tilted the derby hat onto the back of his head and strolled jauntily toward the elevator, Henry hovered behind. He was twisting a limp black forelock with nervous fingers.

"I hate to bring this up, Mr. Duluth," he stammered. "But living in New York's turned out to be a lot more expensive than living at home. The five-hundred-dollar option you let me have is gone. I was wondering whether you could advance me another five hundred on royalties."

"Sure," I said. I was mildly surprised that the parsimonious Henry should run through five hundred dollars in less than two months, but I was used to impoverished authors. I scribbled a

68

check in the living-room and brought it out to him. After all, I was anticipating breaking box-office history. A five-hundred advance to Henry seemed like a pretty safe bet.

He took the check with a sudden, rather attractive smile. "Thank you, Mr. Duluth. You—you don't know what this means to me."

As he spoke, I happened to glance at Kramer. He had strolled back and was standing quite close to us, whistling softly through his teeth. There was a peculiar smile on his lips and he was staring straight in our direction.

It gave me suddenly and furiously to think when I realized that he was not looking at me. He wasn't looking at Henry, either. Those smug, piggy eyes were fixed greedily on the check in his nephew's hand.

Chapter Eight

I WAS SURE THEN that Henry Prince himself was not going to get one cent of that five-hundred dollar check, that it was Uncle George who had wanted the money and had somehow forced the boy into borrowing it from me. The more I saw of Mr. Kramer, the more sinister he became and the more emphatic became my indignation at Lenz for injecting him into my company.

I found the doctor sitting placidly in the living-room, lost behind the *New York Times*. I went into a tirade. I told him what had just happened about Henry and the check. I told him how Mirabelle had reacted to Kramer last night. I pointed out that he was an associate of the man I feared more than anyone on Broadway—Roland Gates. It wouldn't have been possible to choose a worse person to add to the company, particularly now when we were all pretty jittery anyway.

Dr. Lenz laid the *New York Times* on his large knees and smiled at me benignly. "I agree with every word you have said," he remarked. "Mr. Kramer struck me as an extremely unpleasant type of person. It also occurred to me that he is more than likely to have been connected with the disturbances which took place last night at the Dagonet."

I stared. I said: "Then why the hell . . . ?"

Dr. Lenz brushed the sentence away uncompleted. "You have every right to know my motives for urging you to cultivate Mr. Kramer. In medicine we frequently administer what is known as a provocative dose. When we believe a patient to be suffering from a certain disease and yet have no means of verifying our diagnosis, we inject into his system a certain drug which we know will aggravate the symptoms of the disease in question, should the disease be actually present. Adapt that to our own problem.

We believe that there is something vitally wrong at the Dagonet. We know that certain members of your company have reacted abnormally to Mr. Kramer. By putting them into close and constant contact with him, we may be able to force a crisis—provided Mr. Kramer does have some connection with the disturbances. Should his presence at the Dagonet bring about violent reactions, we shall have a far greater chance of putting our finger on the focus of infection. If, on the other hand, he is accepted without friction, at least we shall be able to eliminate him as an irritant factor."

He produced his spectacles and pointed them at me. "Perhaps you understand now, Mr. Duluth. Mr. Kramer is to be our provocative dose."

That, of course, was satanically ingenious. But I wasn't entirely sold. There was danger for the play.

"It's like giving somebody strychnine," I said, "to find out whether he'll die."

At that moment the telephone shrilled. It was answered by Iris who had been lurking in the kitchen, pretending she hadn't been listening to Lenz's conversation. She kept the receiver to her ear for a few moments and then passed it to me.

"Wessler," she said. "And ready to explode."

She was right. My Austrian star was calling from his apartment He was fighting mad. He had just returned from the Dagonet where he'd gone to get his hat and cloak which he had left there the night before. The one thing I'd hoped wouldn't happen had happened. He'd got to his dressing-room before Eddie had been able to repair the damage. He had found the crushed statuette and the cracked mirror.

"Who is thees who come into my room, spoils my dolls and the mirror break?" he asked with an indignation which did odd things to his English. I could visualize him at the other end of the wire, a heroic bearded figure towering over the telephone. "That dressing-room I take special because the mirror suits. Now she is broke."

I tried to calm him down, but all the time I was thinking how

Kramer must have been wrong on one point, at least. Wessler didn't break that mirror himself.

"It was just an accident," I concluded feebly.

"Accident?" He tossed the word back to me. "You need not tell me an accident. Because I know. They do it, I know. They crush my leetle doll; they take my clay too. Yesterday the clay from which I the dolls make it was in the dressing-room left. Now it is gone and special from Wien I have it sent. They steal that too."

I knew exactly who Wessler meant by "they." He was too much of a gentleman to accuse Mirabelle and Gerald outright, but he, like Theo, thought they were back of it. I struggled to think of something soothing to say. I hadn't the slightest idea who could have stolen his modelling clay. Finally I promised to have Eddie Troth look into the matter.

"Thank you." Wessler's voice was cold, unappeased. Then, suddenly, it changed; it lost all its aggressiveness. He sounded like a frightened little boy. "What then is *mit dem Dagonet Theater los?* Why must it always with mirrors be?"

That was a question I wished I could answer.

I was just about to wheedle him off the wire when Dr. Lenz rose from his seat and took the receiver away from me. For the next five minutes he was pouring grave German polysyllables into the mouthpiece. My German was extremely rusty. I had not the slightest idea what he was talking about.

Finally Lenz abandoned the telephone. "Mr. Duluth, I have promised Herr Wessler to go around to his apartment before the rehearsal. Will you accompany me?"

I was due at my office for a conference with my publicity agent but I decided to let publicity go hang. This was a crisis.

Lenz explained what I had never thought to ask him, that his main object in coming to New York last night had been to discuss with Wessler the condition of his half-brother, Wolfgang von Brandt. Although I had known nothing about it, Lenz had obtained Wessler's permission to have Von Brandt transferred from the Thespian Hospital to his own private sanitorium.

It had been at my request that Lenz had interested himself in

72

Wolfgang von Brandt and I was glad to hear he was following it up. The doctors at the Thespian Hospital had more or less given up hope of restoring Wessler's half-brother to sanity, but I'd had a hunch that Lenz, if anyone, might be able to help him.

The story of Wessler and Von Brandt was one of the most tragic in the history of the stage. For years they had been the leading figures in the Viennese theater. Wessler, of course, had been universally accepted as Austria's most celebrated actor. Von Brandt had been business manager, secretary, understudy and general factotum to the Great Wessler. He had even written several vehicles for him. The two of them had been inseparable, a twentieth-century Castor and Pollux.

Some people claimed that Von Brandt had always wanted to act, that he had as much genius as his brother. They said that Wessler had deliberately held him back, had dominated him by the force of his own aggressive personality. I didn't know about that. I only knew what the world knew, that Wessler had been ready to give up his entire career for Von Brandt's sake.

On that most notorious day in current history when Hitler decided to give himself Austria for a birthday present, Wessler had been playing to enormous business in one of his brother's shows in Vienna. Overnight, when ardent Nazis were springing up like toadstools and Hitler was wondering if he dared drive across the border, an hysterical wave of anti-Semitism surged through the Theater and the news spread like wildfire that Von Brandt's father had been a Jew.

He was through, just like that. He was hounded out of the theater by people who, a few hours before, had been applauding his dialogue. His home was despoiled; he was just one of a hundred thousand refugees.

If Wessler had wanted to, he could have denied his half-brother and retained his enormous prestige. He could probably have received a crown of bay leaves from Der Fuehrer himself, for his own heredity was more Nordic than the dramatis personae of *Die Walküre*. But Wessler wasn't that sort of man. In one of the last broadcasts before the radio was stifled, he told millions of listeners-in exactly what he thought of the rape of Austria and what it would mean to the theater, art and culture generally. He then smuggled his brother across the border into Switzerland. The two of them had come triumphantly to the States only to meet with the tragic airplane accident.

That had been some time ago and every bulletin from the Thespian Hospital on Von Brandt's condition had been bad. It had been a shattering blow to Wessler. That was why, apart from anything else, I was so desperately hopeful that Lenz might be able to help.

As a taxi threaded us through the tangled cross-town traffic toward the Austrian's hotel, I ventured to ask Lenz if he had an opinion on Von Brandt's chances.

Lenz smiled his serene, Godlike smile. "It is still early, Mr. Duluth, but I am not unhopeful. It is an extremely interesting case and I have a feeling that the trouble is possibly far more psychological than it is pathological. If I am right and if my proposed treatment brings results, Herr Von Brandt may well be a cured man in the fairly near future."

That was the best news I had heard in a long time.

"You know, of course, Mr. Duluth, that Von Brandt's chief delusion lies in the fact that he has lost his own identity and believes himself to be his own brother. The intimacy between the two of them and the circumstances of their removal from Austria makes such a confusion of identities perfectly understandable. At the moment I am fostering his belief that he is in fact the Great Wessler. He is even learning Wessler's role in *Troubled Waters*. He finds the English difficult and it is a good mental exercise."

That didn't make sense to me. But it wasn't meant to. It was Lenz's pigeon.

The taxi eased to the curb outside Wessler's old-fashioned hotel and the elevator took us up to his suite where an Austrian valet let us into a large living-room whose ponderous luxury was reminiscent of the days before the gilt had been knocked off the

74

gingerbread of interior decoration. Wessler was sitting at a table, wearing horn-rimmed spectacles and working with nervous concentration on a new clay statuette.

As soon as he saw us, he fumbled the spectacles hastily into his pocket and moved to join us, his beard and his striking shock of blond hair gleaming in the light from the window.

He gripped Dr. Lenz's hand. I shall never forget that titanic moment when beard met beard. It was like Jupiter and Wotan getting together at some celestial convention.

Apart from their brief encounter at the Dagonet, they had never met before. Wessler was peering into Lenz's face.

"I am right, yes," he said excitedly. "Last night I feel I have seen you before. Now I remember. On the train to Salzburg in 1935. We share the same compartment."

I had meant to warn Lenz of Wessler's extraordinary memory for faces. But it wasn't necessary. He took that remark in his stride.

"Indeed, my friend. I remember it well. You were good enough to recommend to me the excellent cuisine at the Patzenhof. But at that time I did not realize I was traveling with the great Wessler. You were, I believe, employing another name?"

Wessler seemed a trifle taken aback to find himself confronted with a memory that rivaled his own. Then he beamed: "*Jah!* Always I use incognito when I journeys make. When one is well-known to the peoples it can be tiresome with the autographs. But tell me of my beloved Wolfgang. He is with you. You make him again in the head well, yes? Those doctors who say he is always to be sick. Fools! And I see him soon. You let me, yes?"

"I do not think it would be wise at the moment," said Lenz gravely. "But later—perhaps."

"You tell me all, no?" Wessler pulled him across the room to a Recamier couch where they sat very close together, shaking their beards at each other and talking in rapid, enthusiastic German.

In a chair discreetly apart, I glanced around that long, overstuffed room. I had been there several times before and it suddenly dawned on me that something was different—something

75

seemed to be missing. I couldn't pin it down until I noticed that the two side walls were bare. In the center of each was a large square patch where the brocade wall-paper was several shades less faded. I remembered then.

When I had been there last, a couple of days previously, there had been two full-length mirrors hanging over those patches. Wessler had had them both removed.

It was only too pathetically clear that he'd gotten rid of them on account of what had happened the night before at the Dagonet.

To some people, that might have seemed ludicrous—a man of Wessler's stature getting so scared of mirrors that he couldn't endure having one in his apartment. But I understood. For a long time after the conflagration which killed my wife, I'd been the same way about fire. Even now, occasionally, the very thought of flames could get me in a cold sweat. I knew how it was having to fight against a blind, irrational phobia like that.

And it started me worrying about the Dagonet all over again.

The German duologue was still going full steam when the buzzer rang and the valet let in Gerald Gwynne. My juvenile was looking very young and blasé in a deliberately clumsy tweed suit which some expensive tailor had built around his personality and his Pennsylvania Dutch side-whiskers. If there'd been any women along, he would have brought out their worst instincts.

He grinned at me, gave Wessler an ironical Nazi salue and I introduced him to Lenz.

"A remarkably hirsute bunch, Peter," he murmured. "You ought to grow Dundrearies and be in the swim."

Wessler was staring suspiciously. "What is it you wish?"

"I've come to retrieve Mirabelle's brandy." Gerald's long lashes drooped with a diffidence which was slightly derisive. "She was tactless enough to leave it here when she came home with you last night. Knowing that you look upon liquor as a snare of the Devil, she sent me around to remove the temptation."

Wessler's lips tightened but he didn't say anything.

"And to make amends," continued Gerald, "for having left you exposed to the Devil all night, Mirabelle wants me to tell you that she renounces all claim to the first stage dressing-room. From now on it is officially yours. And she hopes that the mirror will continue to suit you."

Behind the thin veil of flippancy, Gerald's manner was unnecessarily insulting, and his reference to the mirror had most unfortunate undertones. I waited uneasily for the sparks to fly.

They flew.

Wessler rose to his full interminable height. "So Miss Rue hopes the mirror suit me, yes? After what she had done, she sends her— her . . . she sends you to insult me with impertinences?"

"Not to insult you with impertinences—just to retrieve her brandy."

"Brandy!" Wessler's eyes paled to a light, dangerous gray. "Perhaps you say this to Miss Rue and her brandy. She is an actress—yes. A good actress. Were that not so, I would never permit her to play in the same theater with me. In Austria decent peoples have a name for such a woman as this who all the time liquor drinks, who keeps company with boys young enough to be her . . ."

"I'd stop that sentence just where it is if I were you." Gerald had flushed a deep crimson.

For a moment I thought someone simply had to sock someone. Then Gerald said stiffly: "If you'd tell me where to find Mirabelle's brandy, I will stop darkening your door."

Wessler stood absolutely still. "I see no bottle of brandy here."

"Mirabelle left it in the hall last night."

"I see no brandy."

"But perhaps you see a hall?"

Wessler jerked his head toward the door. Gerald disappeared. In a few moments he was back, holding a bottle in his hands.

He was smiling. "As you observe, you did have the brandy. Thanks. And I'll make a point of delivering your message to Mirabelle. I think it should amuse her."

As he moved to the door, I noticed a rather curious thing. The bottle which he had in his hand was more than half full. Last

77

night when Comstock had died, when I had asked Mirabelle for some brandy, she had told me the bottle was empty.

"Is that the brandy Mirabelle had at the Dagonet last night, Gerald?" I asked.

"Yes." The boy's smokey eyes were suddenly on guard. "Why?"

"Oh, nothing," I said.

Gerald stared at me a moment longer, then with a vague smile at Lenz he left.

I don't know why, but that whole brandy situation was beginning to worry me. I was worried at the bottle's ability to empty and fill itself mechanically. I was also worried that Gerald should have been sent all the way cross-town to collect it. But then, I was worried about the whole set-up. The three-way Wessler-Mirabelle-Gerald feud seemed to be getting out of control. I'd known motiveless feuds in the theater before and I'd seen just how much havoc they could play with a show.

I seemed to be getting more than my share of havoc.

Wessler and Lenz talked for a while longer, but Wessler's thoughts were obviously straying. He looked glum and exhausted as if his dog fight with Gerald had taken an awful lot out of him. He was still brooding when we left.

As soon as we were out in the street, I asked anxiously:

"Well, what do you think of Wessler? I mean, what kind of shape d'you think he's in?"

Lenz smiled, a brief comforting smile. "I would say he is as sane and healthy as any man I know," he said. "If I were his physician there is only one thing that would give me cause to worry."

"You mean his mirror phobia?"

"You may perhaps know, Mr Duluth, that I have a strong aversion to psychiatric catch-phrases. I believe that all so-called phobias have a pathological explanation, especially when the subject is as sane as Herr Wessler."

I tried to look intelligent.

"You have doubtless noticed how he peers into every face; how he is eager to recognize a person that he may have seen before."

I nodded.

"You may also have noticed his spectacles and how quickly he put them away when we arrived. That, coupled with his dislike of mirrors . . ."

"Proves he's going nuts like his half-brother?" I threw in nervously.

"It proves nothing of the sort." Dr. Lenz's voice was severe. "It proves one thing only. Mr. Wessler is far more short-sighted than he would have us believe. He is worried about it. That is why he is so anxious to assure himself—and incidentally others—that his sight is as good as his memory. And that is why he could be very easily upset if anything he saw—in a mirror for example—was different from what he expected to see."

As he spoke Dr. Lenz waved an unexpectedly frivolous pair of wool mittens at a passing taxi.

"Where are we going now?" I asked.

"With your permission I would like to visit the Dagonet before the rehearsal." Lenz drew the mittens over his fingers. There was a strangely forbidding gleam in his eye. "In the light of what we have learnt this morning, it seems clear to me now what must have happened last night in that dressing-room to cause Mr. Comstock's death."

While I was still gawping, he opened the door of the taxi and bowed.

"After you, Mr. Duluth."

Chapter Nine

As the taxi took us to the Dagonet Dr. Lenz sat very erect in his seat, large hands on knees, gray eyes fixed with apparent interest on the meter. After a duly dramatic interval he asked: "Perhaps you would be good enough to refresh my memory on exactly what you and Miss Pattison noticed in the way of tangible disturbances last night when you searched backstage."

I ran through the tangible disturbances, the broken mirror and the crushed statuette we had found in Wessler's dressing-room, and the shattered panel of glass in the passage.

Dr. Lenz nodded as if extremely satisfied. "And this morning Herr Wessler reported the loss of his modeling clay."

He seemed even more satisfied by the lost modeling clay. I was completely at sea.

And the sight of the Dagonet itself wasn't particularly a sedative. By daylight it contrived to look even more evil that it had at night. Several fat pigeons were perched on the bosoms of the caryatids. They were cocking their heads and peering down at the traffic. They annoyed me intensely. And weren't they omens of disaster? Or was I getting my birds mixed?

I pushed open the forbidding iron grille for Lenz and preceded him down the cavernous alley to the stage door and past the doorman's room where Mac was stooped over his table with the Siamese cat squatting at his side.

I'd forgotten that damn cat and the ominous label which I had removed from its neck and which was still lying crumpled up in my pocket. After a moment's thought, I decided that the cat qualified as a tangible disturbance. I told Lenz about it and showed him the label.

That seemed to faze him as if it did not fit to some pattern he was arranging in his mind. He paused in his majestic ascent of the stone stairs, a furrow wrinkling his forehead.

"I can only suppose," he said very gravely, "that this was another manifestation of the malicious influence which I cannot but believe is at work against your production."

Which wasn't a very exhilarating remark.

When we reached stage level, I saw at once that Eddie Troth had already started one of his regular fixing-up jobs. The fragments of the glass panel which had been broken the night before were swept into a neat pile in a corner and a new panel was propped against the wall, ready to be inserted in the door.

Lenz seemed interested in the pile of fragments. He stooped over them, examining them. At last he picked one up with extreme caution. He was considering it when my stage manager swung down the passage toward us, grinning one of those healthy prairie grins which take up so much footage in Wild West movies.

He nodded at Lenz. "Been down under the stage setting traps, Mr. Duluth," he said cheerfully. "Seems the rats are mostly concentrated down there. With any luck, I'll clean the place up in a couple of days and save you the expense of having this old barn fumigated."

He made no references to the events of the night before, for which I was intensely grateful. He started whistling and fiddling with the new panel just as if he was any stage manager in any theater.

Lenz glanced up from the splinter of glass in his hand and said suddenly: "Mr. Troth, would you be good enough to loan me that panel for a few moments?"

Eddie looked surprised but murmured "Sure," and handed him the sheet of glass.

"Thank you." Lenz turned to me. "Now, Mr. Duluth, perhaps you would take me to Herr Wessler's dressing-room."

I moved down the passage followed by Lenz, the new panel and the broken fragment of glass.

We reached the dressing-room and I shut the door behind us. Although Eddie had been too late to keep Wessler from discovering the broken mirror, he had, by some miracle of fixing, now acquired a new glass which hung over the dressing-table. In the far corner, the large wardrobe exhibited its own full length mirror. There was something rather sinister about that wardrobe. It was old enough and dreary enough to be the actual closet in which Lillian Reed had disposed of herself back in 1902.

Lenz was pottering around, opening the door of the wardrobe, gazing inside, closing the door and turning to the mirror above the dressing-table. He looked like a magician on the verge of producing a bowl of goldfish from behind his left ear.

Eventually he paused in front of me, holding up the panel of glass between us. "Mr. Duluth, I want, with your assistance, to make a little experiment. I am going to ask you to leave this room and to enter it again when I call. I want you to think of yourself as an actor coming back to his dressing-room after rehearsal—an actor who has imperfect vision and who has reason to fear mirrors." From his pocket he produced his horn-rimmed spectacles. "I am a trifle far sighted, Mr. Duluth. If you wear my spectacles, it should help with the illusion."

I took the spectacles, completely docile.

"One thing more, Mr. Duluth." Lenz crossed to the dressing-table, picked up a stick of red grease paint and drew with it two bold lines across the new glass. "I want you to imagine this mirror to be cracked, as it was last night. With that assumption in mind, I want you to act exactly as you would imagine this hypothetical individual to act." He paused, adding gravely, "And, please do not be alarmed at anything you may see."

A slight gesture of the hand dismissed me out into the passage. I shut the door. Eddie Troth was still loitering around. Feeling distinctly foolish, I put on Lenz's spectacles which instantly blurred my vision into a weird, uncomfortable kaleidoscope. I waited until I heard Lenz's voice from the dressing-room call: "Mr. Duluth."

That was my cue. I groped toward the door and pushed it open.

The first thing I noticed was that Dr. Lenz had disappeared. That drab, musty room seemed empty. I paused on the threshold, trying to throw myself into the role Lenz had asked me to play.

An actor coming back from rehearsal—his first instinctive movement would be toward the dressing-table. I went to the dressing-table. In front of me, swimming out of focus, was the new mirror scrawled with Lenz's grease paint which was intended to give the impression of cracks. As I peered, my own reflection peered back at me, grotesquely distorted like the reflection in the side of a convex silver coffee pot. It was worse than what I used to see in the glass in my hang-over days.

Once again I tried to assume a superstitious actor's reaction. He would have recoiled from the broken mirror and turned to the other one in the wardrobe. I crossed to the wardrobe and gazed through Lenz's spectacles into the full-length mirror inset in its door.

I had, of course, expected to see my own reflection again, cock-eyed as it had been before. But, instead of the familiar face of Peter Duluth staring back at me, I saw something quite different —another face which couldn't possibly have been mine, a strange, inhuman face, something out of an attack of D.T.s, peering balefully from unblinking gray eyes.

For a second I was right off my guard. I felt as if the whole world had gone nuts. At the best of times a disembodied face on the wrong side of a mirror is not an attractive thing to meet up with.

I tugged off the spectacles and the spell was broken.

I saw at once that the closet door with its inset mirror was open, pushed back flat against the side wall, and that I was looking not into a mirror but straight at Dr. Lenz who was standing inside the wardrobe, holding the panel of plain glass in front of him. His hands, keeping the glass in place, were concealed behind the woodwork of the door frame. The illusion of a mirror was most convincing.

It was a trick, of course, which could have worked only on someone with bad eyesight or someone in a thoroughly nervous state of mind—but under those circumstances it would have worked like hell.

Lenz was stepping out of the closet now. He propped the pane of glass against the wall.

"A childish ruse, Duluth, but I think it would have had a profoundly alarming effect upon Herr Wessler with his poor eyesight and his fear of mirrors."

"Wessler!" I had more or less guessed he'd been working around to that. "Then you think Theo had the right idea, that it was meant for Wessler and Comstock barged into it by mistake?"

Dr. Lenz nodded. "As Miss Ffoulkes pointed out, no one could possibly have guessed that Mr. Comstock would come into this room. It is far more likely that Herr Wessler was the intended victim." He added sternly: "But while Miss Ffoulkes seems to consider it some harmless, practical joke, devised by Miss Rue, I am compelled to believe that last night's disturbance was caused by someone with a very strong, malicious desire to demoralize Herr Wessler."

That sounded bad.

He continued: "My reasoning, of course, is purely hypothetical but it fits with all the facts in our possession. I would like to explain to you what I believe to have happened here last night."

I didn't want to hear. I had an overwhelmingly ostrich impulse to bury my head in the nearest sand and pretend that everything was daisy. But there was nothing I could do.

"I believe, Mr. Duluth, that last night while the rehearsal was in progress on stage, someone came into this room with Mr. Troth's sheet of glass. That person broke the mirror above the dressing-table. I can suggest a reason for his doing that. By breaking the mirror, he would not only have created the atmosphere of superstition and fear he required, he would also have insured the fact that Herr Wessler would turn to the wardrobe and be confronted by the false mirror and the pre-arranged tableau just as you did. This individual then stepped into the wardrobe and employed the sheet of glass in the manner I have indicated. We must assume also that he distorted or disguised his face in some manner so that the manufactured reflection would seem macabre, supernatural." He gave a dry smile. "I also endeavoured to contort my face when I was recreating the illusion for you, Mr. Duluth."

"You did a swell job," I said bleakly.

Lenz acknowledged this compliment with a slight bow. "But last night it would have been far easier to create a ghostly illusion. You tell me Herr Wessler's black cloak was hanging in this wardrobe. With that draped around him, this individual could have made it appear as if his face were detached from a body, floating, as it were, in a void." He turned to the dressing-table and picked up the fragment of glass he had selected from the pile in the passage. "I want you to look at this, Mr. Duluth. Do you notice anything unusual about it—"

I looked. Smudged over one corner of the fragment was a sort of grayish substance that looked like clay.

"Wessler's modeling clay!" I said with an unexpected flash of insight.

"Exactly! How effective to have used the modeling clay to build up an alarming mask; how reasonable that a particle of it should adhere to the glass." Dr. Lenz stroked his beard. "That, Mr. Duluth, is what I imagine to have been the set-up in this dressing room last night. It does not go against the evidence."

It didn't. "But it would have been damn risky," I objected. "All Wessler had to do was to investigate and the person would be caught."

"Certainly there would have been considerable risk, Mr. Duluth. But the fact itself implies that this individual must have been clever enough to realize that a face in the glass was the one thing Herr Wessler would never investigate. One glimpse would have been enough to have sent him hurrying in terror from the room, leaving the way open for escape."

He paused. "Of course, when Mr. Comstock blundered into the trap, everything must have been thrown out of gear. I think we can visualize the actual sequence of events. Mr. Comstock, his mind full of memories of the girl Lillian Reed, came to this dressing-room, presumably from an impulse to visit once more the scene of her suicide. Miss Ffoulkes' account of what she saw upstairs had been a great shock to him. He was in an abnormally keyed-up condition. He moved to the dressing-table, and was confronted with the cracked mirror. That in itself would have come as a shock to any superstitious actor. Assume that he threw out a hand for support . . ." He broke off, adding: "Herr Wessler probably left the figurine of Miss Rue on the dressing-table, didn't he?"

I saw then. "You mean Comstock might have grabbed the statuette by the neck?"

"That would seem to explain the condition of the little figure," agreed Lenz placidly. "Imagine Mr. Comstock staring at the thing in his hand, the figure of a woman, her head lolling to one side. That would have added to the cumulative effect of horror. Then, just as you did, he turned to the mirror in the wardrobe. He saw the tableau which had been staged for Wessler." He shrugged. "The face, distorted by the clay, would have seemed to him the face of someone long dead. Naturally he would have connected it with Lilian Reed."

This hypothesis, coming from anyone but Lenz, might have seemed fantastic. But Lenz contrived to make it sound as practical and foolproof as an algebraic equation.

"Let us, for a moment, Mr. Duluth, return to the individual in the closet. The wrong person had fallen into his trap. It was a most embarrassing situation. He must have started to move from the closet with the intention of revealing himself and possibly of explaining the whole affair away as some innocent prank."

I whistled. "So that was why Comstock said it came *out* at him—out of the mirror. He thought he was seeing the ghost of Lillian Reed actually stepping through the glass."

"That is my belief." Lenz had all the answers. "Overcome with the panic which was precipitating his fatal heart attack Mr. Comstock dropped the statuette at the foot of the wardrobe and dashed from the room. It is easy to guess what followed. Fearing Mr. Comstock would insist on an immediate investigation, the individual in the closet must have run from the room and attempted to replace the sheet of glass in the passage, inadvertently dropping and smashing it. As it happened, we were all so concerned with Mr. Comstock's collapse that, although we heard the tinkle of breaking glass, we did not follow it up and he was able to make his escape."

By now Lenz seemed to have everything matter-of-factly buttoned up. Then I remembered something. "But how about Lillian Reed's first appearance? What the hell was it Theo Ffoulkes saw upstairs?"

Lenz smiled. "As a man of the theater, Mr. Duluth, you know surely that a dramatic performance often requires a rehearsal."

"You think Theo broke in on a rehearsal?"

"It is possible, Mr. Duluth. It is also possible that it was a prologue, a curtain-raiser, as it were, to put you all into the right frame of mind with regard to the Lillian Reed legend. For I am sure that the person responsible for this disturbance was familiar with that story and consciously exploited it. Does that not seem to be the only reasonable explanation of what occurred?"

It did. I said so and then asked dismally: "But who on earth could want to pull a trick like that on Wessler? Do you suppose it's your provocative dose, Mr. Kramer?"

"It may have been Mr. Kramer. It may have been anyone, including those members of your own company who were not on stage at the time. From Miss Ffoulkes's description it would seem that a woman, at least, was involved." Dr. Lenz looked with extreme concentration at his own thumbnail. "Were any of the ladies in the cast wearing a light tan fur last night?"

I made a rather jittery mental check-up—Theo, tweeds, no fur; Mirabelle, a chocolate-colored mink; Iris, Persian lamb.

"None of them," I said.

"In that case, we shall have to consider the possibility of an outsider, a woman whom we do not know, who managed to slip past the doorman."

As he stopped speaking the wardrobe door flapped shut with a dull click. It seemed the only sound in that whole dreary theater. My nerves, which had been all set to act up for some time, started off down the straight.

I said hopelessly: "Well, what do we do? Hand everything over to the police and call it a day?"

"Come, come, Mr. Duluth, there is no need to take so defeatist an attitude." Dr. Lenz's voice was light but it was a lightness I knew of old—the everything's-going-to-be-all-right tone which he used on the more refractory patients at his sanitorium. "After all, however unfortunate the circumstances, we have proved, have we not, that Mr. Comstock's death was the result of an accident. No malice was intended toward him *per se*. There is no real case for the police—as yet."

Once again, Dr. Lenz had qualified one of his professionally encouraging remarks with a very ominous—*as yet*.

"There are no entrances to this theater at the moment except through the stage door?"

"Not that I know of—not unless somebody has keys."

"In that case—" Dr. Lenz was very positive—"I suggest that you question the doorman to discover whether any unknown person could have come in through the stage door last night. Especially you should stress—"

"I know," I said gloomily. "A woman with a light tan fur."

For a few minutes we stood there in that stuffy dressing-room, staring at each other in silence. Then the door was thrown open and the lanky figure of Eddie Troth crossed the threshold.

'Finished with that pane of glass?" asked my stage-manager cheerfully. He looked at me and then at Lenz. "What the hell's been going on here?"

I glanced at Lenz. He shook his head.

"Oh, nothing, Eddie," I said. "Dr. Lenz has just been teaching me a conjuring trick. It'd be a riot on a party. It's all done with mirrors."

Chapter Ten

Having given his amazing reconstruction of last night's alarums and excursions, Lenz seemed to feel his responsibilities at an end. He produced his watch, claimed an immediate engagement with one of the other Four First Beards of Psychiatry and left me alone in the dressing-room with several thousand apprehensions and Eddie Troth.

But Eddie was a swell person for elbowing out apprehensions. He started talking about his traps as if rats were the only things in the world that mattered. He said he had bought the cage variety because the doorman, exhibiting unsuspected personality, had threatened to report him to the S.P.C.A. if he used the breaknecks or poison which might damage the Siamese cat.

"Don't like the cage trap so well," concluded Eddie, talking with the assurance of an expert, "but I didn't want to get in wrong with the doorman and I'm having swell results. They've only been set a couple of hours but I've caught a lot of those babies already."

He started to blush and shuffle like a nervous kid and finally plucked up courage to ask whether I wouldn't like to see the rats he'd caught. There was something engaging about a grown man being excited over rat catching. Although it was almost rehearsal time and I had my vital session with the doorman ahead of me. I said I'd go with him—just out of a general impulse of chumminess.

We went downstairs, turned left at Mac's alcove and pushed through a shabby pair of double doors which led beneath stage. I had never been there before. If possible, the Dagonet was even less pleasant below stage than it was anywhere else. There was a century-old smell of greasepaint and grime. The only light, seeping from grilles at street level, cast grudging illumination on

ancient packing cases, left by long-forgotten productions, molder-
ing bits of scenery and all the other flotsam of the theater.
Eddie's newly installed wind machine loomed in a corner. Every
now and then it gave a sort of faint groan as if someone were
dying in unspeakable agony.

With conscious pride, Eddie led me around that limbo of lost
plays, pointing out trap after trap, most of which were suitably
tenanted with a rat. It was really remarkable that he had caught
so many so quickly.

Presumably, after a few months in the Dagonet, even the
vermin got to feeling suicidal.

I asked if he wasn't going to drown them right away but he
said no, caught rats were like ducks, they acted as decoys.

"I'll have six in each trap by tomorrow."

"Maybe they'll escape," I suggested.

Eddie was shocked at such ignorance. He gave me a long
technical lecture on how it was impossible for rats to escape
from traps.

I took his word for it.

He grinned. "Sure, Mr. Duluth, I'm going to save you the
expense of fumigation."

It was rather touching, having him so determined to save Peter
Duluth, Inc. that particular outlay.

Once we were out of the cellar, I left Eddie and started down
the passage to the doorman's room. People were arriving for
rehearsal. Theo passed me with Wessler. She seemed tickled
pink and called out something about Lenz's codeine helping her
cough. Then Mirabelle and Gerald erupted together through the
stage door. Mirabelle looked white and angry. She didn't
acknowledge my greeting and I heard her mutter to Gerald:

"You can't do that to me and I'll be damned if I'll let you."

I wondered vaguely what new trouble was brewing.

When I entered the doorman's room, Mac was brooding over
his scrap-book. The Siamese cat saw me first and turned on me
two distinctly derisive blue eyes.

I did my best to ignore the feline gaze. But with one of those ill-timed feline impulses she leaped at me and clawed her way to my shoulder where she settled down to a steady session of purring.

That made Mac conscious of my presence. He looked up, his toothlessness showing in a senile smile. He said: "She's a fine girl, she is. Mr. Troth wanted to put arsenic down but I wasn't having any arsenic around where Lillian could get it. No, sir."

"Lillian?" I echoed. To me it seemed a little late in the day to protect the long-departed Lillian Reed from arsenical poisoning. Then I saw the doorman's admiring gaze was fixed on my shoulder. "My god," I said hollowly, "you mean you're calling the cat Lillian?"

"Why not?" asked Mac concisely.

It was a question with no obvious answer. I hastily changed the subject and, following Lenz's instructions, asked the doorman whether any outsiders could have gotten into the Dagonet last night.

Mac blinked. He said: "Well, there was that fellow Kramer. Seemed like a real nice guy to me. Not a bit stuck up. Looked at my scrap-book. Said it was the dandiest he'd ever seen. Fine fellow, that."

I might have known the doorman's taste in people would be as indifferent as his taste in pets. I said: "I don't mean Kramer. Was there anyone else?"

"There was that woman that came just after you and Miss Pattison," said the doorman somberly, "the woman I thought was Miss Rue. I'd never seen Miss Rue before, not in the flesh. She hadn't never acted at the Dagonet. And, since she was the only woman on Mr. Troth's list who hadn't come, I figured this woman was her, see?"

"No," I said. "You mean it wasn't Miss Rue?"

"No, it wasn't Miss Rue. She came much later on." He smiled a sentimental smile. "No mistaking Miss Rue when she came— just like a beautiful dream."

"But there's no other woman in the company," I said, feeling rather queer. "Didn't she give you her name—say anything?"

"She didn't say nothing." Mac's rheumy eyes were fixed on

my face. "Ran straight past me, she did. Didn't even say good-evening. Just like she was in a real hurry." He leaned forward and added dismally: "Just like she didn't want to be seen—almost."

Lillian, perched on my shoulder, started to purr louder.

"What did she look like?"

"My eyes ain't so good as they were. And her face was all muffled up in her coat like. But I did kind of glimpse it. That's why I knew she wasn't Miss Rue. That woman wasn't pretty like Miss Rue. Her cheeks were all white and sort of drawn like she was sick."

I tried to keep my voice casual. "When did she leave?"

"I didn't see her leave."

I stared. "You're trying to tell me this woman went into the theater and never came out?"

"I didn't see her leave," repeated Mac stubbornly. "Maybe she snuck out, though. When Mr. Gwynne brings me down Lillian, he said she'd maybe want some milk so I ran over to the drug-store to get her some. Maybe this woman snuck out then. Guess she did. Guess she wanted to leave without being seen just like she came."

He stopped there suddenly, didn't say any more. We looked at each other. Almost deliberately. I had kept until last the most crucial of all my questions.

"Did you happen to notice," I said very slowly, "just what this woman was wearing?"

Mac flicked his scrap-book shut. "Guess I'm not one for noticing what women wears. Wait a minute, though. Sure, I remember something—something she had over her arm like."

I didn't have to listen. I knew damn well what was coming next.

"Guess I do remember what she had over her arm, too," said the doorman in a voice that sounded far away and unreal. "Seems it was a sort of a fur—a light tan fur."

Chapter Eleven

I STARED AT the doorman who returned it without interest. The most alarming fancies were scudding through my mind. That unknown woman, clasping a fur to her throat, had not been just a prop for Lenz's theorizing; she was real; she'd actually crept past the doorman into the Dagonet last night and had crept out again—God knows when.

I tried to think of something to say. But I gave up. I merely smiled a sickly smile and withdrew.

I was half way up the stairs to stage level when Iris caught up with me. She was looking very pleased with herself and a new kind of Garbo haircut which flopped around her shoulders. As a matter of fact it was a particularly successful haircut and I stopped feeling depressed—just like that.

"So that's what you've been doing while Rome was burning," I said. "Having your hair fiddled with."

Iris slipped her arm through mine. "And I've been pulling strings at City Hall," she said.

"City Hall! What on earth were you doing at City Hall?"

She smiled rather guiltily and did something to a strand of hair that had gone a bit too Garbo. "Finding out about marriage licenses," she said. "It's really awfully elementary, Peter. All you have to do is . . ."

That time I didn't have to nip the propaganda in the bud; she nipped it herself. She looked at me with eyes that were suddenly worried.

"What's happened, darling? I can tell from your face. Have you found out anything else about last night?"

There's nothing you can do against feminine intuition. I said: "Yes, I found out something about last night. There's a new woman in our lives; a woman with a light tan . . ."

I broke off as Henry Prince hurried to join us, looking very hot and flustered.

"Mr. Duluth, my uncle may be a bit late. He wants to take the candid camera shots this morning. Is that all right?"

I said it would be all right. But I didn't feel it. I added, in a mood of sudden and complete dejection, "Henry, would you describe your uncle as a woman with a light tan fur?"

He looked startled. "No," he said, "I wouldn't."

"Neither would I," I said.

We went onto the stage.

Everyone was there ready for rehearsal. But the atmosphere was prickly as a porcupine. Gerald was smoldering alone in one corner; Wessler was being stiff and withdrawn in another, while Mirabelle was hurtling back and forth across the stage, taking sips of brandy and kicking at props which presumably she felt were in the wrong position. Even the good-natured Theo Ffoulkes was being objectionable. I heard her damping poor Eddie's enthusiasm for his rat traps and telling him he'd never rid the Dagonet of vermin unless he had the place fumigated with hydrocyanic gas.

I put a stop to the general waspishness by calling the rehearsal to order. Since Kramer hadn't arrived, I started them on the second act which, in my opinion, packed the biggest wallop of any second act Broadway had seen in seasons. But from the gun everything went sour. The whole company sogged down like beer without yeast and I couldn't do anything about it. I was patient, I was sarcastic, I was indignant, I was fighting mad. Nothing helped. I was almost ready to dash to the nearest bar, get utterly pie-eyed and let the whole Peter Duluth come-back roll merrily to hell.

And then, on top of it all, Kramer arrived. He slipped unobtrusively over to Henry and me, his plump face more than usually self-satisfied, his shoulder draped with a miniature camera in a case. He said did I want him to act right away or could he take some shots first.

94

I said: "Take as many shots as you like. And use a machine-gun."

Mr. Kramer thought that was funny and gave a fat giggle. As he moved rather furtively up into the wings I held onto the arms of my seat, waiting for violent reactions to the "provocative dose."

None of the actors had noticed Kramer. They were too absorbed with the task of giving the worst performances of their various careers. Theo snapped her exit line and flounced off stage leaving Mirabelle and Gerald alone together to go into one of their more intense scenes. While Kramer took up a strategic position and fiddled with his camera, Mirabelle's back was turned to him. But, just as he was set to click the shutter, she spun round and stared at him, her arms stiff at her sides. She must have stayed that way for a good five seconds. Then she swept downstage to the footlights.

"Peter, what's that man doing here? Get rid of him. Send him away."

Beneath the vivid red of her hair, her face was white as a Chesterfield packet. Her eyes were blazing. Gerald had moved to her side, looking very young, very handsome and ready to bite anyone that crossed her.

"Get rid of him, Peter," she said shrilly. "I'm damned if I'll have photographers at rehearsal."

Mirabelle had never been temperamental about photographers before. With a certain sinking of the heart, I realized that the "provocative dose" was beginning to work already. I went up on stage. I explained rather ruefully that Kramer had my permission both to take candid camera shots and also to make a stab at the Comstock role.

While I spoke. I watched Mirabelle's face. Only once did her eyelids flicker. Then, very quietly, she said: "If any photographs are taken at rehearsal. I shall leave the cast."

"That goes for me too," put in Gerald, sticking out his jaw.

So far as I was concerned, that was that. Whatever Lenz's plans with regard to Kramer were, I wasn't going to sacrifice

Mirabelle and Gerald. I was all set to tell Kramer to get the hell out when his bright, unwinking eyes fixed Mirabelle's face and he said softly:

"You surely don't mean that, Miss Rue. Rehearsal photographs are swell publicity for my nephew's play. You're interested in the play's success aren't you?"

His tone was distinctly insolent. I waited for Mirabelle to flare up, but to my amazement she didn't. She just stood there without saying anything.

Kramer moved across stage, poured a glass of brandy from that damn bottle and brought it to Mirabelle. "Here, Miss Rue, drink this. You're on edge—tired." His plump lips folded away from each other in a smile. "I know I'll get good results. The pictures I've taken of you in the past have been the most successful of my career, haven't they?"

Mirabelle took the brandy with fingers that shook. She drained the glass. "All right, Kramer," she said. "Take all the damn photographs you want." She tossed the empty glass to Eddie, turned her back on Uncle George and said: "Come on, Peter, let's get down to it again. God, what a lousy performance."

Kramer held the field triumphantly. For the next twenty minutes he crouched and lay in the wings, clicking his shutter.

At length the second act wound to its miserable end and I put them straight back to the first without a break. Things didn't improve. Wessler was apathetic, almost ponderous. Even Mirabelle managed to get strident in her first big entrance. I was ready for the worst possible type of catastrophe when Kramer's scene came.

But the unexpected happened, as usual. Kramer took his cue, entered, spoke his two lines, died and let himself be lowered into the coffin. He stayed there patiently with the lid down for about ten minutes until Wessler and Gerald carried him and the coffin off-stage. No one made a fuss. And, which was even more surprising, Kramer did a very professional job. He had all his business down pat; he made the scene far stronger than it had been with Comstock.

As a director I should have been delighted. But I wasn't. My last excuse for removing Uncle George from the Dagonet had been taken away from me.

When the act was over, I called a halt and sent them out to get something to eat, with instructions to be back by six.

I kept Iris behind. She was still inexperienced in the theater and a bad rehearsal affected her much more than the others. As soon as the stage was cleared, I put her through one of her entrances which she'd been slipping up on badly.

I made her enter and walk across the stage ten times. It was still wrong. Finally my frayed nerves got the better of me.

"For the eight hundredth time—slouch!" I said. "Walk as if you'd been up since three in the morning milking cows. Haven't you the remotest conception of the part? Watch me."

I vaulted up onto the stage and was just going into a passionate demonstration when the swing-door was kicked open and Eddie Troth strode in. His face, normally so cheerful, was white and hard with anger. He didn't seem to be conscious of Iris. He just gripped my arm and said: "I want you to see something."

He was so intense about it that I followed him. He led me down the stairs and through the double doors again below the stage.

The atmosphere was as thick as it had been before. The frugal light from the gratings still spotlighted odd corners of crowded theatrical junk.

"Look!" Eddie was pointing first at one trap, then at another. "See what I mean?"

I was beginning to see. When I had been there last, a rat had been caught in each of those traps. Now there were no rats.

"They're empty," I said.

"Sure. They're all empty—every damn one of them." Eddie led me from trap to trap, muttering: "You saw for yourself. There were dozens caught. Now they've gone. And I wanted to save you the expense of fumigation."

I said: "I told you they'd probably escape if you didn't drown them."

"Escape!" Eddie snorted. "They couldn't have escaped—not out of those traps." He bent low over one of them. A trembling

97

finger pointed to a wire gadget which was detachable so that the rats could be taken out. It was hanging loose. "See that? It's been tampered with. So've all the others."

I stared with a certain amount of incredulity. "Are you trying to tell me someone deliberately let those rats out?"

Eddie's eyes were gray as slate. "Someone came down here, Mr. Duluth, and let out every one of those goddamn rats. That's what he did."

"But why should anyone do a thing like that?"

"I don't know why." Eddie hitched up his pants. "But I've got a pretty good idea who. And I'm going to fix his feet. You're a witness. That's all I want."

He strode out of the cellar. Since there was so much blood in his eye, I felt I'd better follow. As I emerged into the corridor, I was just in time to see him disappear into the doorman's room.

And I heard his voice right away. It was hoarse with fury. He was accusing Mac of having sabotaged the traps for the entertainment of the Siamese cat. He was threatening to strangle the unfortunate Lillian if there was any more funny business.

I saw no good reason why the doorman should be blamed. I went to his aid, but Eddie was beyond himself with rage. There was nothing I could do to calm him down.

Finally I got tough with him. I called him out in the passage. I said: "There's enough trouble around this place without you getting temperamental too. I don't know who buggered up your traps and I don't care. But I do want this place free of rats. If you can't work it with traps, we'll have to get the fumigators in and do it thoroughly."

"But . . ." Eddie's mouth was suddenly sulky.

"I know you wanted to save me the expense. I don't give a damn about that." I wasn't used to Eddie's being obstinate and it made me mad. "Get the fumigating people on the phone right away. Tell them to come round as soon as they can and blast this place wide open with hydrocyanic gas. Tell the cast there'll be no rehearsals until it's safe again. At least I can get the Dagonet efficiently deloused."

For a moment I thought Eddie was going to come back at me, but he must have sensed that I was dangerously near the breaking point. He strode back into the doorman's room, dialed a number and passed my orders on tersely to someone at the other end of the wire. He slammed down the receiver.

"The squad'll be round this evening. I'll tell the cast rehearsals are postponed indefinitely."

He shot me a savage look and stalked away.

I wondered why he was taking it so hard.

As soon as my stage manager had gone, Mac ventured to emerge from his sanctuary behind the table, clutching the placid Lillian to his breast.

"I didn't let no rats out of them traps, Mr. Duluth," he implored. "He ain't got no right to strangle my Lillian."

Although I had nothing but distrust for Lillian personally, the old man's affection for her was rather moving. I assured him I'd prevent Eddie's strangling her and that I was convinced he'd had no share in releasing the rats.

With moist eyes and trembling lips, Mac crushed my fingers in a horny hand and said he'd never forget my kindness, no sir, he'd never forget it.

Then a queer, crafty look came into his eyes. "You was asking me about people that came to the theater last night when they had no right," he said. "Like that woman with the fur over her arm."

"Yes," I said, instantly alert.

"Guess I could tell you something that'd interest you." He cocked his head on one side like a sinister vulture. "I said I wouldn't tell. Promised, I did. But you've been good to me. I'd like to do right by you."

I didn't say anything. I waited for him to go on.

"I'll tell you how it was, Mr. Duluth." he said. "Quite a while after the gentleman with a beard came last night, I thought I'd take a bit of air. So I puts on my coat, picks up Lillian and goes down the alley to the grille that leads to the street. Kind of cold, but I like to see the people go by. And, boy, did Lillian make a hit? Almost everyone asked me what she was and several ladies stroked her." His old face registered sentimental pride. "Lillian's real friendly. Let 'em all stroke her. Yes, sir."

There was some more about Lillian's friendliness.

"I'd been down there about five minutes when I first saw this guy, hovering around, his collar up and his hat tugged down, see? I thought once he was coming up to talk to me but Mr. Troth came out of the stage door and passed me, saying: 'Rehearsal's almost over. The rest'll be out soon.' When he saw Mr. Troth, this guy kind of slips away. And the same thing happened a couple of minutes later when Mr. Gwynne and Miss Ffoulkes came out." Mac leaned forward furtively. "But soon as they're gone, this guy comes up again, sneaking up to the grille. He puts his hands through the grille toward Lillian and says: 'Hi there.' "

He paused, nodding his head. "Lillian had been so friendly with the others. But soon as she saw this guy, she pressed her ears back like she was scared and struggled and fought and jumped out of my arms and dashed back to the theater. I ran after her; I comes in here into my room. And she was hiding—" he pointed —"right there under the table. I was calling to her when I looks up and there's this guy again, right in the room, kind of smiling."

Mac bared his few teeth in an imitation of his strange visitor's smile. " 'I'm afraid it ain't no use trying to get that cat out while I'm around,' he says. 'Cats hate me. My wife used to like 'em a lot but she couldn't never keep them while I was around.' I asked him what he thought he wanted, coming into the theater like that. He didn't say nothing. He just took out a five-dollar bill and waved it and said: 'Guess you're feeling pretty thirsty. How about taking that cat over the street for a milk or a beer?' "

Mac's voice faltered a trifle. "Well, maybe I shouldn't of. But five bucks is five bucks. I ain't so rich I could pass it up. I tried to find out what he wanted but he wouldn't say. So I takes the five bucks, gets Lillian and goes for the beer."

"Exactly what time was this?" I asked.

"Just after Mr. Troth and Mr. Gwynne and Miss Ffoulkes left. I didn't stay over the bar for more'n few minutes. When I got back, you'd come down and was waiting here for me, telling me to 'phone the ambulance for Mr. Comstock."

"And you don't know what this man wanted?"

"I don't know nothing. When I leaves for the beer, he was standing right here. When I comes back, he'd gone."

"And," I said, "what did he look like?"

"Guess he was about middle height, dark with eyes that sort of went up at the sides. Come to think of it, he gives me his calling card. Didn't pay much attention. But I got it here."

He fumbled and produced a card which he handed me. I might have guessed it. In flourishing copperplate engraving the card said:

"Roland Gates."

First the mysterious woman with a light tan fur, then Mr. Kramer, "the provocative dose," then Mr. Roland Gates. That was all—nothing more than that.

I gulped. "I see," I said.

But I didn't. I didn't see one damn solitary thing.

Chapter Twelve

I LEFT THE doorman's room. Even if he did have more crucial information up his shabby sleeve, I was in no fit state to hear it. Immediately outside, looking very beautiful and inquisitive, was Iris.

"You still here?" I asked.

"Of course, darling. You were going to teach me to slouch." She drew me through the stage door, out of the doorman's range of hearing. "I listened," she said. "So Roland Gates was here at the theater last night."

"Everyone was here at the theater last night," I said drearily. "Everyone except Santa Claus."

"And those rats, Peter, did someone really let them out of Eddie's traps?"

"If anyone mentions rats I'll scream," I said. "I'm having the place fumigated. At least I don't have to worry about rats."

"But who could have let . . . ?"

"Listen," I said ferociously, "we are going to Sardot's; we are going to have something to eat and we're going to discuss the sex life of the bee."

At Sardot's Iris tried half-heartedly to discuss the sex life of the bee, but all too soon the conversation reached the birds and flowers stage and through that to our own sex lives and City Hall. Out of sheer self-protection, I had to change the subject.

After we'd eaten, I abandoned Iris to put in a belated appearance at my office. Now that rehearsals were suspended I had some time to catch up on the business side of my production.

Things were going at their usual hysterical high pressure when I reached Peter Duluth, Inc.'s new and very swank offices on Fifth Avenue. The waiting-room was stuffed with its normal quota of histrionic hopefuls who were told at regular intervals by

Miss Pink, my indomitable secretary, that Mr. Duluth was out of town, that he wasn't doing any casting, that he was in conference.

I strode through the serried ranks, trying to look as if I were out of town and not casting and in conference. Behind me I heard the telephone shrill, heard Miss Pink's bright voice proclaiming:

"I'm so sorry. Mr. Duluth is in conference. No there's no casting today, no . . ."

I shut the door on her and dropped into a chair behind my desk, starting to glance through the mail. Instantly my business manager materialized from nowhere and began to shout at me about some calamity concerning electrical equipment; then my publicity agent arrived brandishing newspaper clippings and outlining a new press campaign. Like a series of punctuation marks in an interminable sentence, Miss Pink slipped in and out, being brisk and bringing checks to be signed. I signed them, all of them, and started shouting back at my business manager and my press agent. We all got very hot. But it was oddly comforting to find that here at the office, at least, *Troubled Waters* was being treated like an honest-to-goodness piece of merchandise that had to be peddled on Broadway, instead of a Grand Guignol vehicle for ghosts, rats, murders and women with light tan furs.

At last I was left alone with the mail again. I was struggling with it when the door from the waiting-room burst open onto a whirlwind which seemed to consist largely of a mink coat, flying hands, red hair and a borzoi wolf hound. They all precipitated themselves at me.

"Peter, darling, I thought you'd be here, I've got to see you. It's utterly important. The most terrible thing . . . Dmitri, darling, be an angelic dog and sit in the corner . . . you've got to do something about it, Peter. If he goes through with it he'll be ruined as an actor, absolutely ruined . . . Don't you agree?"

For the next few seconds the room was all Mirabelle and borzoi. One of them started barking, presumably the borzoi. I sat in patient silence while chaos reigned and then, somehow, the dog got chased into a corner where it squatted, lean and reproachful, its aristocratic nose supported on two thin paws. Mirabelle said,

"Darling dog," she tugged off her gloves, tossed back her hair, made a rush at me and seized both my hands.

"Darling, you mustn't let him tear up his contract." The husky voice torrented words at me. "You may say I'm selfish; that I want him for myself. I adore him, of course. But it isn't that. It's not even the play, though God knows what we'll do if he walks out on us now. It's Gerald himself. He's too young."

She dropped my hands, perched herself on the edge of my desk and lit a cigarette. Long before I'd recovered my breath, she was gripping my shoulders, gazing at me from ocean-green eyes, the amazing red hair swirling around her shoulders. She looked like something out of a myth—a dynamic dryad or a super-charged water nymph.

"Peter, darling, we've got to *do* something."

I said meekly: "Mirabelle, what are you talking about?"

"But, my angel, I *told* you! The wire came in this morning. Hollywood's offering Gerald fifty thousand for one picture. He has three days to make up his mind." Mirabelle's hands did something beautiful and dramatic. "Don't you see how Hollywood will ruin him? He's only just out of a small town, Peter. I lived in a small town once. My God, I was even married in one before I came east to be an actress. I guess you never knew that. But it's true. And I know how something glamorous like Hollywood, coming on top of that, completely demoralizes you. Gerald's career means everything to me—everything. He's being stubborn as hell. He won't listen to me. He says he has some reason for having to get out of New York right away." She looked earnest and rather dangerous. "But you've got to make him see sense, Peter. You've got to be tough as hell and hold him to his contract."

I had recovered my breath now only to lose it again. Pelion seemed to be piling itself on Ossa that afternoon. As if things weren't hellish enough without Hollywood's trying to wheedle away my juvenile on the eve of the opening night!

"He can't quit now," I said. "It'd be damn disloyal to me. And it would be crazy anyway. If he holds out till we're through with *Troubled Waters*, he'll get a far bigger offer. I'll talk to him." I added without conviction: "I only hope he'll listen."

"Of course he'll listen, angel. Everyone listens to you." Mirabelle kissed me and started weaving around the room again as if every care in the world had slipped from her shoulders. That was typical of her. One second she was bowed to the earth with tragedy; the next, she had the earth under her arm. She said conversationally: "Didn't Gerald mention anything about it to you when he saw you at Wessler's this morning?"

"He didn't tell me anything," I said. "He was too busy being stinking rude to Wessler."

I had meant that as a mild admonition and she took it that way. She threw away the cigarette and stared me straight in the eyes.

"You think I'm being damn childish about Wessler, don't you? I am. I admit it. But I just can't help it. Everything about him makes me see red. He's so respectable and solid and enormous and—and that damn memory of his. It drives me crazy. There isn't a face in the United States he hasn't seen before—not a single face except mine." She tossed her head derisively. "This morning he started remembering Henry. Henry! That unmemorable, subdued little chipmunk. But he doesn't remember seeing *me* before. Oh, no. And I've only been plastered over the stage magazines for twenty years. That's all, just twenty years."

So her vanity was piqued because Wessler hadn't gone through his "where-have-I-seen-you-before" routine with her. I wondered if that could possibly be the reason back of her dislike for him.

"But he's a wonderful actor, Peter," she was going on rapidly. "He plays better than I do. Maybe that's why I'm so loathsome about him. Every time we're on stage together, I feel he's stifling me, obliterating me. I feel if I don't fight back, there won't be anything left, that I'll be swallowed up."

"Baloney!" I said. "You know you can stand up against anyone in the theater."

"Peter, you're divine to say that, but it's not true." The sting had gone out of her somehow. She looked pinched, rather frail.

"He does something to me. He makes the play real. It follows me away from the theater so I can't sleep at night, can't get that damn voice of his out of my mind. I think I hate him." She broke off, a strange catch in her voice. "God, I'm being neurotic."

I'd never see Mirabelle like that before. Usually, even in the darkest days after the divorce, she would have died rather than let anyone see her without control.

I said: "Darling, no one's going to stop your hating anyone, if that's the way you feel." Since I seemed to be in a didactic mood, I added: "But I do think it might be a good idea to pipe down a bit. There wasn't any point in sending Gerald around to be deliberately bad-mannered."

She looked up sharply. "You mean this morning? When he went to get the brandy? Darling, I didn't mean him to be bad-mannered. I swear it. I wasn't trying to be nasty. It's just that—that I wanted the brandy."

"Yes," I said, "I noticed the bottle was half full."

Her reply came too quickly, too breathlessly. "And I said it was empty last night, didn't I, Peter? I know it. I've been feeling terrible about it. But, Peter, when Lionel—Lionel died like that, it was so sudden. My nerves went. I didn't really know what I was doing, I was thinking of what he said about the mirror, all that. I was shot, Peter. That's why I said the bottle was empty. I really thought it was."

She sounded perfectly truthful. What she said made perfect sense. I wondered why I didn't believe her.

She was still staring at me, her eyes remembering back. Then her expression changed, her mouth tightened as if she had something to say and was scared of saying it. She said abruptly:

"About Comstock's part, Peter, why did you get that man to play it?"

I didn't quite know what to say. I could hardly explain Lenz's theory of Mr. Kramer and the "provocative dose." And yet I was curious to find out just what was wrong between Mirabelle and Kramer.

"He's Henry's uncle," I said guardedly. "And he offered to take over." I added: "You know him, don't you?"

Mirabelle's eyes widened—a little too far. "Me know that man? Darling, don't be too absurd. How could I know him?" She flushed slightly as if it had occurred to her that she was maybe protesting too much. She added quickly: "But, Peter, apart from anything else, you don't want that man in the play. That's what I came to tell you."

"Not want him?" I echoed, agreeing fervently in my heart. "But why should we get rid of him? He did the part well."

"I don't give a damn how he played the part." Mirabelle clutched my arm impulsively. "It's just the part itself that's wrong. You know it's unlucky to have a coffin scene on stage. Comstock played it and he died, didn't he? It's jinxed. I know it's jinxed. I want you to cut the role out altogether."

"I may be superstitious," I said, "but not that superstitious."

"It's not just superstition." Mirabelle's voice was urgent. "It's a bad part, Peter. It's melodramatic. It makes the first act top-heavy. It's unnecessary."

She started to tell me why. Mirabelle was always electric when she discussed plays, but this time she discharged as much dynamic energy as the T.V.A.

As a tempestuous climax to her argument, she snatched copies of the script from the table, dragged the impervious Miss Pink from the outer office and made us all three act the scene through, eliminating the dying business magnate. Miss Pink was incongruously allotted the Wessler role while I, for some reason, was Iris. Mirabelle played all the other parts.

It was one of those crazy, extemporary things that she did superbly. And she convinced me. Switched around her way with the Comstock character dying off-stage and never appearing, the scene wasn't hokum any more. She'd tightened it where I'd never realized it was sloppy. She had lifted the whole act.

"There, darlings." she tossed back her hair and beamed triumphantly at Miss Pink and me. "Isn't that better? Tell me, darlings, isn't that the way it should be?"

It was. And I admitted it, only reminding her that Henry, as author, had contractural rights to veto any alterations. That didn't seem to bother her.

"I knew you'd realize," she said. "Then it's all right? You can tell that Mr. Marker or Kramer or whatever his name is to get the hell out."

Mirabelle plunged into her old, overwhelming self for a moment, throwing the scripts on the table, kissing me, kissing the exiting Miss Pink and hurling herself at the borzoi who still squatted patiently in the corner.

And yet, I wasn't quite deceived. Her suggested alteration was swell. But I knew she'd had only one reason in pushing it. She wasn't basically interested in improving the first act. She was just desperately, madly keen to get Kramer out of the company—at all costs.

Things weren't getting straightened out. They were just getting more and more tangled.

As soon as Miss Pink had gone, Mirabelle dropped her rather manufactured exuberance. She moved toward me, holding out her hands, her lips half parted, uncertain.

"Peter, we've got a wonderful play. A very wonderful play. We mustn't let anything happen to spoil this."

"How could anything spoil it?" I asked, thinking offhand of at least a dozen answers to that one.

"Oh, I don't know. Sometimes I think it's all too good to be true. At last I've got a part that means everything for me. It's the part I've always dreamed of playing—better than my dreams. You know those damn doctors told me I was crazy to leave the hospital. They said I'd crack if I took on another play. But I knew right away that *Troubled Waters* was one of those things that come and you've got to grab before it's—it's to late. I think I'd die, Peter, if anything happened to prevent me . . ."

She broke off, her hand moving suddenly to her cheek as if to brush away some invisible thing that had stung her. "Peter, there's something I want you to tell me—honestly. I mean,

108

honestly. Am I any good any more? Am I as good on the stage as I was when I was married to Roland?"

"You're far better," I said quietly, meaning it.

"Am I? Oh, am I, Peter? You wouldn't lie, would you? I'd kill you if you lied. You see, I don't really know any more." Her eyes were suddenly naked, panic stricken. "How long did I live with Roland? Seven years. They were seven bad years, Peter. I hated him; I was scared of him. But I was acting well, we were acting well together. I thought somehow that just having him always there, loathing him, helped me—keyed me up so that I could really get into a part. A sort of escape, I suppose. That's one reason I stuck by him so long."

She moved the hand from her cheek and stared at it blindly. "Now I've cut all that away. I'm free. There isn't any more Roland. He's a nightmare that's gone. But something else has gone, too. At least I had roots with him, even if they were rooted in hate. Now I'm cut loose. Peter, you won't understand, but I'm afraid, hellishly afraid."

She'd never talked that way about Gates before—never to anyone. Mirabelle who had always been indomitable, a tower of strength—it was horrible to see all that stark suffering in her and not be able to help. And I knew then that there was something wrong in her life, something far worse than any of us had guessed.

"Mirabelle, darling," I said, "tell me what's the matter. Tell me what you're scared of. Is it Kramer? If it is, I'll see him to hell."

Her lips were trembling; there was a dazed, lost look in her eyes. Then she was in my arms, burying her face against my shoulder, clinging to me like a kid.

"It's nothing, Peter, nothing that isn't inside of me. It's just that I'm scared I'm through. I'm washed up. I can't take it any more."

Anything I could have said would have seemed pretty futile. I just held that small, quivering body and wished with every ounce of my being that someone would start giving us all an even break.

I was only dimly conscious of raised voices in the office outside.

Then one of them definitely became Miss Pink's, loud, executive, saying: "Mr. Duluth's busy. He mustn't be disturbed."

I heard another voice, soft, unrecognizable; then there was a scuffling. The door opened. I heard Miss Pink calling: "Please!" But the door shut her and her voice out. The man who had entered stood with his back to it, his hands in the pockets of his black overcoat, his black hat tugged down over black, sardonic eyes.

He looked at us. "Dear me," he said, "what a dramatic entrance."

I had never been less prepared for anything than I was for the appearance of Roland Gates at that particular moment. My arm instinctively tightened around Mirabelle's waist. I said quietly: "You better get out of here, Gates—right away."

Roland Gates didn't move. I hadn't seen him since the divorce and his ignominious retreat from Broadway. He looked exactly the same—like a handsome, dissipated lizard. He laughed a thin laugh.

"Come, come, Peter, surely I'm permitted to bring messages of good-will to my ex-wife—even if she is in the arms of my ex-producer."

Mirabelle hadn't heard him until then. I was sure of it. But that laugh must have seeped into her confused, racking thoughts. I felt her body tense suddenly in my arms.

It was a bad moment for her to face Gates. I would have done anything to make it easier for her—anything including strangling, as a matter of fact, preferably strangling him. I started to move toward him, but her fingers tightened on my lapel. She whispered: "No, Peter. Don't do anything."

I knew then that she wanted to face the situation herself. If she felt that way, it was best to let her get it over with. She had to go through with this sometime.

And she did it superbly. For one second she didn't move. She stood with her back to him, staring at me, her face twitching slightly, completely out of control. Then, like some trick shot on the movies, I saw her expression change, saw the amazing transformation which turned her in a flash from that broken, haunted creature into the Great Mirabelle Rue.

When she wheeled around to Gates, she was completely poised. Her eyebrows, tilting upward, registered mild surprise. "Why, Roland, I didn't notice you. But then you always sneak into rooms, don't you?"

I could tell Gates was a little nonplussed, He'd thought he had caught her with her hair down and he'd been hoping to extract every ounce of satisfaction out of it. His eyes, green and flat as an iguana's were watching her.

"You're looking rather under the weather, Mirabelle," he said.

"Do I? I'm feeling particularly fit." Mirabelle glanced at me indifferently. "Aren't you going to ask Roland what he came for, Peter? He always comes for something. I expect it's money."

I felt absurdly exhilarated. Mirabelle had done such a sweet piece of table turning.

"Yes, Roland," I said, "want me to write you a check?"

"Thank you, Peter, but I'm financially solvent. I'm glad to hear you are, too. Last time I saw you, you were rather too solvent— alcoholically." Gates strolled to a chair, perching himself on the arm and lighting a cigarette. "As it happens, I came here because I'm intensely interested in your and Mirabelle's future. I understand you've been having some trouble down at the Dagonet?"

Mirabelle's eyes widened. "Trouble, Roland? Why, no, we haven't had any trouble."

"I'm glad I was misinformed." Gates blew two jets of smoke from his nostrils. "Even so, I'm a little worried for you. They tell me you're running Wessler without an understudy. You're taking a big chance, you know. He's very undependable, and he's got in wrong with the Nazis. If anything happened to him—well, that'd probably be the end of your come-back, wouldn't it?"

I knew what he was working up to. Gerald had warned me of it the night before. But Mirabelle's hand on my arm kept me from saying anything.

"Go on Roland."

"It has occurred to me that I'm the person to help you," continued Gates. "Give me a copy of the script, let me learn the Wessler role. When—I should say, *if*—he cracks up, then I can take over. I feel it's a part that would interest me. I also feel it would be amusing for Mirabelle and me to team up again." He flicked ash on to the floor. "How do you feel about it, Mirabelle?"

Mirabelle gave him one long, curious look. Then she turned her back on him as if she had completely banished him from her consciousness. She held out both her hands to me.

"I promised Gerald to have cocktails at five, Peter. I'll have to fly."

Very slowly and deliberately she picked up her gloves, fixed her crazy hat at the glass, moved to the forgotten borzoi, looped the lead around her arm and coaxed the animal forward.

She brushed past Gates, came up to me and kissed me. "Eddie'll call me when the theater's ready for rehearsal again, won't he? Oh, and the script alteration, you'll take it up with Henry?"

'Yes," I said.

"And Gerald, too. You won't forget what we decided about Gerald? I know you'll be able to do something."

She moved to the door leading to the outer office and threw it open so that we were in full view of my business manager, my press agent, Miss Pink and about a dozen nondescript callers.

Just as she reached the threshold, she veered round suddenly and offered Gates one gloved hand. He took it.

"Good-bye, Mirabelle"

"Good-bye, Roland."

Then while her audience in the outer office watched in expectant silence, Mirabelle withdrew her hand from his, peeled off her gloves and tossed them into the scrap-basket.

"Oh, Roland, you asked me a question. You wanted to know whether I thought it would be amusing to have you playing with me at the Dagonet." Her smile was sharp and glittering as an icicle. "I don't think it would be very amusing, Roland. I don't think it would be amusing at all. Besides, the theater's being fumigated. It wouldn't be safe for you."

Chapter Thirteen

THAT WAS WHAT I called a thoroughly devastating remark.
But it didn't devastate Roland Gates. Nothing did. He just
moved to the door, closed it on the departing figure of Mirabelle
and drawled:

"Surprising how women bear grudges—like elephants or is it
rhinoceroses?"

"Rhinoceroses," I said pointedly, "are the animals with the
tough hides."

Gates sighed. "I presume you share Mirabelle's exaggerated
sentiments about me? You don't want me to understudy
Wessler?"

"I don't," I said bluntly. "You ought to know my opinion of
you. I expressed it fairly forcibly at the time of the divorce."

"Yes, as I remember, you were a little shrill." Gates was
watching me with a blank, sardonic stare. "You think I'm a
wicked, wicked man, don't you, Peter? I'm afraid that sojourn of
yours in the nut-house made you rather smug."

I looked at that neat, masklike face, thinking back to some of
the unspeakable things that came out in Mirabelle's divorce
testimony. I said: "It's made me smug enough to feel a very
strong desire to throw you out of this office. Before I do, however, it might interest you to know that the doorman told me
you slipped him five bucks to let you into the Dagonet last night."

Gates took that very calmly. "I expected him to pass on the
good news. In fact, I left my calling card to make sure he'd get
the name straight."

I was in a damn awkward position. I wanted like hell to find
out what Gates had been doing at the Dagonet the night before.
But it was vitally important to keep him from knowing exactly
how much trouble we were having.

While I was thinking of something to say, his mouth twitched in a quick reptilian smile. He continued. "It's a waste of time trying to be discreet, Peter. I know what happened at the Dagonet last night."

That was not so good, but there was just a chance he was bluffing.

He wasn't. "Yes, Peter, I met an old acquaintance of mine at Sardot's—a Mr. George Kramer. After we'd sent his little nephew home to bed, we had a couple of drinks. Kramer told me all about Theo's intriguing experience in the upstairs dressing-room."

I'd guessed, of course, that there was some sort of tie-up between Kramer and Gates. I might have known this would have happened. Although I made a feeble attempt to go on being nonchalant, it was impossible to fool Gates. He was enjoying himself immensely.

He said: "You're probably dying to hear what frightful abominations I perpetrated in your theater last night. But I'm afraid you'll be disappointed when you hear the truth. I went there with the simple and benign intention of finding out whether my ex-wife had received a little present I'd sent her. I was a mere onlooker in the melodrama."

He crossed to a chair and sat down again on the arm, lighting a cigarette. "I'll tell you just what happened to me. Having disposed of the doorman I went upstairs to stage level and down the corridor to the first star dressing-room which I presumed to be Mirabelle's. I was just going to the door when it was hurled open from inside and a man—that old fellow Comstock—dashed right past me and staggered toward the stage. He was gasping and wheezing and gibbering something that sounded like *Lillian* —as if he'd just met up with all the fiends in hell. Distinctly pulp, Peter."

Gates tossed his cigarette on to my carpet and watched it smoldering a few seconds before he crushed it. "I was quite non-plussed. By all the laws of fiction, I should have squared my jaw and gone into that room to investigate. But I'm afraid I didn't. I turned tail and ran."

His pink tongue came out like a chameleon's after a fly. "Action continued in the best dramatic tradition. When I was about half way down the stairs I heard a crash of glass behind me. I glanced over my shoulder. Up on the landing I saw a man hurrying away from that same dressing-room. I only had the briefest glimpse of him. But that was more than enough. I accelerated and was out of the Dagonet as rapidly as even you could have wished."

I had quite forgotten it was Roland Gates who was telling me that story, quite forgotten that I loathed him and was supposed to be putting up a front. I could only think how amazingly this fitted in with Lenz's theory; how the man Gates had seen must have been the person who had staged that fantastic tableau in the wardrobe, the person who had used Eddie's pane of glass and smashed it, the person who was at the root of all the major and minor disturbances at the Dagonet.

And the craziest part of it was that this person had been a man. Presumably the woman with the light tan fur had been thrown in as a bonus.

"Did you recognize him?" I said uneasily. "Did you see his face?"

"Did I see his face?" Gates glanced up, his small, pointed teeth showing in two level lines. "That's the purplest patch of my story, Peter. I didn't see his face—because he didn't have a face to see. There was nothing but a pair of eyes staring out of a grayish, featureless blank."

He said that so suddenly, with such calculated calmness, that he threw me completely off balance. A woman with a light tan fur, a phantom sabotager of rat-traps and now a man without a face—all massed together in one afternoon. Things had gone so very, very far beyond a joke. I felt a violent nostalgia for the good old alcoholic days in Lenz's sanitorium where the worst that could happen to me would have been a chance encounter with a homicidal maniac. What were homicidal maniacs to the ordinary, run-of-the-mill visitors at the Dagonet Theater?

Gates was saying: "That, Peter, is my little anecdote. As experiences go, it was interesting and certainly worth the five-dollar outlay."

I wasn't listening to him. My mind was beginning to function along rational lines again. I forced myself to visualize the large, comforting form of Dr. Lenz. And Dr. Lenz made me think of Wessler's lost modeling clay. Lenz had suggested that the man in the wardrobe might have distorted his face with the clay. There was a reasonable explanation for Roland Gates's apparition.

That made me feel a little better, but not very much.

Gates had crossed to the desk and was leaning over it languidly. He said: "I read in this morning's paper that Comstock brought the drama to a fitting climax by dying on stage. You claim to shudder away from my morals, Peter. But even I am shocked by what that implies. It isn't at all savory to frighten an old man with a weak heart to death." He paused, smiling that fixed, flat smile. "In fact, I imagine that in a court of law it would come under the heading of murder."

I was still too confused to catch on to the way things were going.

"Yes," continued Gates, "I think it certainly rates as murder in the first, second, or third degree. Even if it doesn't, it's something that should intrigue the authorities. I'll be extremely interested to hear the police verdict."

I started to see exactly what he was planning in that cold, saurian mind of his. I said: "You know I haven't told the police."

"You haven't? You're conniving at a felony?" His eyebrows slid upward. "I suppose I see your point. It would be unfortunate for your come-back production if the police took over at the Dagonet, wouldn't it? You'd probably be kept from opening indefinitely. Lucky I didn't report what I saw last night." His small hand with its femininely pointed nails reached past me and picked up a copy of the script of *Troubled Waters*. "Don't you think it might be a sound idea for me to learn Wessler's part after all?"

"So you want that part in exchange for holding back on the

police," I said, trying to keep myself in control for just a little while longer. "This is a stick-up."

"Stick-up?" echoed Gates. "My dear Peter, be civilised. The police mean nothing to me. I think they are a tiresome institution. They would, however, seem even more tiresome if I felt I was part of your company. I see no reason why I shouldn't be frank. Mirabelle was ill-bred enough to wave our dirty linen under the noses of the sentimental public and has done a certain amount of damage to my reputation. The surest way to repair that damage is to show the public that Mirabelle and I are reunited again— on the boards, at least. Your play seems to me to be the ideal vehicle for my rehabilitation."

He twisted the corner of the manuscript. "I shall only appear on stage, of course, if Wessler should be indisposed. I can learn the part and I need not intrude myself at rehearsal. There won't be anything official about it." He slipped the copy of the script into his overcoat pocket. "Is that okay by you?"

He knew and I knew that he held all the cards.

"Anything's okay by me," I said softly. "You can learn the part; you can learn it backward, forward and sideways; you can have more fun. But there's just one little formality I'd like to go through first. It may possibly make you change your mind."

I doubled my right hand into a fist; I swung; I slugged him very hard and square on the jaw.

I hadn't done anything like that since my prep school era. But, apparently, it's a trick you don't forget.

The only thing I had enjoyed that day was the sight of my business manager, my press agent and Miss Pink removing Roland Gates from the carpet.

Chapter Fourteen

B UT MY MOMENT of elation was very short lived. After Roland Gates had been removed, restored and sent on his way, I slid into suicidal gloom. It wasn't just the fact that I'd been either successfully or unsuccessfully blackmailed into taking Gates on as Wessler's unofficial understudy—though Heaven knew, that was bad enough. It was the cumulative effect of all the shattering things that were happening to my play, and my own ability to make any sort of sense out of them.

Miss Pink came in again with letters to sign. I started signing them, then I stopped. Instead of adding "Peter Duluth" to a chatty letter for the editor of *Stage*, I turned the notepaper over and began scribbling with furious abandon on the back.

This is what I wrote.

REASONS WHY TROUBLED WATERS CAN'T CONCEIVABLY SEE THE LIGHT OF DAY

(1) A homicide concealed from the police.
(2) Roland Gates.
(3) Uncle George Kramer.
(4) A malignant Siamese cat.
(5) A lady with a light tan fur.
(6) A gentleman with a mask of modeling clay.
(7) Someone who lets rats out of traps.
(8) Gerald Gwynne who wants to go to Hollywood.
(9) Mirabelle Rue who's scared of something, who's got a damn phoney brandy bottle, who'll probably have a nervous breakdown.
(10) Conrad Wessler who's almost blind(?), who's the probable victim of some obscure plot, who's probably going nuts like his half-brother.

(11) Theo Ffoulkes who's got a cough and will probably die.

(12) Peter Duluth who at any minute is going to order a case of Scotch, lock himself in a padded cell and burst into tears.

I stared at that document for a long time, wallowing in self-pity. I didn't attempt to think or to plan. I just brooded.

Then a sluggish memory of my promises to Mirabelle seeped through the gloom. I could see Gerald before rehearsal at the Dagonet and try to stop him from walking out on us. But Henry Prince probably wouldn't show up at the theater. I told Miss Pink to get Henry on the wire. That, at least, showed the germs of constructive action. If I could get Henry to agree to Mirabelle's script alteration, there was a fighting chance of eliminating Mr. Kramer from the cast as a step toward eliminating him from our lives.

Henry's voice sounded on the phone. I told him Mirabelle's suggestion for switching around the first act to cut out the business magnate role. With unexpected fluency, I urged on him the obvious dramatic advantages of such a move. I had put several other script changes up to him in the past and he had been meek as a lamb about okaying them. I fully expected him to give way on this point.

But I might have known. His voice went suddenly stiff and stubborn. He said he had written the play with the Comstock-Kramer role as an essential factor. He would not dream of consenting to its removal.

He went on and on like that, showing a tenacity I'd never before suspected. He concluded in a tone that wasn't quite so emphatic: "Besides, Mr. Duluth, however I may feel, I can't have the role cut because I have promised Uncle George to—let him play it."

That gave the whole show away, of course. Henry didn't really want the part left in any more than Mirabelle wanted it out. Neither of their reactions had anything to do with the play itself. They were connected solely with Mr. George Kramer. Mirabelle was so scared of him that she was desperately eager to get him out of the cast; Henry was so scared of him that he was desperately eager to keep him in.

I rang off. I thought of the five-hundred-dollar check which Kramer had forced Henry to borrow from me that morning. I picked up my black list.

With a despairing flourish. I added a thirteenth item to the category of disaster. I wrote:

(13) Henry Prince who's completely under Uncle George's thumb and is probably being blackmailed by same.

While I was writing that, I suppose I should have been conscious of someone standing behind me, reading over my shoulder. But I hadn't the slightest sensation of not being alone until a voice said:

"Read that, Peter."

I started. I glanced up to see Iris with her Persian lamb looking Park Avenue and very determined—a sort of over-privileged Joan of Arc. She was holding out a piece of paper.

"Read that," she said again.

I took the paper. I read: "Dear Sir, With regard to your shipment of electrical . . ."

"The other side," said Iris.

I turned the thing over. The back was covered in Iris's round, school-girlish script.

She had written.

REASONS WHY TROUBLED WATERS CAN'T
CONCEIVABLY FAIL TO SEE THE LIGHT OF DAY
(1) Dr. Lenz
(2) Iris Pattison
(3) Iris Pattison
(4) Iris Pattison
(5) Iris Pattison
(6) Iris Pattison

I folded both pieces of paper and put them in my pocket. I got up. I kissed Iris. She smelt of something very faraway and nice.

"Do you know who you are, darling?" I said.

Iris said: "No."

"Pollyanna of Sunnybrook farm," I said.

She disengaged herself from my arms, looking at me from purposeful eyes. She said: "Darling, the theater's being fumigated. There won't be any rehearsal till tomorrow. Now that we've got the time, let's hire a car, drive south, cross the Maryland state line and . . ."

"No," I said.

"Why not? Why the hell not?"

"Because I know myself," I said, meaning it more than I'd ever meant anything. "I'm not just stalling, because of Lenz. That's not it. You're something I'm making myself work for. It's only because there's you at the end that I can get through this bedlam and make *Troubled Waters* a success. If I got you before I rated you, I'd be sunk."

"I see, Peter." Iris was watching me from quiet, thoughtful eyes. "Okay. Cut Maryland. We'll do something else—something gay."

"Such as?"

"Well go to the movies," said Iris.

We did. We went to the Astor and then to the Paramount and then to the Music Hall, plunging headlong from one movie to another. A sort of harmless jag. But it didn't work. The Dagonet stayed at the back of my mind. After the third show, we staggered into the Pennsylvania Drug Store for a sandwich. We didn't discuss our next move, but instinctively, when we left the place, we headed for Forty-fourth Street.

I guess it was sheer morbidity that took us past the theater that night. But we happened to strike it just as the men from the fumigating squad were arriving. Eddie Troth, very sulky and curt, was supervising the proceedings with Mac hovering in the background, peering at the hermetically sealed cylinders of hydrocyanic gas discoids with a sort of wary anxiety as if he, along with the rats, was scheduled for immediate annihilation.

While the squad took the theater over, shutting all windows and vents, the chief fumigator was chatty with Eddie and me. He explained how the discoids were spread over the floor space and how the gas, slowly vaporizing, impregnated the air and left a harmless residue behind. He told us cheerfully that every living thing in the theater would be destroyed. Even a human being, exposed to that insidious, odorless gas, would lose consciousness in thirty seconds and die in less than five minutes. Although his squad wore gas masks, they had to work in quarter-hour shifts only, otherwise the gas would seep through their clothing, get under their skins and poison them that way. Hydrocyanic gas seemed the most efficient of exterminators.

I hoped it would remove, equally efficiently, all ghostly faces in mirrors, women with light tan furs and men with masks of modeling clay.

Just after the auditorium itself had been shut off and the laying of the discoids had begun, Mac injected drama into the situation by reporting the loss of Lillian. Despite a warning from the chief fumigator, the old doorman rushed crazily up to the first-floor dressing-rooms, which were still uncontaminated, calling: "Lillian, Lillian."

Eventually he returned, the Siamese cat clasped under one arm, beads of sweat standing out on his forehead.

"I got her," he said. "I got my girl. I saved her."

I couldn't work up a great deal of enthusiasm. So far as I was concerned, Lillian could very easily have been spared from my cast.

Iris and I left then, just as the men had started pasting paper over the cracks around the doors. They said we would be able to rehearse again at noon the next day and I told Eddie to call the company for twelve-thirty.

When we reached my apartment, we discovered Lenz seated in the largest and most comfortable arm-chair. Beside him, on a table, was a glass of soda-water.

He looked up. "Since you were not here, Mr. Duluth, I took the liberty of making myself at home and taking a little refreshment."

"Grand," I said.

His eyes were fixed intently on my face. "My main object in returning, Mr. Duluth, was to inquire whether there have been additional disturbance at the Dagonet today."

I dropped into a chair, letting myself sag. "Yes," I said, "there've been infinite additional disturbances. The whole Dagonet Theater is one gargantuan, diabolical disturbance." Gloomily I added: "I wish I was alone on a desert island with three coconut palms, the Encyclopedia Britannica and a camel."

I could see from Dr. Lenz's expression that he was recording that remark as definite evidence of a manic depressive psychosis. He made no reference to it, however. He merely said: "Perhaps you will tell me everything that happened."

I did. It made as sorry a tale of woe as I had ever heard.

Lenz did not speak right away and Iris broke in brightly: "In any case, what happened today proves Dr. Lenz's reconstruction one hundred per cent right—I mean about the man making a mask of clay and hiding in that closet. I think it's amazing the way Dr. Lenz figured that out."

"More amazing the way you can hear through key holes," I said. Iris waved away this malicious interruption with an impatient shrug.

I continued: "If he could just explain the difference between the woman with the fur and the man with the clay mask, he'd go to the top of the form."

We both waited for Lenz to speak. Finally, after his fingers had traveled up and down his imperial, he said: "I must confess that the situation is becoming considerably confused. Unquestionably there have been reactions to the 'provocative dose'. But they have not been at all the reactions I anticipated." He paused. "If you remember, Mr. Duluth, I suggested that there was more than one thread of mystery at the Dagonet. Now I'm beginning to feel there must be several—several, perhaps, which have no immediate connection with each other."

That was the last straw. "Several threads!" I repeated. "We've got a notion counter full of them. There's—"

Iris broke in: "Show Dr. Lenz your list, darling. It would be far less painful that way."

Obediently I produced my list of the thirteen disasters and handed them to Dr. Lenz. As he read it, his expression remained serene and Olympian. He passed me back the list.

"That is very interesting, Mr. Duluth. But I think you exaggerate a trifle. Tomorrow I will give the matter some serious thought. I have every hope that we will be able to formulate an adequate explanation. Meanwhile, it is late."

That, of course, was one of Lenz's typical don't-get-worried-little boy edicts. But, almost for the first time since I'd known him, he didn't carry conviction. In spite of his supernormal placidity, I knew damn well that he had no more hope of formulating an adequate explanation than I had.

When I'd finished kissing Iris good-bye, Dr. Lenz had retired to a bathroom from which issued the vigorous sound of teeth being brushed. Eventually he emerged, resplendent in the gray woolen nightshirt.

I had never seen him so imposing.

He stared at me gravely and said: "Last night, Mr. Duluth, I found my room slightly restricted for my evening exercises. Perhaps you will permit me to perform them in here?"

I permitted him, of course. As I went off to my own room, I

caught a last glimpse of him lying on his back on the floor, his legs weaving solemnly to and fro in the air with a rhythmic motion reminiscent of a six-day bicycle ride.

I have no idea how long he kept it up. But I do know that even in a nightshirt with his legs in the air Dr. Lenz had no difficulty whatsoever in preserving his dignity.

Chapter Fifteen

NEXT MORNING, WHEN Iris and I went down to the deverminized Dagonet for rehearsal, we ran into Gerald Gwynne at the stage door. My juvenile was looking as handsome as ever, but pale and rather sulky. He paid no attention to me. He just shot Iris a queer kind of glance and said:

"Hullo, Iris."

"Hullo," she said.

He was going to push past us when I stopped him. I had promised Mirabelle to get the Hollywood business cleared up. I thought it would be best to do it out there where the others couldn't get involved. I chose the tactful approach. I didn't remind him of his obligations to me; I just treated him like the kid he was and pointed out it was pretty dumb to take up the first movie offer that came his way.

He listened rather impatiently. He said: "I don't give a damn about the offer. I don't give a damn about Hollywood either. I told Mirabelle that. It's just that I've simply got to get out of New York. I can't stay in this dump any longer."

It struck me as odd, his saying that. The other night, when he'd called me about Roland Gates, he'd been so stubbornly eager to stick by Mirabelle.

"Why do you suddenly want to leave New York, Gerald?"

He pushed out his jaw. He said, "That's my own business."

I lost my patience with him then. It so obviously wasn't his own business whether or not he quit my show. I told him a hell of a lot, the general drift being that I needed him badly, that I wouldn't dream of letting him break his contract for no reason and that if he tried any funny business like walking out on me, I'd sue him.

I concluded: "And, if you had any loyalty to me or Mirabelle, you wouldn't ever have brought the matter up."

He flushed a very deep red. I couldn't tell whether it was because he was angry or because he was ashamed.

"If that's the way you feel, that's the way you feel." His eyes, dark, unruly, found Iris's again. Then they turned to me, staring straight at me. I was astonished at the change in their expression. Gerald and I had always been pals. But at that moment he looked as if he was hating me like hell. "Okay, Peter, you can have me if you want me. I'll stay. But I'll tell you one thing. If I knock someone's block off or burn up the theater or—well, don't say I didn't try and get out while the going was good, see."

He swung away, and disappeared through the stage door.

I couldn't make any sense out of that. I turned to Iris. Somehow I had the hunch that she knew what was back of it all. But she wasn't answering any questions. I could tell that.

She slipped her arm through mine, a strange sort of pitying look on her face.

"Don't mind him, Peter. Poor kid, he's so young. It's hell to be so young."

She said that almost tenderly. And I was suddenly, unreasonably jealous of Gerald Gwynne.

Perhaps it was my imagination, but the Dagonet smelt, looked and felt far more wholesome after its night with the hydrocyanic discoids. The clearing of the air had a marked effect upon the company, too. They were almost cheerful. Theo, her cough less insistent, was puffing at a Goldflake, striding about the stage, pointing out to Eddie the small piles of whitish residue left by the discoids, and extolling hydrocyanic gas and codeine simultaneously. Wessler, squatting on a wooden box in the wings, was fiddling contentedly with a clay Rhine maiden and playing his where-have-I-see-you-before game with Gerald and Henry.

Even the stage looked far more as if we were getting somewhere. I'd wanted to rehearse some of the entrances and exits with an actual door and Eddie had fixed up a provisional tormentor from some junk he'd found below stage. It stood there just like a regular piece of scenery, making dress-rehearsal time seem excitingly close.

I was moving to join Wessler when the swing-door opened on Mirabelle, and she swept me away into a corner. She was radiant and vital as ever. If her encounter with Gates had taken anything out of her, she showed no signs of it. She asked breathlessly: "Peter, angel, tell me about Gerald—is it all right?"

"Yes," I said. "I twirled my black mustaches and threatened to foreclose. He isn't going to Hollywood."

"Thank God for that." Then she added in a queer, tentative voice: "And is—is Henry willing to cut the Kramer role?"

I told her what had happened. Her eyes clouded over. Her small gloved hands closed into fists and then opened again. "So Henry's being difficult, is he? I'll have to see about that."

I was going to ask what she meant but at that moment George Kramer himself appeared from the house and started towards us. Mirabelle hurried away and went into a huddle with Gerald.

George Kramer came right up to me. For a few seconds his pouchy eyes watched Mirabelle. Then they slid over to me. "Miss Rue's kind of nervous, isn't she? High-strung. I guess that's the way with most of the big-time actresses. She takes a swell picture, though. My candid shots were very successful yesterday."

"They were?" I said.

"Sure. And the magazine goes to press tonight. Unless you need me, I'd like to leave right after I've done my part and rush some prints through to catch next month's issue. Is that okay?"

"It's okay," I said, only too glad we'd get rid of him that much sooner.

I called the rehearsal to order then. The show went beautifully until the moment of Kramer's entrance when, as the half-drowned business magnate, he was carried on stage by Wessler. Mirabelle had been playing superbly but at that point she went completely off key. There was nothing I could put my finger on; she said her lines; she went through her business; but there was a sudden exaggeration, a very subtle burlesque which brought out all the latent hokum in the scene.

For a moment I was bewildered; then it dawned on me that Mirabelle was putting on a deliberate act for Henry's benefit. Since I had failed to persuade him into cutting the Kramer part she was making a stab at it herself. Only too gladly I gave her her head.

She took full advantage of it. All the time the script had her emoting over Kramer, watching him die before her eyes and recoiling in disgust from his dead body, she managed by brilliantly unobtrusive over-playing to guy the entire scene. Gerald started to clown too while he and Wessler carried Kramer to the coffin, lowered him inside and closed the heavy lid on him.

Wessler was obviously baffled by what was going on, but he continued playing straight and he did it so well that he almost managed to lift the scene single-handed. He exuded tremendous force of personality when, as the iron-willed farmer, he ordered the others around the coffin, forced Mirabelle to her knees at the head and went into a prayer. In spite of Mirabelle's final "Three Orphans" clutch at her throat, he brought real dignity to the moments when he and Gerald lifted the coffin, Kramer and all, and carried it through the door in Eddie's tormentor offstage.

But as soon as they had exited, Mirabelle swirled down to the footlights and gazed at Henry.

"Mr. Prince," she said dramatically, "at last you can see for yourself."

Henry pushed at a lock of lank black hair which drooped over his forehead. "See what, Miss Rue?"

"That scene, of course. Perhaps it seemed all right on paper but when it's acted, it's ludicrous, perfectly ludicrous. You'll have the audience rocking in the aisles. There's only one thing to do. You've got to cut it out."

Henry's eyes slid nervously toward the tormentor behind which Uncle George and the coffin had been deposited. "I—I don't see anything bad in the scene if it's played right."

"Played right!" Mirabelle's voice was suddenly ominous. "Just what do you mean?"

"Well, didn't you overact slightly?" murmured Henry, flushing a deep crimson.

129

"Overact! Me, overact!" Mirabelle flung herself into an instant and terrifying rage. "Did you hear that, Peter? He's accusing me of overacting. *Me*. . . . Isn't he satisfied? Perhaps he can play the part better himself. Is that what he's trying to say? All right, let him play it; I don't give a damn. Let him play it. To hell with him and his lousy melodrama."

She hurled herself past Wessler and Gerald and stormed toward the swing-door. Henry, completely flustered, jumped up and called after her:

"Miss Rue, please, please, don't go. I didn't mean that. You know far more about these things than I do. If you really feel that way, of course we'll cut the scene."

In a second Mirabelle was back at the footlights, smiling a dazzling smile, stretching out her two hands to Henry.

"I knew it!" she cooed. "Didn't I always say Henry was the most intelligent author I ever worked with, Peter? Didn't I say that? Of course, too sad having to tell your uncle to leave, but the play must come first, mustn't it? Why not make a clean sweep, Henry? Why not tell him now?"

"I . . . well . . ." stuttered Henry limply.

"He said he'd be leaving right away. He's probably gone," I cut in. "Eddie, go see if you can catch him."

My stage-manager disappeared and returned to report Kramer had left. The show started off again smoothly.

Mirabelle's victory had been overwhelming and unconditional.

At three-thirty I broke the rehearsal. The women had to go for costume fittings and Wessler was giving a couple of press interviews. I told Eddie to have them all back by seven and left the theater with Iris for a late lunch.

We had passed the doorman's room and were strolling down the alley when I heard a mournful miaow. I turned to see the diabolical Lillian running along a ledge behind us, her tail erect, her whiskers trembling with emotion.

For no apparent reason, she gave me a look of infinite tenderness and leaped onto my shoulder. I made an irascible move to throw her off, but she stuck. She sat there, purring and pushing a rasping chin against my cheek.

"I think," I said, "that I hate this animal more than . . ."

I broke off because of the look on Iris's face. She was staring at me with a sort of wild excitement.

"Peter," she said, "don't move. Stay there. Don't touch the cat."

"What . . ." I began.

"Peter, what fools we've been. What incredible fools. Do you know what you've got on your shoulder?"

Vaguely alarmed for her sanity, I said: "I have on my shoulder the cat of the doorman."

"No," she said. "You haven't. Look at it—the colour of its fur. It's weaved around your throat. It's light brown. Don't you see?"

She leaned toward me, grabbing my arm. "That isn't a cat, Peter, it's a light tan fur."

Chapter Sixteen

I PUSHED THE cat off my shoulder. It scuttled back through the stage door.

I said: "So our cat's been masquerading. But where does it get us?"

"It gets us to this," said Iris firmly. She had it all figured out. "Last night you asked Lenz why on earth there should have been two unknown people in the theater—the man with the mask and the woman with the light tan fur. Don't you see the explanation now? Theo only thought the face she saw was a woman's because of the fur. Now that the fur's a cat . . ."

"The person who carried it might just as well have been a man," I finished. "In other words, those two people can be merged into one. But where else does it get us?"

"Nowhere," said Iris blandly. "But we can think about it while we eat lunch."

We did think about it over lunch without progressing any further. We were still thinking about it when an apologetic rustling at my side drew my attention to Henry Prince. My young author was twiddling his hat in thin fingers; his solemn spectacles were aimed at my face.

"They told me you'd be here, Mr. Duluth," he said.

I asked him to join us at lunch but he said he wasn't hungry. Could he talk to me, he said. I nodded and he dropped into the third chair next to Iris.

"Mr. Duluth," he faltered, "I want you please to do me a favor. Will you break the news to Uncle George, I mean about his not being needed for the part any longer?"

"Sure," I said. "If you'd rather not do it yourself."

Henry picked up a piece of bread and pulled off random crumbs. "It's all very worrying. I was so afraid Miss Rue would walk out that really before I knew what I was saying, I'd given in about that role." He looked lost and pathetic. "I shouldn't have done it. I don't know what will happen."

There was no mistaking his distress.

"What's on your mind?" I asked.

Henry glanced at Iris who said politely: "Shall I take my fruitcup to another table?"

"No, no. I don't mind your hearing. It's a relief to be able to talk. I've been so worried, so—so alone." Henry squeezed crumbs into a bread pellet. "I think you guessed, Mr. Duluth, that I didn't really want that scene kept in. It was just that Uncle George wanted to play it and—well, I have to do what he tells me."

It was an immense relief to have someone let down at last and give me some dope on Uncle George Kramer.

"We suspected as much," I admitted. "Has Kramer been black-mailing you?"

"Oh, no, I couldn't say that. I'm sure Uncle George is being this way just because he thinks I'm going to be successful and rich. He thinks I can afford it."

"What's he got against you?" I said.

Henry hesitated. "It's just that he knows something about—about my family. He used to be so kind about it until he found out that my play was going to be put on. Then, that first night when he came to the Dagonet, he was quite different, kind of sneering and threatening. He told me he wanted to get that photo-graphic assignment and when I explained I didn't have the authority to give it him, he—he said he'd tell everyone what he knew."

"So he railroaded you into making me give him the photo-graphic work and that part in the play?"

"Yes. You see, Uncle said he had a particular reason for wanting to be in your play. And the five hundred dollars I borrowed from you . . ."

"That went to Uncle George too. I thought as much. Maybe I'm a suspicious New Yorker, Henry, but that sounds damn like blackmail to me. I guess you're scared now we've got rid of him that he'll tell the world what he knows?"

"I am, Mr. Duluth. I'm terribly afraid. But I don't think Uncle George is really bad. If only you could help me." Henry sniffed and blew his nose on a serviceable handkerchief. "It would be the end of everything if Uncle George told about Father."

For the first time in our acquaintance I started thinking of the shy, naïve Henry as a human being. I was sorry for the poor kid. He was so very much at the mercy of any cheap chiseler.

Iris leaned forward. "What is it he knows about your father, Henry?"

That was a question I had not felt justified in asking, but I silently cheered Iris's nerve. Henry looked at his hand miserably.

"It's not only Father—it's me, too. You see, Dad was the bank-manager in Karsville where I was born. Everyone respected him and he was a fine person. But last year there was trouble. Some company went bankrupt. The bank had a great many shares. Dad and all his depositors were faced with ruin. He took desperate measures to try and save the bank. I don't really understand those things or what he did. But the inspectors found out and—and put him in prison. He's there now."

We didn't say anything and he went on: "I'd been training to be a doctor at the time. But, of course, I had to give it up. We didn't have any money left and I had to support mother somehow. I tried to get a job but I couldn't until Uncle George turned up one day and said he could get me into the Thespian Hospital. It wasn't much of a salary but I'd have taken anything and my medical training was useful."

He was watching me with worried eyes. "All the time, in my free moments. I was trying to write a play. Dad had always wanted me to do it. I finished it at last and sent it off to you. Your reply came back accepting it and asking me to come to see you. I was so excited I threw up my job right away before pay-day. I didn't have a cent in my pocket. I always sent most of my salary back to Mother. I had to get to New York. Uncle George's car was there outside the hospital. I just got in it and drove up here. I didn't mean to steal it. I was going to drive right back, but seeing you and hearing about the play made me forget everything. The police traced the car and delivered it back to Uncle George. I didn't really think I was doing wrong, but when he came to the theater that night, Uncle George told me he could still have me arrested if he wanted to for taking a stolen car over a state line. That's—that's how he made me get him into the play and everything."

I stared at him. "Henry, is that all Uncle George has got against you—that your father's in jail and that you borrowed his car?"

"But think what it would mean to me if it all came out now just when I'm beginning to be successful. My father a jailbird; me a thief and . . ."

"My dear Henry—" I felt very paternal in the face of so much rural simplicity—"New York's a little different from Karsville. In New York your father can be in jail, your mother can be in jail, your grandmother can be in jail and everyone gives three cheers. As for the car-stealing—if that's all you're worried about, forget it." A sudden idea came to me. "On the contrary, we won't forget it. This is swell. Why didn't I think of it before? I'll get my press-agent to slam the story all over the theatrical columns. *Eager young author steals car to keep appointment with producer.* It'll make dandy publicity."

Henry was gazing at me half in astonishment, half in relief. "You really mean it wouldn't matter—not even if Uncle told?"

"Your Uncle George," I said, "hasn't a leg to stand on. And you and I are going right round to his studio and we're going to fix his feet so properly that he'll want to creep away and curl up and die."

I was excited. I had a lever on Mr. Kramer at last. With any luck I could use Henry's pathetic little problem to rid the Dagonet of disturbances permanently. For I knew Kramer to be a small-time blackmailer; I was positive that all the trouble at the theater had been mere manifestations of Uncle George.

When Iris went off for her fitting appointment, I bundled

Henry into a taxi and drove around to Kramer's studio-cum-apartment, somewhere in the East sixties. An elevator took us to the third floor and a door bearing the legend: "George Kramer, Art Photographer."

I knocked peremptorily. There was no reply. I knocked again.

"Perhaps he's in the dark-room." suggested Henry. "Try the door."

I did. It was open, and we walked in.

A narrow hall led into a large studio furnished with chairs, spotlights, hanging backcloths, cameras and a few surrealistic blocks of wood which were obviously used to inject Art into the photography. Several tin cabinets lined the walls; their drawers all gaped open, revealing an untidy mass of scattered studio portraits.

Henry moved to a door in the rear wall calling uncertainly: "Uncle George! Are you there? It's Henry."

When there was no reply, he muttered something about looking in the bedroom. Left alone, I moved to the photograph cabinets. It seemed odd to me that Mr. Kramer should have left them in so singularly haphazard a condition. I glanced into the first drawer. The photographs inside, mostly portraits of theatrical celebrities, were crushed and bent as if someone had been furiously searching through them, completely indifferent to the havoc caused. The more I looked, the more certain I became that the searcher, whoever he was had not been Mr. Kramer himself.

Most of the photographs were, or had been, in folders, each of which was marked with the particular name of the actor or actress. As I passed to the next cabinet, I noticed a folder labelled *Mirabelle Rue*. I pulled it out and opened it.

It was empty.

That started me thinking. Then, just as I was throwing the file back, a most extraordinary picture, half concealed by a dis-lodged profile study of Tallulah Bankhead, caught my eye. I tugged it out for closer inspection. It must have been about twelve inches by fifteen—the life-size image of a face. And it was an incredibly shocking face—the face of a man with dead, staring eyes, blistered lips and cut, distorted cheeks. A man without identity, a Grand Guignol fantasy.

As I gazed at it in revolted fascination, Henry reappeared, murmuring: "Uncle must be taking the candid shots round to the magazine. I . . ." He came up to me, pausing by my elbow. "My God!"

I glanced up. The change in his appearance was amazing. His lips were half open; his eyes were fixed incredulously on the photograph in my hand.

"What on earth's the matter?" I asked.

"That photograph!" he breathed.

"Its fairly unpleasant, but . . ."

"But it's not just a photograph." Henry twisted his fingers together. "I mean—don't you know *who* it is? It's Wessler."

"Wessler!"

I gazed down at that appalling travesty of a face.

"Wessler," repeated Henry. "Just after the airplane accident."

I could see it then. Once it had been pointed out to me, I could just realize how this thing could be Conrad Wessler. The matted hair was blond, the eyes, though lusterless, were the same eyes. It was shocking to think that anything so basically perfect as Wessler's face could have disintegrated into something as grotesque as this.

I turned back to Henry. "But how do you know?"

"Uncle George told you about these photographs he took for the plastic surgery people at the Thespian Hospital," he faltered. "When Wessler found out about them, he asked to have all the negatives destroyed. Uncle kept this one. He showed it to me back in Karsville. He enlarged it—just the face. He said then it might be valuable. I didn't understand what he meant. I didn't know he—he still had it."

I hardly listened; I was too busy thinking. At last we were getting onto Kramer's real racket. A man with an entree into an actor's hospital taking pictures of actors when they were sick and holding them up with the negatives when they were cured—that was as low and unsavory a brand of blackmail as I had ever come across. And it explained so much. Mirabelle had been at the Thespian Hospital, too. Probably Kramer had been trying to blackmail her with some photograph of this sort. That was why she'd been so anxious to get rid of him and yet so obviously scared of him.

And then this picture of Wessler—it opened up a new vista.

"Listen, Henry," I said, "this is important. That first night when Kramer came to the theater, you left almost immediately. You went to have a drink together, didn't you?"

"Why, yes."

"But after you left the theater, were you with Kramer all the evening?"

Henry looked rather dazed. "No, I wasn't, Mr. Duluth. After we'd been at Sardot's about half an hour, Uncle George met a friend of his—Roland Gates. They sent me away. They said they had something private to talk over."

Everything was fitting in far more reasonably than I'd imagined possible. With blinding clarity, I saw what must be the solution to our mystery. Kramer had in his possession this picture of Wessler. On the night that he'd come to the theater he'd probably had it in his portfolio, intending to use it to extort money from Wessler. That would explain his eagerness to force Henry into getting him a place in the company.

And then he had met up with Roland Gates. Gates wanted like hell to play opposite Mirabelle. He wanted like hell to get Wessler out of the cast. After they had sent Henry away, the two of them could so easily have pooled resources and worked out a plan for frightening Wessler out.

Kramer knew about the Austrian's fear of mirrors; he'd seen the doorman's scrap-book and from it could have learned the Lillian Reed legend. They had all the cards. One of them could have brought the light tan fur cat in earlier and staged the prologue. Theo saw them later. While Roland Gates got rid of the doorman and kept watch downstairs, Kramer could have slipped into the dressing-room and engineered the trick with the false mirror.

And, for the first time, I realized just how diabolically cruel that trick must have been. Kramer had this photograph of Wessler. If he had modeled his clay mask on it, Wessler would have been confronted not with just *any* frightening face, but with a ghastly travesty of himself as he had looked in those terrible days after the accident.

The more I thought, the more logical it all seemed. The plan failed; instead of frightening Wessler it killed Comstock. Then, with typical bravado, Gates had gone on trying to achieve his object and tried to blackmail me by threatening to expose to the police a crime which he himself had committed.

I felt an absurd exhilaration. All I had to do was to let Kramer and Gates know I was wise to their racket, and scare the daylights out of them. Then there'd be no more trouble at the Dagonet.

The case was solved.

I folded the photograph of Wessler into my pocket, thanking God I'd managed to confiscate it before it could do any more damage. In a burst of enthusiasm I slapped Henry on the back.

"Henry," I said, "the Dagonet is no longer jinxed. The waters have stopped being troubled. We have nothing more to worry about."

I meant it. I really thought it. But that was probably the rashest statement ever made by any human being.

Chapter Seventeen

My mood of exhilaration did not flag. It lasted through a couple of hectic hours at the office and was still bubbling when I reached the Dagonet. Now that I was convinced the Kramer-Gates combine had been back of everything. I was in no hurry to bring matters to a head. My only immediate precaution was to leave a note for Kramer with the doorman. The note informed Uncle George curtly that his services were no longer required and that, if he came to my office next morning, he would be paid his rehearsal salary to date. That, I figured would keep him away from the Dagonet and ensure his appearance at my office where I could tell him forcibly what I thought of him.

I was looking forward to that moment.

I managed to check an impulse to pass on the good news to my company. By that time I was cagey enough to hold back until I was one hundred percent sure of my ground. But Iris noticed something had happened to me. Just before I got the rehearsal started, she said: "Peter, what's the matter? You look as if you'd just created the world."

"I have," I said. "I've created a new heaven and a new earth and they're both completely devoid of ladies with light tan furs, blackmailers, faces in mirrors and corpses. Okay, everyone—let's get going. We play the first act according to Mirabelle's altered script."

I'd been excited about that rehearsal before it began. I was wowed when it started. Something, presumably the absence of George Kramer, had given the company that extra fillip of assurance which makes all the difference between brilliance and competency. I sat there in the auditorium watching, admiring and feeling smug.

And it seemed perfectly justifiable for me to feel smug. As the first act zipped forward, I started totalling up exactly what I'd accomplished. A few months ago, I had been a futureless has-been just out of a nuthouse; Henry Prince had been a small-town nobody; Iris had never even walked across a stage; Wessler, his career apparently at an end, had been moping over his half-brother and his own synthetic face; and Mirabelle had been struggling on the brink of a nervous break-down. A few months ago we had been just that—a bunch of ciphers, making loud noises in a void.

And now we were the *Troubled Waters Company*; we were a high-power, beautifully efficient unit; we were heading straight to the top with all flags flying.

And we'd done that despite every sort of obstacle. We'd been through hell and we'd proved we had enough guts to rise like a flock of phoenixes from our own ashes.

We rated all the luck that was coming to us.

That's the way I was thinking as I sat there in the house watching my players putting on the star performances of their careers. Wessler was immense. Gerald, Theo and Iris gave one hundred percent support. Mirabelle made her entrance and lit the whole dreary theater up like a flame.

I knew Mirabelle would go all out to justify her script altera-tions. And she did. When the act went into the new scene she kept the tempo keyed up by the sheer force of her own personality. Even though the others were a bit uncertain with their business, she took the whole responsibility off my shoulders. She was really directing and acting at the same time, something that no one in the theater could do as impressively as Mirabelle.

And, in spite of the fact that it had its origin in a simple desire to get rid of George Kramer, the revised scene was an infinite improvement on the old sequence. It had a slashing, exciting speed. Wessler and Gerald went out to search for the body of Mirabelle's "friend" in the flood. While they were gone, the three women sat around the stage motionless, exchanging only a few terse sentences until the men came back again carrying the coffin.

Those moments had a simplicity, a starkness that had never been there before.

I leaned forward in my seat, watching as Gerald and Wessler laid the coffin reverently on the boards. Without a word, Wessler crossed to Mirabelle, took her arm and dragged her to the casket.

She stood there, her head tilted defiantly backward, her hands on her hips. Wessler was glaring at her. For a split second they held that pose—the tough honky-tonk girl and the tyrannical patriarch facing each other and hating each other over the body of the girl's elderly pick-up.

Then, very slowly, Wessler stooped; his huge hands moved to the catches; he swung open the lid of the coffin.

My attention was riveted on Mirabelle as she shrugged contemptuously and glanced down into the coffin. It was a superb piece of playing. She had that character down pat—to the last flicker of an eyelash. I was thinking how Brooks Atkinson was going to rave and Gilbert Gabriel and Wolcott Gibbs.

And then, suddenly, everything went mad. As I watched, I saw the blood drain out of Mirabelle's cheeks; I saw her eyes narrow to needle points of horror; saw her lips drop open and stick in a white, meaningless smile.

Wessler gave a thick gasp. Then he was at her side, his great arm sliding roughly around her waist, supporting her.

It was horrible seeing them both that way, as if they had switched into some utterly different play, some drama of panic outside my comprehension.

Gerald and Iris and Theo had broken the scene and were running toward them.

"Mirabelle," I began, "what the hell . . . ?"

But her eyes were still fixed on the coffin, staring blindly down. She didn't look up. She didn't seem to be conscious that anyone was near.

Then she laughed, a high, strangled laugh.

"We changed the first act. We changed the first act to get rid of Kramer. That's what we did. And he's still here! My God, Kramer was here all the time . . ."

For the first second that amazing speech meant nothing to me. I jumped from my seat and sprang up onto the stage with Eddie following. The others were all clustered around the casket. Some-one screamed—I think it was Theo. I heard Iris calling: "Peter, look!" I pushed roughly through to Mirabelle and Wessler. I stared straight down into the coffin.

The shock of what I saw came before I was ready for it. It didn't seem real. It was something impossibly grotesque, devised by the imbecile mind of the Dagonet Theater.

That coffin was not empty. Stretched inside it, plump hands clasped peacefully over his vest, lay Uncle George Kramer.

I didn't move for a moment. I didn't speak; I didn't think; I didn't feel. I just stared in fascination at those plump, white hands, at the round plump face which stared unwinkingly back from wide, sightless eyes. There was a smile on George Kramer's lips, a stiff idiotic smile as if his mouth were held up at the corners by pins. His skin was tight and glossy like wax; there were bluish patches like spattered ink.

And he was lying there with no visible wound, no visible sign of struggle—just straight and rigid and horribly dead.

Chapter Eighteen

My voice, when it came, sounded like the whine of a mosquito. "Eddie, help me get him out of the coffin."

My stage-manager was there at my side. I saw his strong arms slide into the coffin and under Kramer's arms. I got hold of the legs. We lifted. While the others backed away, we slung Kramer out onto the stage.

He lay there, his legs sprawled crazily sideways. I dropped on my knees. Feverishly I pushed him upward so that we could see his back. There was no sign of a wound there. Eddie took his shoulders, lowered them. My hand groped for the wrist, feeling for the pulse.

There wasn't any, of course. I'd known that. From the beginning I'd known he was dead.

Dimly I became aware of the others—Mirabelle's face drawn and haggard, Theo, her lips gripped between her teeth; Iris and Gerald. . . . I seemed to see them like blurred shadows thrown on a screen.

"Gerald," I called. "Get the women away. And Wessler! All of you get away."

I tried to say something else, but suddenly the words wouldn't come. I seemed to be drifting into some warm, sickly miasma.

Then I heard Iris's voice like a faint scratching on my eardrums. "Eddie, get Peter away! Get him away from that coffin. Don't you see? It's the gas—the fumigation gas!"

I felt arms around me, dragging me. I made an enormous effort to move my legs forward. Right, left, right, left. Something scraped past me and then slammed back—the swing-door. I was out in the passage, lying limply against Eddie's shoulder. Gradually things began to slide back into focus. First the iron banisters of the passage, hard, gleaming, then a hand, curved over my sleeve; then Iris's face, white and anxious, close to mine.

"Peter, are you all right? Tell me."

"Sure I'm all right. But . . ."

"It was that hydrocyanic gas. It must have been. Some of it must have been left in the coffin," said Iris urgently. "The hydrocyanic gas, it almost killed you—and it killed Kramer."

Someone opened the door to Wessler's dressing-room. We all trooped in. I sat down on one of the bare wooden chairs. I felt better sitting down. Eddie put a cigarette into my mouth. He was gazing at me ruefully.

"Feel pretty groggy myself," he said. "I guess Miss Pattison's right. It was that hydrocyanic gas."

"But Kramer!" said Theo bleakly. " We ought to go back on stage and get Kramer."

"It's no use," said Eddie. "He's dead. Better not touch him any more than we can help. He must have died a couple of minutes after we put him in the coffin this morning. That damn stuff must have been hanging around in the upholstery. It works instantly. Even—even when we were looking for him to tell him we didn't want him around any more, even then I guess he was dead. Naturally, I never thought to look in the coffin."

For a second or two we all stood and sat in that small dressing-room, staring at each other.

Then Mirabelle whispered: "But what shall we do?"

It seemed only too evident what we had to do. "Get down to the doorman's room, Gerald," I said, "and call the police."

"The police!" echoed Iris.

"Of course the police. We've got to bring the police into it now." All of a sudden it struck me as funny, savagely, tragically funny. I'd had the mystery sewed up. I'd had Kramer as the villain of the piece. Everything was in the bag. The play was saved. And now this—Kramer dead, asphyxiated by hydrocyanic gas in a coffin!

Gerald still stood by the door.

"What are you waiting for?" I said. "Get the police. And—

call headquarters, try to get Inspector Clarke. God knows, I haven't the slightest idea whether you can get any policeman you want. But he's a pal of mine. It would be better to get him."

Gerald slipped out of the room. He was back soon. He said he had contacted Inspector Clarke and that he'd be right over. If it was possible for anything to improve the situation, that did. Clarke had been on a case once before when I'd been involved. I knew he'd take care of my interests as far as he could.

That indeterminate period of waiting covered some of the worst minutes in my life. None of us talked. But it was more than obvious what the others were thinking. I was thinking it myself. There was no getting around it.

George Kramer had been a blackmailer. Only that afternoon I had learned just how real a menace he might have been to almost anyone in my company. In spite of our efforts to get him out of the cast, he had stuck; he'd hung around where he wasn't wanted. And now he was dead.

I kept telling myself that it was an accident. Somehow that deadly gas had collected in the coffin; somehow it hadn't evaporated; merely by chance Kramer had been carried in the coffin behind that tormentor where we couldn't see whether or not he had climbed out. I tried to pretend to myself that this was the way it had happened. But I couldn't, because I knew too much. I knew about the other things that had occurred at the Dagonet. I knew that someone had deliberately let the rats out of Eddie's traps.

That little fact, which had seemed so ridiculously meaningless, now took on alarming proportions. No one bothers to let rats out of traps without a good reason. Now I could see an incredibly sound reason for that deliberate piece of sabotage. If someone had been eager to have the Dagonet fumigated, if one of the many people who wanted Kramer out of the way, had already thought out an intricate plan for staging this "accident" to cloak a . . .

I didn't use the word "murder"—not even to myself. I didn't dare burn my boats so irrevocably. But, inside me, I was sure as I had ever been of anything that murdered was the word for Kramer.

And the police were coming. In a few minutes they would be there, asking questions for which there were no answers except the answers that would reveal so much that we had been trying to keep dark.

Less than half an hour ago, I'd felt on top of the world, with success spread out at my feet, real and positive as Manhattan Island from the Empire State Building. Now we had this on our hands—something far too big for us to cope with ourselves. The whole flimsy card castle was crumbling. It looked like the end of *Troubled Waters*, Peter Duluth, Inc. and my come-back.

And for me—what?

I suppose we'd been sitting around in that dressing-room for about fifteen minutes before we heard footsteps ascending the stairs outside. Mirabelle started. Wessler gazed fixedly at the door. Iris, her voice very low and husky, said:

"The police."

Still pretty unsure on my feet, I crossed to the door. I hadn't the slightest idea what I was going to say to the police. I opened the door and closed it behind me. I looked down the corridor, thinking: "This is the end."

Then a faint hope stirred inside me. It was not Inspector Clarke of the Homicide Squad who was moving up the stairs. It was Dr. Lenz.... Dr. Lenz who always appeared miraculously when I needed him most.

I went up to him I clutched his arm. I said: "Thank God you've come."

His gray eyes were placid. "What is the matter, Mr. Duluth?"

Swiftly I told him everything.

Not once did that steady gaze flicker. He merely said:

"And Mr. Kramer is on the stage?"

"Yes. But you can't go near. The gas . . ."

"The gas should have dissipated by now." He patted my shoulder. "Please try not to distress yourself more than you can help. Join the others. I will be with you immediately."

147

He eased me toward Wessler's dressing-room. Before I shut the door behind me, I caught a glimpse of his wide, black-coated back disappearing onto the stage.

Less than five minutes later he joined us. His bearded face was grave but it showed absolutely no sign of concern.

"I have examined Mr. Kramer," he said. "It seems to me there is no doubt but that he died from hydrocyanic gas poisoning." He paused, regarding his thumbnail. "In fact, I was able to look into the coffin itself. I saw there a whitish residue such as is left by the fumigator's discoids. It is clear what must have happened. Last night, during the fumigation, a discoid must have slipped into the coffin. Since it was cool inside and there was little ventilation, the process of evaporation would have been considerably slowed up and what gas there was would have become absorbed by the upholstery. When Mr. Kramer was lowered into the coffin, the warmth of his body speeded up the vaporization of the discoid. Almost immediately, before he had time either to realize what was happening or to struggle, he must have lost consciousness; in a short time, he must have died. I can see no reason why anyone should be blamed."

His solemn gaze moved to each of us in turn.

"I feel sure that the police must adopt the same attitude as I. It was an unusual but a very understandable accident."

I stared at him. "You really think it was an accident?"

"But, of course, Mr. Duluth." Lenz's raised left eyebrow indicated mild surprise. "What reason is there to believe otherwise?"

I could have told him a dozen reasons. But I didn't. For I realized what he was doing then. He was doing what none of us had the nerve to do. In so many words he was saying: *"Keep your mouths shut and maybe we'll get away with it. It's our only chance."*

He didn't put it that crudely, of course. But I'm sure there wasn't a person in the room who didn't get his meaning, when he added: "I'm certain you all agree that this play means a great deal to each one of us. We have already had trouble—very

148

unfortunate trouble with Mr. Comstock. It is a difficult situation. One is apt to imagine foolish things—that the two accidents, for example, must necessarily be connected. I suggest that we all banish fancies of that kind from our minds. I also suggest that we should only cause a great deal of confusion if we told the police anything more than the bare facts of what has happened tonight."

It was unscrupulous, of course. It was anti-social and immoral and downright criminal. Lenz was a wonderful man.

His serene gaze traveled around the room.

"Is there anyone who disagrees with me?"

I looked at the others. I knew that it was just as vital in their lives as it was in mine to save the show.

"No," I said, "there isn't anyone who disagrees with you."

"There certainly isn't," said Iris firmly.

Which seemed to set the stage for the arrival of the police.

There was a whole carload of them, Inspector Clarke himself, quiet and alert, a medical examiner, a photographer and several plainclothesmen. For a couple of hours they swarmed over the theater. Lenz appointed himself mouthpiece for our faction. He explained about the fumigation; he pointed out the remnants of the discoid; he told an extremely convincing story for the accident theory, with all the weight of his massive reputation behind him.

Inspector Clarke seemed suitably credulous. Although he was one of the smartest men in the squad, he had worked with Lenz on a homicide case before and it must have been almost impossible for him to suspect that so important a personage would hold back a deliberate murder from the police.

Finally I was questioned. I didn't lie because I wasn't given the opportunity. I merely said that Kramer was a member of my company; that his role had made it perfectly natural for him to have been left unnoticed in the coffin; that I knew next to nothing about his private life. I did, however, hold back the fact that Kramer had been Henry Prince's uncle. Although I was sure my author would be only too willing to join our conspiracy of silence, I would have hated like hell to have him thrown up against one

149

of Clarke's concise interrogations. Guile was not Henry's long suit.

Finally everything seemed over. The medical examiner had borne out Lenz's theory as to the cause of death and the probability of its being accidental. The police were ready to go.

Believing fervently in Santa Claus, I went downstairs with Inspector Clarke. He was extremely pleasant. He chatted about our friendship in the past and offered messages of good luck for my future.

But at the stage door, he paused. His young, shrewd eyes watched me curiously.

"That's a pretty darn good fumigation company you employed, Mr. Duluth. It's kind of surprising they'd have done something as careless as dropping one of those discoids in that coffin."

"Y-yes," I said. I'd never thought of it from the viewpoint of the fumigation company.

Clarke shrugged. "Of course, I'm not an expert but I'd have thought any discoid put in that coffin last night would have been harmless by the time you started rehearsal. But Lenz says the gas could have got soaked into the upholstery. Guess he knows." He paused. "I believe that stuff's pretty easy to obtain—that hydrocyanic gas. Anyone can buy it in some form or other at the drug store, can't they?"

"I don't know," I said.

"Well, I'll take the whole business up with the fumigating people right away. Guess I'll know more about the set-up then." He paused a moment. "Having kind of bad luck around this place, aren't you, Mr. Duluth? First that old fellow Comstock—and now Kramer."

Until then no mention had been made of Comstock.

I said as casually as I could: "Yes, Comstock had a heart attack at rehearsal. Poor old guy. Lenz was around at the time but there was nothing we could do."

"Dr. Lenz was around, eh? He's a fine man." Clarke glanced up. "They tell me he's backing the show."

"Yeah. He is."

Clarke's eyes widened very slightly. "Sort of useful person to have around in an emergency." He moved into the alley, whistling under his breath. Then he turned. His smile wasn't at all encouraging.

He said: "I'd kind of like to drop in on a couple of your rehearsals. No objections, I suppose?"

"Of course not," I said uneasily. "Be delighted to see you any time."

"Thanks." Clarke was still whistling. "It'd be interesting to see how well you folks can act on stage—particularly after tonight. So long."

"So long," I said.

All of a sudden I had stopped believing in Santa Claus.

Chapter Nineteen

IT'S AMAZING HOW you can take almost anything, when your fiber's toughened to it. In spite of the horrible circumstances of his death, I didn't feel the least twinge of pity for George Kramer. I didn't give a damn, either, who had killed him or why. Nothing mattered except my passionate determination that, in spite of murder and a suspicious police force, *Troubled Waters* was going to open on the scheduled date.

As soon as Inspector Clarke and his men had gone, I started systematically and shamelessly to block all channels through which Clarke might learn the truth. I began with the doorman. I retrieved from him and destroyed the note I had written telling Kramer his services were no longer required. I warned him against mentioning the trouble with the rat traps, hinting that if Clarke found out about it, he would most certainly suspect Mac of having a hand in Kramer's death. That worked like magic.

Upstairs on the landing I had a short conference with Lenz. I said: "That was just a stall of yours about the accident, wasn't it? You do think he was murdered?"

"I'm afraid one must admit the possibility." Lenz smiled ruefully. "In view of all the evidence, it seems unlikely that we should have a second mere accident on our hands. It would have been simple, disarmingly simple, for someone to have slipped some form of cyanide into the coffin and to have made use of the fumigators to cover his tracks." He paused. "If it did happen that way, I regret to say I feel partly responsible. It was I who introduced Mr. Kramer into your play. My 'provocative dose' seems to have succeeded only in eliminating itself."

"Kramer had it coming to him," I said. "But so long as you suspect murder, too, I know where we stand. Clarke's not satisfied with the accident. We've got to keep him from getting any wiser."

I went into Wessler's dressing-room where the company still sat around in bleak silence. I gave them a very tough spiel, saying in so many words that we were all in it up to the neck and that our only chance was to present a united front. They got on to it all right. I was confident there'd be no trouble from them.

My next assignment was Henry Prince. Promising Lenz and Iris to join them later at the apartment, I took a taxi to my author's place. I found him at home and gave him the bare facts of his uncle's death. I had not intended to let him guess we even suspected murder. But he was smarter than I thought.

As he listened, his lips went very pale. At last he faltered: "The police, do they think . . .?"

"No," I cut in. "It was an accident."

"You're just saying that. You don't believe it." Henry gripped my arm urgently. "After—after all that's happened, with Uncle George making everyone hate him, it can't be an accident. Somebody must . . ."

"Okay, I'll admit it," I said. "We do think he might have been murdered, but we're trying to hold it back from the police. If you want your show to open, I advise you to keep your mouth shut."

"Keep my mouth shut!" Henry gave a rather hysterical laugh. "Can you imagine my going to the police? I told you this afternoon Uncle George had been getting money out of me, pestering me. What would the police think if they knew that? They'd—they'd think I murdered him."

"Guess they would," I said.

Henry was scared stiff. I thought it best to leave him that way. So long as he was worried about his own skin, he could be relied upon to keep quiet about ours.

I went back to the apartment and reported my activities to Lenz and Iris. I said wearily: "This is a swell situation. I started off trying to produce a play and now I'm trying to protect an unknown murderer from the police. Soon we'll all be cutting each other's throats for the sheer fun of the thing."

"I agree that we have been forced to adopt a very anti-social

attitude," said Lenz placidly. "But I think we may justify ourselves a little if we remember that Mr. Kramer, from all we know
of him, was no great loss to the world."

"You don't know the half of it," I said. I added bleakly, "A
couple of hours ago I had everything figured out. Now my
theory's blown higher than a kite."

I told them everything I'd thought out in Kramer's studio. I
showed them the photograph of Wessler.

"Kramer was a blackmailer," I said. "And Gates is a blackmailer plus. I thought it was just that the Dagonet had become
a blackmailer's convention. But now . . ."

The buzzer shrilled. I went to the door. Gerald Gwynne came
in, his young face drawn, his eyes dark and smouldering.

"I've got to talk to you, Peter," he said.

He went into the living-room and sat down on the couch
next to Iris.

I followed and said: "What is it?"

"It's about Kramer. Mirabelle says I've got to tell you something." He looked up. "He was a filthy blackmailer."

"We know that," I said. "We know all about his racket—
selling embarrassing photographs to actors and actresses. He was
trying something like that on Mirabelle, wasn't he?"

Gerald's lips tightened. "He was, the swine. Mirabelle thought
you'd better know otherwise you'd be wondering just why we'd
been trying to get him out of the cast. That's what was back of
it. He'd taken some beastly photos of Mirabelle when she was
in the Thespian Hospital—when she was sick and didn't know
anything about it. Ever since she came out, he's been threatening
her, trying to get money out of her." He gave a savage laugh.
"Seeing him dead in that coffin tonight was one of the
pleasantest experiences of my life."

I asked: "And Mirabelle paid up?"

"She paid up, of course. She couldn't have pictures like that
going the rounds. But, later, when he came to the Dagonet,
Kramer changed his tack. He started trying to force her into
making you ditch Wessler and take on Roland Gates."

That came as a shock. "My God, what an unspeakable thing to do!"

"Unspeakable's putting it mildly. Kramer let her have three days to make up her mind. Those three days stopped this morning." He added suddenly: "You and Henry were at Kramer's studio before rehearsal tonight, weren't you?"

"How do you know?" I asked, surprised.

"I know because I was there too, I heard you coming; heard your voices outside and managed to scram down the fire-escape." Gerald stuck out his jaw. "I'd gone there to give Kramer Mirabelle's reply. I'd gone there to tell him very sweetly that she'd see Gates in hell before she played with him and that if Kramer didn't give us back those photographs I would murder him. That's what I'd gone there to say."

He threw out his hand. "It so happened I didn't have to murder him. I guess he was already sewed up in that coffin. Seems like he was a damn sloppy person though. The door was open. I just went in, and rummaged around in his photographs. I found the ones I wanted. Thank God, I destroyed them. If the police had gotten on to them, they'd be asking some pretty damn awkward questions by now." He paused. "That's all Mirabelle or I had to do with Kramer. Mirabelle said I was to tell you."

For a while, after he'd stopped speaking, we sat around in silence. Then Iris turned to Gerald and said quietly:

"There's one thing more we've got to ask. And don't mind about telling us. You know we'd be on your side. Did you or Mirabelle actually kill Kramer?"

That question seemed to floor him for a second. Then he looked at her steadily and said: "No, we didn't kill Kramer."

He got up as if he were going to leave. Just as he reached the door, he paused, swinging back to us, a queer expression on his face.

"You really meant what you said just now?" he asked. "You wouldn't blame anyone for killing Kramer?"

155

I looked at Lenz. He was sitting on the couch, calmly inspecting his fingernails. "Can you imagine us blaming anyone?"

Gerald said: "In that case, I'm going to tell you something else. I haven't even mentioned it to Mirabelle. But I guess, as you said, we're all in it together; we all ought to know—everything. This afternoon when I went to Kramer's place, someone else was just coming out. She knows I saw her. She didn't even try and hide."

"Who was it?" I asked.

He looked down at the carpet. "Theo Ffoulkes," he said. "I don't know what she was doing there. If you're interested, you'd better ask her. But I do know something. As she went by me, she was shutting her handbag. I caught a glimpse inside."

Very slowly, he added: "Inside that bag she was carrying a revolver."

Chapter Twenty

W HEN I HEARD that I almost wished Gerald hadn't told me. There were more than enough potential suspects for Kramer's murder already in my cast. I hated the idea of having Theo involved too. But I had to follow it through. After Gerald had left, I called Theo's place and asked if I could go round.

Her voice, vague and very tired, said: "Of course you can come, darling. I'm in bed but that doesn't matter, does it?"

"No," I said.

I got into a taxi right away and drove over. She lived downtown in a sort of actor's club. I went up to her floor and knocked on her door.

From inside she called: "It's open darling."

I went in. She was sitting up in bed, wearing very severe white pajamas. She looked rather wonderful, like Lady Gwendoline Marchbanks, the haughty British heroine of a pre-war romance.

She said: "I'm not trying to be glamorous, Peter. It's just that I'm worried about my bloody cough. I'm keeping it warm." She leaned over to the bedtable and took a pill out of a small bottle. "I'm living on Lenz's codeine pills. They'll either kill or cure me by the time we open."

I sat down on the edge of the bed watching her. She gave a queer, crooked smile.

"I'm talking about opening just as if there hadn't been a couple of dozen major catastrophes. Are we going to open Peter?"

"We are," I said.

She took one of my hands in both of her own, squeezing it. "I know just how much hell all this is for you. I think it's pretty grand the way you're bearing up."

"I'm just trying to get along," I said.

"On a not very even break." She added quietly: "How about that policeman, Clarke? I didn't trust him. He's too bright. He suspects something, doesn't he?"

"I think he does. We're just hoping he'll give up being suspicious." Her hands were still on mine. They were very cold. I said: "But there's such a hell of a lot of things to be suspicious about—if he gets onto them."

"I suppose there are."

"That's why I've come, Theo," I said bluntly. "Gerald tells me . . ."

"That I was round at Kramer's studio this afternoon with a gun," she cut in. "I expected he'd tell you."

I said: "I guess Kramer's been trying to blackmail you, too?"

"Me! Good God, no." Her thoroughbred profile tilted upward. "That poisonous piece of vermin had nothing against me."

"Then why did you go there? Why the gun?"

She didn't speak for a while. When she did, she took her hands away; there was an awkward flush on her cheeks. "I wouldn't tell anyone but you, Peter. You're the only one who knows just how much of a bloody fool I am. And I don't mind your knowing, somehow. I went round to that studio fully prepared to riddle Mr. Kramer with bullets. But it wasn't because he'd done me any harm personally. It—it was because of Wessler."

I might have guessed that.

"This morning at rehearsal before you came, Kramer started talking to Wessler in German. I picked up some German when I played Shaw in Vienna. I listened. It was all very veiled and subtle. Kramer said he had some photographs Wessler might be interested in and couldn't he bring them round sometime? I thought at first it was just one of those 'feelthy picture' rackets; then I started to think just how queerly Mirabelle and Gerald and Henry had been acting about Kramer and it dawned on me that he was up to some real dirty work—like blackmail. Wessler didn't get onto the idea at all. He was just polite and Austrian.

But I understood and suddenly I thought Kramer was probably back of that first blasted scheme to scare Wessler. I thought if— if I went round to his place and forced him to speak the truth, I could get things straightened out for Wessler."

"So that's what you were doing at the studio."

"Yes. Kramer wasn't there, of course. I didn't go in." Theo stifled a cough and made a little grimace. "The gun was a typical piece of theater. I bought it. I didn't have the faintest idea what to pull or anything. That's all I know. I was probably being damn stupid; but then I'm damn stupid about Wessler anyway."

We neither of us spoke for a while. We just sat there, Theo half lying back against the pillows while I perched on the edge of the bed.

Suddenly she said: "Peter, have you ever been in love with the wrong person?"

"Often," I said smiling.

"Then you haven't been." She shook her head very slowly. "You can only be really in love with the wrong person once. I'm so mad about Wessler that I'd commit murder for him. And it's all caged up inside me like a thousand rats gnawing my vitals." She laughed rather harshly, trying to mock herself. "That's what it's like being in love with the wrong person. You can only go through it once."

I moved up the bed closer to her; I put my hands on her shoulders and kissed her cold, firm lips.

"Do you know something, darling?" I said.

"No."

"You handed me exactly the same line last year when you were hopelessly in love with that waiter at the Waldorf who had red hair and a wife in Hackensack."

She looked up at me, her gray eyes slowly crinkling at the corners. She said: "Peter, you're a louse to bring that up. And it wasn't Hackensack, it was Jersey City."

I left her then without asking any more questions. But as a taxi drove me home again, I couldn't help checking up that, in the past few hours, at least three members of my company had expressed an almost indecent relief that George Kramer was out of the way.

When I got back to the apartment, it was in darkness. Iris had departed and Lenz, presumably, was asleep in bed.

I was just going to follow suit when the phone rang.

The quiet, alarmingly pleasant voice of Inspector Clarke said: "I called thirty minutes ago and they told me you were out. Keeping kind of late hours these days, aren't you?"

"I was out at a friend's house," I said.

"You were? Well, I thought you might be interested in how your little accident's working out. I talked to the fumigation people. They think it's mighty queer that one of those discoids managed to get in that coffin."

"That makes two of us," I said, trying to sound blasé.
Inspector Clarke placidly ignored the interruption.

"Sure. Kind of indignant when I suggested it. But I guess that's what happened. Don't see how there could be any other explanation, do you?"

"I don't," I lied.

"Just one thing more. They're holding the inquest ten thirty tomorrow morning. Afraid you and Lenz will have to attend." His voice suddenly changed. It was flippant, far too flippant. He said: "Don't get het up, though. It'll be just routine. No one's going to ask you—awkward questions, not yet anyway. Goodnight."

"Goodnight," I said.

But it didn't seem at all a good night to me.

Next morning at ten-thirty, Lenz and I turned up for the inquest. I was jittery as hell but tried not to show it. I don't know what Lenz was feeling. He gave the appearance of being a rather impatient important personage, compelled to waste valuable time ona mere matter of red tape.

There were quite a few people at the inquest. I don't know what they came for. Lenz and I sat up front, close to the coroner and the jury. Clarke was there, deceptively quiet and innocuous; with him was a red-faced angry man who turned out to be the representative from the fumigation company.

Clarke started the ball rolling with a flat report of his activities at the Dagonet. I was called next. I answered curt questions from the coroner. I said we had decided to fumigate because the rats were bad; I explained Kramer's role and the exact reasons why he had to be left in a closed coffin; I mentioned the provisional tormentor which had made it impossible for us to notice whether or not he had emerged from the coffin when the scene was over. I also pointed out that Kramer had said he was leaving right after he'd finished playing and that consequently his absence had not seemed strange.

Eventually Lenz took my place. He was magnificent; using a great amount of dignity and words of at least six syllables, he explained his own reactions on examining the body and expressed it as his expert and weighty opinion that an unfortunate accident had occurred. He wowed the jury.

In fact, they were so impressed that they paid very little attention to the indignant representative from the fumigators who, although admitting the possibility of Lenz's theory, quoted lengthy chapter and verse in an attempt to prove that his company had never been guilty of negligence before.

The coroner summed up and, very shortly afterward, the jury gave its verdict. The verdict was accidental death caused by hydrocyanic gas absorbed and retained in the upholstery of the coffin. They added a rather bad-tempered rider, censuring the fumigation company for negligence and censuring me for not having arranged more efficient ventilation in the coffin itself.

I was sorry for the fumigation company. This probably left a black mark on their reputation. But by that time I had become far too caught up in my own affairs to have much sorrow left over for anyone else.

I would have felt almost cheerful if it hadn't been for the glance thrown at me by Inspector Clarke just as the jury had given its verdict.

It was a very unnerving glance—amiable, congratulatory, but distinctly sardonic.

I had left the courtroom and was moving down a dreary corridor in the direction of daylight when a voice behind me drawled:

"Good morning, Peter."

I swung round. Roland Gates stood behind me, his small hands tidily sheathed in kid gloves, his eyes watching me, bright, amused. With a certain satisfaction, I noticed a large, bluish bruise on his jaw.

"You must permit me to congratulate you on your performance in the courtroom, Peter," he said. "You have an unexpectedly convincing stage presence."

I said: "What the hell are you doing here?"

"My dear Peter, aren't I entitled to a little curiosity? George Kramer was something of a friend of mine. I was shocked to hear of his lamentable demise." He paused. "Now that I've attended the inquest, I'm even more intrigued. Really, Peter, you seem to be doing the most bizarre things at the Dagonet."

"I thought," I said coldly, "that you and Kramer between you were responsible for whatever bizarre things may have happened at the Dagonet."

"Peter, how interesting." His waxy eyelids flickered. "I'm afraid you over-estimated my ingenuity. I confess I indulged one rather childish whim. I did procure that singularly repellent cat. . . ."

"You got that cat into the theater?"

"But all in the spirit of innocent fun. I wouldn't have had the temerity to do it if I'd known what I was competing against." He cast a quick glance down the bleak passage. "But we shouldn't be talking this way in a hotbed of law and order, should we? So far as the authorities are concerned, everything seems to be explained away. I don't want to put ideas in anyone's head."

He added: "About the Wessler role, Peter. It might interest you to know that I've learned most of it, and it fascinates me. Just the sort of part I like." One of his small gloved hands moved to the bruise on his cheek. "After your pugilistic display the other day, I almost decided to let everything drop. But now—I've made up my mind to forgive you. I can't resist that second act."

There were a thousand and one things I wanted to tell Roland Gates. I wanted to tell him that I knew how Kramer had worked on Mirabelle to let Gates into the play; I wanted to tell him I knew that he or one of his satellites had been in that upstairs dressing-room when Theo had been scared by the face in the mirror; I wanted to tell him that my fondest wish was to be attending his own inquest in the very near future. But I wasn't going to give him the satisfaction of knowing he riled me that much.

"There's one thing I forgot to ask you the other day," Gates said suddenly. "I seem to be news at the moment—America's ranking Krafft-Ebing husband. You won't have any objection to my informing the press that I'm definitely connected with Mirabelle's show, will you?"

I didn't see any way I could stop him. He still had all the cards. I told him so.

"Thanks, Peter. Thanks a lot." Those flat, dark eyes were staring at me with absolutely no expression in them. "I'm developing a very genuine admiration for you. You're the only theatrical producer in Broadway history who's managed to get away with murder—twice in one week."

He stared at me insolently. I stared back.

My fingers were itching. But I couldn't sock him again—not in the city morgue.

Chapter Twenty-one

I DROVE STRAIGHT to the Dagonet where the company was waiting, very restless and on edge. They flocked around me nervously and Mirabelle asked the question that must have been in all their minds.

"What—what was the verdict, Peter?"

"Accidental death," I said. "Looks as if it's going to be okay."

I didn't tell them about that one, sardonic glance Inspector Clarke had thrown at me; I didn't tell them about Gates, either. But I couldn't forget them myself. Even if Iris had been right last night, even if the disturbances were going to stop now Kramer was dead, we were not out of the wood by a long way. There was not only the menace of Gates; there was the menace of the police. On one side *Troubled Waters* was still exposed to lawlessness; on the other side, it had to be prepared for a flank attack from the law.

That wasn't a very promising set-up.

Although my news from the inquest had brought a certain amount of relief, the company was still pretty shaken. Eddie informed me that the coffin had been rendered one hundred percent safe again; but, even so, its very presence on the stage was enough to remind us all of the Dagonet's mortality rate.

I got the rehearsal going at last, ready for the worst. But you can never foresee things in the theater. For some cockeyed reason that rehearsal kicked up its heels and galloped off down the straight as sweetly as if the play were in its second year instead of its second homicide. It was only Mirabelle who worried me. In spite of the flawless technique, there was something wrong, something very deep down—a lack of conviction that she was playing right. Once she had to break the action to pour herself a jigger of brandy and her hand was trembling when she put the empty glass back on the table.

Maybe she had made a point of flourishing the liquor habit in the past just to irritate Wessler. But I knew she wasn't doing it on account of Wessler then, she needed that brandy badly.

But she picked up as the play went on. By the time I called a halt at six, she was almost back in her stride. And later that evening, when I got them to work again after dinner, she was running on all six cylinders.

In fact, she was alarmingly good. The whole flood of her antagonism to Wessler, which seemed to have dropped during the Kramer interim, was back in her playing. She had all her Wessler scenes keyed up to snapping point, so that at any minute I expected the atmosphere on stage to crackle and shoot out blue sparks.

The others reacted to her. Everyone played with a sort of added intensity. Particularly Wessler. I'd never seen him put the role across with such violence.

The rehearsal reached its climax in the big second act scene between Mirabelle and Wessler. It was a scene with a hell of a punch in which Mirabelle used a lot of tough language and where the outraged Wessler finally cut her short with a slap in the face.

From the moment when the others slipped down into the house and left them alone on the stage, Wessler and Mirabelle were dynamite. Mirabelle went into her denunciation. I saw Gerald watching her with cautious attention from his place in the aisle. I noticed Theo, too, staring fascinated at Wessler as he stood facing Mirabelle, the very essence of ominous contempt.

Then the time came where the script had Mirabelle's dialogue break, had her come forward, grip Wessler's arms and shake him. She did it marvelously. You could see the murder in her eye. And you could see murder in Wessler's eye, too.

He jerked his arm free; he lifted his hand. In rehearsal, I cut the slap. But that night Wessler seemed carried right out of himself. With sudden violent force he brought his great hand down square on Mirabelle's cheek.

She gave a little cry, staggered backward and stumbled onto her knees.

I knew she was hurt. I knew, too, that Wessler had meant to hurt her. I sprung up onto the stage, but Gerald reached her first. He dropped onto the worn boards beside her, slipping his young arms around her, supporting her.

"Mirabelle, darling, are you all right?"

He lifted her small body. One of her hands was pressed tight against her cheek. She seemed half dazed.

"It's—it's all right, Gerald. Really . . ."

Gerald swung round to Wessler, his face white, the veins in his temples standing out hard and thick.

"You dirty German swine," he said.

Before any of us moved, he had carried Mirabelle to the swing-door and off the stage.

Wessler stared after them blindly. "I do not know what I do," he whispered. "It is just that Miss Rue, she is that woman in the play. She make me forget. I do not know what I do." He turned to me, his bearded face haggard, miserable. "I must go to her, tell her how I am sorry, how . . ."

"I'd leave her alone," I said curtly.

For a few seconds we stood around doing nothing. Then I happened to notice Mirabelle's brandy bottle and her empty glass. She'd be needing something to pick her up. I poured brandy from the bottle. There was just enough to make about three inches in the glass. I took it with me offstage.

The door to Mirabelle's dressing-room was shut. I suppose I should have knocked, but I never thought about it. I knew Mirabelle so well.

I pushed open the door.

"I've brought the brand . . ." I began.

But I didn't finish the sentence. Mirabelle and Gerald were standing close together by the mirror. Gerald's arms were still around her; Mirabelle's face was pressed against his shoulder, turned away from me. Her body was quivering.

Gerald was saying: "Darling, you don't have to worry. I'll

never leave you. What the hell do my problems matter compared to this? We'll fight it together. It'll be all right."

"Mirabelle," I said, "isn't there anything I can do?"

She didn't answer. I don't think either of them had noticed me until then. But Gerald wheeled round, sharply, his eyes blazing.

"Get out of here," he said.

"But, Gerald . . ."

"Get out, I say." His voice was savage. "For God's sake, leave us alone."

I went. As I shut the door behind me, I heard a faint, strangled sob, I knew then that Mirabelle was crying—crying with the dull, numbed despair of a woman with no hope.

Chapter Twenty-two

THAT WAS ONE thing too much. I'd been struggling like hell to get through that nerve-racking day without giving up. But this brutal eruption of the Wessler-Mirabelle volcano swept me right off my precarious foothold.

I stood there in the corridor, alone with Mirabelle's brandy glass. There couldn't possibly have been a worse moment for a retired drunk to be left alone with a glass of brandy. I'd given Lenz my solemn word never to touch liquor; I'd given it to Iris too. Until then I'd been able to resist temptation. But I couldn't resist it any more. Five seconds after I had left that dressing-room, I had taken a large swig of Mirabelle's drink.

I would probably have drained the glass if it hadn't been for the taste. At first I thought it was just me, that I'd avoided alcohol for so long that I'd forgotten the way it tasted. Then I took another sip, let it rest on my tongue. Yes, it was like brandy and yet it wasn't. There was a bitter flavor—something wrong.

For a moment I stood there stone still, trying to fight back the thoughts that were coming into my head. I remembered the various episodes in which Mirabelle's brandy had featured. It had stayed over night at Wessler's; Gerald had come all the way crosstown to pick it up; Kramer had poured some for Mirabelle at his last rehearsal. This was that same brandy. And it tasted wrong.

I didn't know what to do. I looked at the veins on my left wrist. They were twitching. And the thoughts that I tried not to have rushed up so that they were blazing like neon signs in my mind. The crazy, inexplicable menace at the Dagonet was not over. Someone had fixed Mirabelle's brandy. Someone had poisoned Mirabelle's brandy.

I stood there, twisting the glass, completely without constructive thought. Heavy footsteps sounded behind me and I turned to see Dr. Lenz, immensely impressive in his black hat and black topcoat. He gazed at the glass with a slight furrowing of his forehead. I knew what he was thinking. He was thinking he'd caught me out deliberately backsliding.

I faltered: "Mirabelle's not—not feeling so hot. I was taking her a drink."

He listened gravely while I blurted out what had just happened on stage. All the time I talked, my mind was working furiously, trying to decide whether or not to pass on to him my insane suspicions about Mirabelle's brandy. I almost told him. Then I didn't. I didn't have the nerve to admit I'd tasted the drink. I didn't have the nerve, either, to let my psychiatrist think I was cuckoo enough to believe what I did believe. I shirked it.

But I had an idea. As Lenz moved toward the stage, I followed. Just as he pushed through the swing-door, I slipped the glass of brandy behind a red fire-bucket. I had a friend who was a chemist. I could get him to analyze it right away. Then I'd know just where I was—what I was up against this time.

I wasn't sure whether Lenz noticed what I had done. If he did, he showed no sign.

Back on the stage, rehearsal enthusiasm had decidedly dwindled. Wessler still looked shaken. He was listening with absent politeness to Theo's far too hearty attempt to be conversational, while Eddie and Iris stood around disconsolately.

I couldn't bear to have any more time wasted. I took Iris and Theo through a couple of scenes in which they figured alone together. Eventually Gerald appeared, pale and tight-lipped. Mirabelle was resting, he explained. She'd be back again in a few minutes, ready to go on rehearsing.

And she did come back, her eyes too bright, her lips slashed red across a clown-white face. But she was wonderfully in control. She went straight up to Wessler. She held out her hand.

"We should have rehearsed that slap before, Herr Wessler. It's hard to get it the right strength."

Wessler's mouth relaxed its miserable line. He smiled brokenly. "You mean, it is forgiven?"

"Of course." Mirabelle smiled a brief, impersonal smile. "Come on, Peter. Let's finish the act."

And after that, surprisingly, the rehearsal went well. Maybe they were putting up a front for Lenz. Or maybe that violent scene had somehow cleared the air.

But it didn't cheer me any. I was too busy thinking about the brandy.

I got my plans figured out. After rehearsal I told Lenz and Iris to go back to the apartment, retrieved the glass of brandy and took it in a taxi to my analyst friend. I didn't tell him anything. I just asked him to find out what was in it and pass on the good news.

With my suspicions still red-hot inside me, I went back to the apartment. Lenz and Iris were both of them relaxed, almost cheerful. Iris talked as if we had nothing more to worry about.

I didn't disillusion her. After all, someone might as well have a few moments' basking in a fool's paradise.

Lenz was suggesting bed when the phone rang. Iris leaped on it before I could get there. I watched her apprehensively.

"Yes," she said. "Oh, hello . . . yes . . . no, I'm afraid I haven't . . . no, I can't imagine. . . . Where? . . . Oh . . . yes, I'll ask Peter, of course . . . sorry . . . isn't it?"

She let the receiver slide back onto the stand. Her lips were rather tight.

Both Lenz and I were staring at her

"Come on" I said. "Tell us the worst."

"Worst?" Iris looked far too casual. "My dear, it's nothing. Only Theo. She called up about having mislaid her handbag. She wanted to know if any of us had seen it. Seems she must have left it at the theater tonight."

"Her handbag?" I said. For a moment that sounded innocent enough. Then I began to see what was bothering Iris. "Do you mean she's lost her handbag with the . . .?"

"Yes," put in Iris. "That's why she's worried. She had a lot of those codeine pills Dr. Lenz recommended. They were in the bag." She glanced at Lenz. "You said codeine was poisonous, didn't you?"

I felt hot and cold all over. Lenz returned Iris's gaze. "Yes, Miss Pattison, codeine is a poison, just as veronal is. That is to say, its cumulative effect may be dangerously toxic if it is taken in excess over any period of time. That is true of all derivatives of opium, though some of them—heroin, for example—are more violent in their action." He smiled briefly. "To relieve your mind, however, I should tell you that one could hardly produce a lethal effect with a single dose."

Iris looked less worried. "Thank God for that. After what happened to Kramer, I wouldn't like to have any violent poisons floating around the Dagonet. But—" she smiled awkwardly—"I guess it's nothing to worry about. Theo's always losing things."

That's where the matter ended. Soon we all went to bed. But I couldn't get that lost codeine out of my mind. It was quite a long time before I went to sleep.

That night I had bad dreams. Ever since the terrible theater fire which had killed my wife, I had been plagued by a periodic nightmare. It always took the same form. I was alone in an enormous darkened theater and I knew, somehow, that it was impossible for me to get out. I was sitting in the highest balcony, miles up in the air and I was afraid—horribly afraid because something told me that within five minutes the place would catch fire.

I was going through it all again that night—only this time the theater was the Dagonet. I was leaning forward in a narrow balcony seat, every nerve in my body waiting for that first yellow flame. And then—a new development in that cyclic dream—the theater was suddenly filled with noise, shrill, throbbing noise, the ringing of a thousand fire-alarms. I sprang from my seat, started dashing madly up the steep aisle toward the exit doors which I knew to be locked. I was beating on them....

And then I was awake, sitting up in bed, beads of sweat breaking out on my forehead. The echo of those nightmare fire-alarms still rang in my ears. Only gradually did they dwindle to one sound—one real sound, the ringing of the telephone at my bedside.

For a moment I did not move. I sat there, staring at the small black instrument until I had shaken off the memory of my dream. The bell had stopped ringing now. Wondering who on earth could be calling at this remote hour, I picked up the receiver.

I heard voices at once—voices which told me that Lenz with his trained doctor's ear for noises at night, had got there first and was answering the call on the connection in the living-room. I was still pretty dazed with sleep. That's why, perhaps, that second voice, the voice from the other end of the wire, didn't mean anything to me at first.

It was soft, husky, like the voice of someone who didn't have any breath in his lungs. I didn't recognize it. But I did recognize the desperate, agonized emotion behind it.

It was asking urgently: "Who is that? Is—is that you, Dr. Lenz?"

Then Lenz's serene voice. "Yes."

"Thank God!" There was a little strangled sob. "You've got to come—come at once. I can't bear it—not any longer. Dr. Lenz, you've got to come— It's—it's killing me."

It was horrible, the stark, tortured quality of that voice. My fingers gripped tightly on the receiver.

Lenz was saying: "I'll come at once. But who is it? Who are you?"

There was a long pause from the other end of the wire. Then that husky, unrecognizable voice again. It whispered,

"This is Mirabelle Rue. . . ."

Chapter Twenty-three

A F T E R   T H A T   T H E R E   was silence, followed by the soft click of a receiver being slipped back on the stand. I jumped out of bed and started to dash around the room, grabbing clothes. In a second Lenz's solemn face appeared around the door.

"There . . ."

"I know," I said. "I heard."

He disappeared. Within a few minutes I had thrown on a shirt, a pair of pants, shoes and an overcoat. I ran out into the hall. Dr. Lenz had beaten me to it. Fully dressed down to the large pearl pin in his tie, he was waiting patiently by the door.

The elevator shot us downstairs and we leaped into a taxi. As it rushed us toward Mirabelle's hotel, Dr. Lenz's gray eyes stared imperviously at nothing. Once he took out his ponderous gold watch, checked the time at a quarter to four and put the thing back in his vest pocket. He didn't say anything.

Which was the most sensible thing to do, of course. What was there to say?

But there was plenty to worry about. I thought of Mirabelle as she'd been that day in my office, broken, gnawed by some fear she refused to share with me; Mirabelle at the rehearsal, acting on her nerves, with Roland Gates always at the back of her mind; Kramer pouring her a glass of brandy. That brandy . . .

I was jittery as hell as we paid off the taxi and hurried into the expensive foyer of Mirabelle's hotel. I knew the number of her suite. Without waiting to call on the house telephone, I bundled Lenz into the elevator and hustled him out at the penthouse floor. I ran down the passage to Mirabelle's door and knocked.

There was no sound from within. I knocked again—more loudly. For minutes, it seemed, I waited there, conscious of

173

nothing but the absolute silence inside the apartment and the uncertain feeling in the pit of my stomach.

I started banging on the door with my fists.

A dog barked inside. Then a second—then a third. The whole floor resounded with that sudden bedlam of barking. I could hear the pad of running paws and a wild scuffling against the door. There was still no sign from Mirabelle.

Lenz joined me. He said calmly: "Try the bell."

I had been too het-up to notice the buzzer. I pressed my thumb against it, setting the dogs off into an orgy of yelps. The buzzer was still shrilling when quick footsteps sounded from within. A voice called:

"Dmitri, Rupert, Zenda—go on back to the bedroom. Naughty dogs."

The commotion subsided. After a few seconds, the door was opened.

Mirabelle was there. I had prepared myself for almost everything except this. She was exactly the same as ever, breath-taking with her chestnut hair pushed back from her forehead and a sort of floating, pale green negligee. She stared at us for an instant blankly; then she held out both her hands, smiling that dazzling smile which had carried so many plays through the summer into their second season.

"Dr. Lenz, Peter—darlings! How divine to see you! But why in the middle of the night and why all the ringing and banging?"

"Mirabelle," I asked hoarsely, "are you all right?"

"All right?" Her forehead puckered. "Of course I'm all right. Why ... ?" Her gaze slid over my unconventional assortment of clothes. "Angel, you've lost your neck-tie and your socks. You've been in a brawl. Are you hurt? Is he hurt, Dr. Lenz?"

Lenz didn't say anything, which made the situation that much more confused.

"We ... I ..." I began, not quite sure whether to be angry or relieved.

"Never mind, darling." Mirabelle slipped her arm through mine

174

and drew me into the hall. "Just so long as you're all right now. That's all that matters."

Before I had time to speak, I was whisked into the living-room and stretched out on a couch. Mirabelle, restless as curtains in the wind, was dashing in and out of the room, bringing cigarettes and glasses of water and keeping up a constant, cooing monologue. Finally she perched herself on the arm of the couch and stroked my hair.

"Now, darling, tell me all about it."

I glanced despairingly at Lenz who had seated himself on a small wooden chair.

He folded large hands across his breast. "There seems to have been a misunderstanding, Miss Rue. We merely came here, the two of us, in answer to a telephone call."

Mirabelle picked up a cigarette, put it to her lips, lit a match, blew the match out and put the cigarette back on the table.

"What telephone call?" she said.

It seemed extremely difficult to believe that Mirabelle could have sent out a despairing S.O.S. and forgotten it again in less than half an hour. Clutching onto the few vestiges of my composure, I explained the situation.

Mirabelle's eyes narrowed. "But how remarkable, darling. How very remarkable."

"You mean," said Lenz, "that it was not you who telephoned to me?"

"But, angel, why should I have telephoned to you? I think you're marvelous and I've always adored your beard, but—well, I've been fast asleep ever since I got back from the theater."

"That is strange." Lenz stroked the extreme tip of his imperial. "I have a keen ear for voices, Miss Rue. I would have been willing to swear on oath that it was you who spoke over the telephone."

Mirabelle went through her business with the cigarette all over again, building up to a climax where she floated across the room in chartreuse clouds and unearthed a silver lighter from beneath a large French doll. She came back to the couch and I noticed her fingers move slowly to her cheek as if she still felt the slap Wessler had given her earlier that night.

"A practical joke, darlings," she said at last. "An absurd, tiresome practical joke. I'm miserable you were dragged out in the middle of the night. But what can we do?"

Mirabelle seemed to have hit the nail firmly on the head. What could we do?

At that moment, an inner door was pushed open to reveal the borzoi and two gigantic great danes. They glared at Lenz and me and moved to Mirabelle. All three of them licked her hand ceremoniously and, with much thumping of tail, arranged themselves in a geometric pattern on the carpet at her feet.

In the face of so much canine disapproval, there seemed nothing for it but to leave ignominiously. We did.

Mirabelle came with us to the door and kissed us both with absent minded affection and a delicate whiff of cyclamen. I glanced back at her standing by the door, twisting the ears of the two great danes while the borzoi sat gazing up at her with aristocratic melancholy. Mirabelle and her dogs—nothing could have been more peaceful.

"Well, what do you make of that?" I said as Lenz and I went down together in the elevator. "If Mirabelle didn't call, who the hell did? And why?"

Lenz's fingers were playing over his watch chain. With cryptic irrelevance, he asked: "What is your telephone number, Mr. Duluth?"

"Lipscombe 3-1916."

"And Miss Rue's calls, I presume, are put through the hotel switchboard?"

I told him I believed so. When we reached the deserted foyer, he moved to the night-operator's hide-out and pushed his head through the grille. "Perhaps you will be good enough to tell me the exact time at which Miss Rue made a telephone call tonight to Lipscombe 3-1916. I am her doctor; it is necessary for me to know."

I stared. The operator blinked and patted blonde hair. It was probably against all hotel regulations for her to answer leading questions like that, but no operator in the world could have stood up against Dr. Lenz.

"The call from Miss Rue to the Lipscombe number went out about three-thirty," she said brightly.

"Thank you," said Lenz.

"You're welcome, I'm sure," offered the operator.

Dr. Lenz was still at the grille. He produced a piece of paper and a large silver pencil and was scribbling absorbedly. When he had covered the page, he folded it, demanded an envelope from the operator, sealed it and wrote Mirabelle's name on the outside. He pushed the letter and a dollar bill through the grille.

"Perhaps you would see that Miss Rue gets this first thing in the morning."

As he moved away toward the swing-door, I said weakly: "Then it was Mirabelle who called?"

"It was, Mr. Duluth."

"And—and she tried to pretend she hadn't. How in the name of heaven did you figure that out?"

"As I told Miss Rue, I have a keen ear for voices. I knew it could have been no one else on the phone."

"But she must be crazy. What's it all about? What's happening? What did you write her that letter for?"

Dr. Lenz's face was pale. I had never before seen him look so worried. "I wrote to Miss Rue to warn her that it is not always wise to be too brave."

I had no idea what he meant. He did not enlighten me.

Chapter Twenty-four

I RETREATED TO my bed that night in a very neurotic condition. Mirabelle's screwy behavior alone had been enough to shorten my already much-abbreviated life; but that Lenz, who was supposed to be on my side, should start being mysterious seemed altogether more than a harmless youngish producer-director should be expected to bear.

At breakfast the doctor added to my anxiety by announcing his intention of returning to the sanitorium. The psychiatric or what-ever-they-were problems of Wessler's half-brother, Wolfgang von Brandt, seemed suddenly to have taken on major importance in his mind. He made no reference to the happenings of the night before and volunteered no explanations. He merely packed his nightshirt and tooth brush, enveloped my hand in his great palm and said:

"If I felt I could be of any immediate use I would stay. But I cannot feel that way at the present time."

He went, leaving me none the wiser and considerably more uneasy.

As soon as he had gone. I hurried downstairs to Iris's room on the fifth floor. I found her in her made-over studio couch bed with a sort of metal fish-net over her hair.

"Hello." She pushed herself up against the pillows and patted the fish-net. "Don't look so disapproving, darling. I won't wear it when we're married."

"Are you telling me?" I said.

Then I poured out to her the incredible history of Mirabelle's telephone call. I knew I should have been the strong man shielding the weak, defenseless little woman, but with Iris and me things seemed to work in reverse.

"And there's something else," I concluded, twisting the pink fold of pajama which had somehow gotten between my fingers. "Something else I've got to tell you about Mirabelle. I haven't dared mention it to Lenz. I was scared he'd shut me up again. But I—I think things are still going on at the Dagonet; I think someone's trying to poison Mirabelle's brandy."

Iris extracted her pajamas from my convulsive grip and smoothed out the creases. She looked very calm and self-possessed, exactly the way I wanted her to look.

"Tell me about Mirabelle's brandy being poisoned," she said.

I told her about how I'd backslid and drunk some of Mirabelle's drink and sent the glass to be analyzed. Her eyes went very dark.

"That," she said, "and then Mirabelle's telephone call later last night."

"Exactly. But what in God's name do we do?"

Iris got out of her studio couch, retrieved two pink slippers from the window sill and moved to the telephone. She held it out to me.

"Call your friend," she said, "and see if he's done the analysis. We can't do anything until we know one way or the other."

That made sense, of course. Feeling very nervous, I took the receiver and dialed. My friend had done the analysis—only too well. I listened to what he said. I put the receiver back on the stand.

Iris's "Well?" was electric.

"He's done the analysis," I said. "I'll tell you just what he said. He said that glass contained a considerable amount of some alkaloid of the morphine group. He said there wasn't enough poison to kill anyone outright but that, taken over a period of time, it might be very dangerous."

"Talk English, Peter. What poison was it? Did he say?"

"He did," I said. "He couldn't be sure. Not yet. But he's almost certain it was . . ."

"What, Peter?"

"Codeine," I said.

We stared at each other in arid silence.

Iris said very softly: "And Theo lost her codeine last night.

Peter, it *is* all starting again. First Wessler, and now Mirabelle. What—what are we going to do?"

"Give up," I said. "Give up and have done with it. Call Clarke."

"Tell him someone's trying to poison Mirabelle just now when we've managed to hold back about Comstock and Kramer?"

"Hell, we can't go on like this indefinitely. We can't endanger Mirabelle's life—just to keep our show open."

"Nonsense, Peter. We've got to. The play's as important for Mirabelle as it is for us. And what good could the police do? They couldn't go around tasting everything she drank before she drank it. They can't do anything we couldn't do ourselves. Someone's trying to poison Mirabelle slowly. We can prevent that ourselves, Peter. We've got to."

"Then—at least, we must tell Mirabelle."

"Tell Mirabelle?" Iris thrust her chin out determinedly. "Peter, you can't tell your star ten days before opening that someone's trying to poison her. Think what it would do to her performance! Think—oh, damn everything. This play was going to do so much for us; it's our life, Peter. We're both tied up with it so tightly now that we sink if it sinks." She gripped my arms. "*Troubled Waters* is going to open, Peter. Even if we all get murdered, it's got to open."

She was gazing straight at me, her lips half parted. It was just like Iris to have that extra crazy ounce of courage that I lacked. "We'll take care of Mirabelle ourselves, Peter. We'll find some way."

Suddenly there was a lot of soft pajama in my arms. "Do you know," I said, "you're probably the most beautiful woman I ever saw?"

Iris said: "This is one hell of a time to start realizing that."

But she took the fish-net off. I was still kissing her when a sharp knock sounded on the door. Iris broke away. She tried to act startled, but she hadn't reached the point where she could fool me with a performance. Too casually she lit a cigarette, smoothed back her hair and said: "Come in."

The door opened and Gerald Gwynne was there. He moved quickly toward Iris. Then he saw me and his dark young face went sullen.

"Hello," said Iris. "Do you want me or Peter?"

From the way she said that I knew she had been expecting him and was giving him the high sign. That came as a real sock beneath the belt, because it implied so much that had never been said. I took a careful look at Gerald. It seemed suddenly important that he was ten years younger than I was and plenty handsomer. I found myself wishing like hell that I'd let him go to Hollywood after all.

He was still watching Iris. He said: "Matter of fact, I came to see Peter. Thought he'd probably be down here."

I didn't tell him I knew he was lying. I let it ride that way. "What do you want to see me about?"

He didn't speak for a moment. Finally he muttered: "It's about Wessler. I think it's pretty damn unpardonable what he did to Mirabelle last night. I've come to tell you that you ought to do something about controlling Wessler, if you want the show to get anywhere."

"Since when have you become so interested in the show's success?" I asked. "Only a couple of days ago you were trying to walk out on us."

He flushed: "Why bring that up? It's over, forgotten. I just demand an even break for Mirabelle. She hates Wessler's guts; it's tough enough for her as it is having to play with him. You ought to see, at least, that he doesn't beat her up at rehearsals."

"Thanks for the swell advice." I was suddenly fighting mad. "What do you expect me to do? Fire Wessler and take on Roland Gates? That would be dandy for Mirabelle, wouldn't it?"

"Don't be a fool. I . . ."

"Cut that out," I said. "Mirabelle got you into *Troubled Waters* because she went down on her bended knees to me to have you hired. You're doing a good job but if it's going to your head and if you start thinking you're a goddamn little prima donna, you can quit. Take up your Hollywood contract and get out."

"Okay, okay," he said. "No need to shoot your mouth off. If you feel that way—okay. Sorry I brought it up. I was only asking. Forget it."

He swung away toward the door. It was bad for my business to let him go that way. But I wasn't going to do anything about it. Gerald had reached the door and was turning the handle when Iris said: "Don't go, Gerald. Not yet."

He turned immediately, moving back to her, his eyes changing their mood. "What is it, Iris?"

She was looking at me cautiously. I couldn't get her drift. It was as if, by coming into the room, Gerald had made it so that Iris was someone quite different, someone I didn't know.

She said: "Gerald, you're fond of Mirabelle, aren't you?"

"You know the way I feel."

"Then you've got to do something for us." Iris came over to me, putting her hand on my arm. "You mustn't tell this to a soul, Gerald. Not even to Mirabelle. That's frightfully important. But you've got to do what we say. We think someone's trying to doctor her brandy. We think someone's trying to poison her."

The skin around his cheek bones was suddenly taut and white. "Poison Mirabelle!"

"We're not sure. We may be crazy. But we can't take any chances. Gerald, you're always with Mirabelle. You've got to watch her brandy. At rehearsal, all the time, you've got to watch it, taste it and be sure it's—it's all right. Will you do that for us?"

"But—but I can't believe . . ."

"You don't have to believe. You've just got to do that."

"All right." Gerald's face relaxed. There was a queer, slightly derisive gleam back of his eyes. "Okay, Iris. If you want me to— I'll do that."

Iris put out her hand, letting him slip his brown fingers over it. "Thank you, Gerald, I . . ."

She stopped because there was a second knock at the door and it swung open almost immediately. Theo Ffoulkes came in, her lean, aristocratic face set in a pale mask. She was completely changed from the amused, resigned Theo who had spilled girlish confidences to me the night before.

"Iris, I've got to see Peter. I've been upstairs. He's not . . . oh, there you are, Peter."

She came right up to me. From under her arm, she brought out a folded newspaper. She thrust it at me, pointing to a certain place.

"You can't have done this, Peter. You can't have done a thing like that!"

Gerald and Iris came up to me, reading over my elbows. I saw the paragraph she meant—right away. It said:

Possibly the most sensational news in the theater right now is a definite statement made by Roland Gates that he has been hired to understudy the male lead in Peter Duluth's forthcoming production of *Troubled Waters*, starring Mirabelle Rue. At the moment the role opposite Miss Rue is being played by the famous Austrian actor, Conrad Wessler. But it is rumored that he has not been at all well and may have to relinquish the part. There is, therefore, a big chance that the public will once again be seeing the famous team of Gates and Rue which everyone supposed to have been permanently ruptured by last year's notorious divorce suit. It is believed in many quarters that to appear with Gates after all that came out during the divorce is probably the most unwise thing Miss Rue could possibly do—if she wishes to retain the sympathy of the public.

After my latest encounter with Gates, I'd been expecting something like that. But the fact that I expected it didn't make it any easier to deal with.

Theo's eyes were cold as steel. "I can't believe it, Peter. I can't believe you'd let them print a thing like that. You know how sensitive Wessler is about the airplane accident. You know what it'll do to him to read in the public press that he's expected to crack up. And Gates for an understudy! You know Wessler would never let anyone understudy him but his brother and . . ."

"Let me have a chance to tell him what I think of him." Gerald pushed her aside and came up to me, his face ready for murder. "Is this true?"

"In a way."

"In a way! You must be mad. You did this without telling Mirabelle? After all that's happened, you hire that filthy swine Gates to . . ."

"Shut up," I cut in. "Shut up both of you, and listen to me. Yes, I let Gates take a script to learn the Wessler part. I did that. Do you suppose I did it because I thought it was a swell idea? Do you think I'm such a fool? Gates knows about Comstock; he knows Kramer was murdered. He threatened to tell the police unless I let him learn the Wessler part and put this notice in the press. That's what happened. I'd like to know what you would have done in my place. Let the show go to hell, throw up your own jobs, I suppose, just to keep Mirabelle and Wessler in cotton padding. After what happened to Kramer, I'd have thought you'd have gotten wise to what's going on. In case there's any misunderstanding, I'm not directing a Broadway production, I'm directing the Sino-Japanese war."

That socked them, all right.

Gerald gave a low whistle and said: "So Gates is taking up where Kramer left off. He's blackmailing us himself."

"He is," I said. "But that's nothing, checked up against the other things that are happening. I don't give a damn about Gates. He doesn't come into the picture unless Wessler cracks up. And it's our job, mine and yours and Theo's, to see that nothing happens to Wessler."

Theo lit a Goldflake. She smiled a little twisted smile, looking miserable and ashamed. "I'm blasted sorry, Peter. Once again I'm the original bloody fool. I ought to have guessed." She paused, adding: "You see, I thought that now—now Kramer's out of the way, there weren't any internal worries. I thought it was just the police we were up against."

"Just a little ray of sunshine," I said bitterly. "How about that purse of yours?"

"My handbag! My God, you don't mean that's tied up with it all. You don't mean my codeine . . .?"

"I don't know what's going on," put in Gerald in a slow drawling voice that had lost all anger or interest. "But I wouldn't get intense over Theo's bag, if I were you. There's nothing at all dramatic about its disappearance."

While we stared, he felt in his side-pocket and brought out a small black handbag.

"I was bringing it around to rehearsal to give it to you, Theo."

Theo took the bag. "Yes, it's mine. But where did you find it?"

"Couldn't say off hand. It was in my pocket this morning. Must have picked it up at the Dagonet last night, thinking it was Mirabelle's."

"But you know it isn't Mirabelle's. You've seen me with it thousands of times." Theo opened the clasp and looked in the bag. Then she stared at me. Her voice came soft, indecisive: "Last night, Peter, my bottle of codeine pills was half full. Now there's hardly anything left."

That brought us up with a jerk. I turned to Gerald. So did Iris and Theo. He was the only one completely in control of himself.

He said: "From what Iris said, I can imagine what you're thinking. It isn't at all true. I haven't been poisoning anyone with codeine."

"But who . . .?" began Theo.

"That's hardly my pigeon," said Gerald. His eyes slid to Iris. They stayed there a moment. Then he gave her a queer little formal bow. "This is where I leave," he said. "Good-bye all."

Theo guessed we didn't want her, either. In a moment she left too and we were alone.

I dropped onto the studio couch, feeling dead to the world.

"Now what the hell have we done?" I said.

Iris said: "About what?"

"About Gerald. What the hell have we done about Gerald?"

"Peter, you can't think . . ."

"Yes, I can. He had Theo's bag. He's the obvious person to

have lifted the codeine, isn't he? And he's the person we've put on to guard Mirabelle. That's funny, that is. That's hellish efficient."

Iris looked stubborn. "Gerald wouldn't do a thing like that."

"You seem to know a darn lot about Gerald. A darn sight too much if you ask me."

"Just what do you mean by that?"

"You know what I mean. I'm not blind. He came here to see you this morning. You were expecting him. My God, aren't things tough enough for me without your double-crossing me too?"

Iris sat down at my side, taking both my arms. "I'm not double-crossing you, Peter."

"Then I'd like to know what you are doing. I don't blame you, mind. What have I got to offer? I'm only a theoretically cured drunk with a foul disposition. Why the hell you stuck to me all this time I can't imagine."

"Peter, don't say that. You mustn't say that." Her eyes were miserable. And I realized it. Although I was half cuckoo with jealousy I realized that and told myself her eyes couldn't lie that way. "I'm for you, Peter—you and me. Gerald, he's nothing. Maybe he thinks he's in love with me. That doesn't matter. You've got to believe that."

"But he is in love with you?"

"He says so. I've been trying to explain it all to you. He told me the night Comstock died. He said I'd got under his skin and there was nothing he could do about it. I didn't pay any attention. I told him he was only a kid. I told him to forget it. But he didn't. That's why he made a fuss about going to Hollywood. That's why he wanted to break his contract and get out of town. But you couldn't spare him, and he—he said he had to see me sometimes, just see me. That's why I said he could come to my apartment every now and then. There's nothing more in it, I swear. But I hate complications. That's why I've been so damn persistent in trying to get you to marry me and make everything tidy again."

186

I knew she meant it. I slid my arm around her, letting my head lie on her lap. I said: "Who'd have thought this was going to be the happiest day of my life?"

Too soon I started thinking again. "Iris," I said, "I've just thought of something. If Gerald's in love with you, what the hell is his relationship with Mirabelle."

"He's crazy about her. He follows her around night and day. He'd die for her."

"And yet he's in love with you. Isn't that rather Eugene O'Neill?"

"Don't be unsophisticated, Peter. Mirabelle gave him his start. She got him into *Troubled Waters*. He owes her everything."

"And maybe she expects too much in return. Maybe she's grabbing and he doesn't want to be grabbed any more." I felt suddenly worried again. "Darling, I wish to hell we hadn't put him in charge of her brandy."

"Gerald's all right," she said firmly. "He's a darn fine kid. We can trust him."

"So could we trust anyone else in the cast. Look where that's gotten us."

As I spoke, the phone rang. I reached over Iris for the receiver. When I heard Lenz's voice I was so relieved I didn't even wait to hear what he had to say, I just poured out the whole story of Mirabelle's brandy and what we'd done about it.

"Iris says it's okay to have Gerald take the responsibility," I concluded.

Lenz did not speak right away. At last he said: "I think Miss Pattison is very wise."

"But," I insisted, "we're putting Mirabelle's life in his hands and for all we know he's the person that's trying to poison her."

Lenz gave an odd little chuckle. "If Mr. Gwynne is trying to poison Miss Rue, you cannot tie his hands more efficiently than by making him solely responsible for her safety."

That made sense, of course.

"I would not worry myself unduly on Miss Rue's behalf," he continued. "I have more than a belief that she can take care of herself. I telephoned you on a completely different matter. The time has come when I feel it wise for Herr Von Brandt to meet his brother again. I've spoken to Herr Wessler and he is prepared to come out to the sanitorium this morning. I would like you to accompany him."

There seemed to be so many more pressing things than Wessler's half-brother. "But . . ." I began.

"I know you are a busy man, Mr. Duluth. I know this means forfeiting a rehearsal. But I cannot stress too strongly the importance of this meeting not only for Von Brandt's sake but for Wessler's also."

What could I say? I said it. "All right, I'll come."

"Thank you, Mr. Duluth." Lenz's voice struck me as curiously excited. "Thank you very much."

Chapter Twenty-five

I CALLED EDDIE and told him to carry on the morning rehearsal as best he could without Wessler and myself. Then I took out my seldom used coupé and drove round to pick up Wessler.

The Lenz sanitorium was about thirty miles out in Westchester County. It was one of those clear, bright days that sometimes happen in November, and I found it an amazing relief to shake New York off my heels and breathe air for a change.

Wessler was elated and garrulous. But I knew this meeting with Von Brandt was going to be an emotional ordeal and I could tell that his almost childlike exhilaration was a nervous camouflage.

For he had never seen his beloved half-brother since the accident. After the first period of complete loss of memory had passed, Von Brandt had seemed almost normal for a while; then he had developed the crass conviction that he was himself Conrad Wessler. Afraid of making him worse, the psychiatrist at the Thespian Hospital had been unwilling to let the two brothers meet. And until now Lenz had kept on the same tack. I hoped like hell for Wessler's sake that Lenz's treatment was going to work.

But, when we finally reached the sanitorium and I swung the car up the long drive, I forgot all about Wessler. Ever since I had been let loose on the world, labeled "Cured," I hadn't been near the place. Seeing those antiseptic buildings and the green, landscaped park, I had a moment of panic, remembering the way I had been in those far too recent days and wondering dejectedly just how soon it would be before I was back again in one of Lenz's politely padded cells.

Inside the building itself, however, my gloom was dispelled. We were met by a new, bright nurse who did not know me as an ex-patient; we were asked to wait in a room which was hardly recognizable since the furniture had been switched around and given fresh slip covers—presumably as part of Lenz's policy of keeping his patients from getting into a rut.

The nurse came back, still looking bright, and led us down a corridor to Lenz's office. Lenz himself was sitting behind his desk. It was an awe-inspiring sight. In his own setting Lenz seemed even more aloof and Olympian.

"Herr Wessler, Mr. Duluth. I am thankful you were able to come so promptly."

Wessler was twiddling his hat nervously in two large hands. He looked flushed and awkward.

"Wolfgang is again well? He know me? At last I can embrace my brother?" He asked eagerly.

"I am planning for you to meet him," said Lenz. "You must understand that it has been a difficult case and I am by no means certain yet of the results of my treatment. Before I ask Herr Von Brandt to come here, I must explain the situation a little more fully."

"Yes, yes, tell." Wessler dropped into a leather chair. I drew a wooden one close to the desk.

"As you know," began Lenz, "your brother's main delusion lies in the fact that he believes himself to be not Wolfgang von Brandt but Conrad Wessler—the great actor, the idol of Vienna. Now that I am familiar with a certain amount of your background, I am not surprised by that confusion of identity. Correct me if I am wrong, Herr Wessler, but I believe that in Austria it was always you yourself who were in the spotlight. You were the nationally known figure; your brother, although he was constantly with you, took a very secondary place. He wrote plays for you, it is true. But largely he acted as your secretary, business manager, et cetera. He attended to all the more mundane details connected with your success."

Wessler's forehead was furrowed as if he were finding it a little hard to follow Lenz's English. "Yes, so is true. It is naturally the one who acts that becomes well-known." He hesitated. "They say, my enemies in Vienna, that Wolfgang can act as well as I; that I keep him down, stop him from acting because I am jealous of my success. That is what they say, mein enemies. But it is not true. Wolfgang, he is my brother; I love him and I know. Perhaps there is in him the sparks of genius; sometimes I feel I see it; but Wolfgang he is always what you say strung up, temperamental. I say: *No, Wolfgang, you must not act,* but I say that because I feel it is bad for him to act. He would too excited get. It was that I am afraid of to act would make him perhaps lose his mind." He threw out his hands. "It is difficult to explain other than that."

Lenz was watching him, his eyes extremely interested.

"I think you have put your finger on the root of the trouble, Herr Wessler. I believe that your brother does have a very strong desire and possibly a great talent to act, latent in him. His is also a rather unstable personality. Your desire to keep him from the stage was admirable. But I feel it is that thwarted passion to be a great actor, bottled up inside him, which has made him confuse his own identity with yours. He wished so much to be what you are that now he believes himself to be you. It is a morbid type of wish-fulfillment."

Wessler said excitedly: "Yes, yes."

"The doctors at the Thespian Hospital," went on Lenz, "came to much the same conclusion. But they tried to do all in their power to shake his delusion, to make him see that he was Wolfgang von Brandt and not Conrad Wessler. I have approached him from the opposite point of view entirely. I have done everything to foster his delusion." He glanced at me. "I have made him believe he has come to America—he, the great Conrad Wessler—to act in a play for you, Mr. Duluth. I have given him, as you know, the script of *Troubled Waters*. I have given him lessons to improve his English and have had him learn the part. He believes he is here in the sanitorium merely because he has been suffering from headaches and insomnia. He is convinced that in time he will appear as the great star on Broadway."

He paused, looking down at his hands. "That may strike you as

191

rather heartless. But I see in it the only way to cure him. I have done my utmost to let his delusion run its full course. I am hoping now that the sudden shock of confronting the delusion with the actuality may restore Herr Von Brandt to normalcy."

Dr. Lenz rose from his chair and pressed a button. "Herr Wessler, please do not be too hopeful of a favourable outcome. But, whatever happens, I must ask you both to make no attempt to contradict anything Herr Von Brandt may say or wish."

Wessler had risen too. He was standing, staring at the door, his mouth a firm, anxious line. There was something very dramatic about those moments of waiting. Even I, who was in no way emotionally involved, felt the tension.

And then the door opened and a man came in, followed by a white-coated attendant. I had never seen Wolfgang von Brandt before. Somehow it came as a shock that he did not look more like his celebrated half-brother. There was a resemblance, but it was more one of expression than of feature. Von Brandt was shorter, slender and graceful, with black hair and very dark, very sad eyes.

For a second he stood in the doorway like an actor deliberately holding his entrance. He showed no sign of noticing either Wessler or me. His sad eyes were fixed on Lenz's face.

He said: "You wish to speak with me, Herr Doktor?"

"Yes," said Lenz. "Here are some visitors from New York to see you."

Wessler moved forward, his face alight with a shy tenderness. He stretched his hands out to his brother.

*"Hier bin ich, Wolfgang."**

Von Brandt half turned to look at him. There was not the slightest hint of recognition in his eyes. With a gesture of mild distaste he drew back from Wessler's outstretched arms.

"Es tut mir so leid. Aber ich kenne Sie nicht."†

Wessler's face dropped. Lenz who had been watching them both carefully said: "But you do know him, Herr Von Brandt. It is your brother."

* "Here I am, Wolfgang."
† "I'm so sorry. But I don't know you."

"My brother!" Once again Von Brandt's eyes moved searchingly over Wessler. Then his lips curled in a smile. "You try to mock me, Herr Doktor. I have but one brother—Wolfgang von Brandt. He is dead in an accident; he is dead from saving the great Wessler's life. I do not wish to talk with impostors. Please to do me the favor of asking this man to leave."

It was pathetic to see the light drain out of Wessler's face. He started brokenly to speak in German but Lenz shook his head and said:

"Perhaps it would be best for you to leave us for a while."

Wessler left, sneaking out of the room like a whipped great Dane.

As soon as he had gone, Wolfgang von Brandt moved toward me, pausing straight in front of me. Over his shoulder he said: "And this gentleman, Herr Doktor?"

Lenz said: "This is Mr. Duluth. He has come from New York to see you."

"Mr. Duluth!" Von Brandt's face lightened. "So at last I see you, Mr. Duluth. Please, please, to forgive for me my so poor English. It is not so in the part. I learn it word perfect. You do not have to worry from rehearsals. I know every little bit, everything. That play— It is my play; it is my child. It is not so good in English as in German, but it is yet good. Soon when I am better from my headaches, my sleeplessness, I leave this place; I come to New York, and we start the production. And I do not know how I can thank you for believing in me and in my play at this so trying time. You help me to fulfill my dearest wish—to act this play to an American audience."

It was rather heart-breaking. I didn't know what to say. Von Brandt's voice ran on excitedly. Over and over again, he said the same things; how perfectly he had learned his role in English, how eager he was to come to the Dagonet; how soon he could be cured of his headaches and sleeplessness.

I didn't contradict him; I didn't by the slightest gesture let him think I knew there was anything wrong. But in my mind I was certain Lenz had been far too optimistic. Wolfgang von

Brandt was charming; he was as courteous and normal as anyone could be.

But the very platform of his sanity rested on his insane conviction that he was Conrad Wessler.

All the time he was talking to me, Lenz watched him with a sort of wary anxiety like a trainer watching his most promising piece of champ material. It was impossible to guess what was in his mind.

Von Brandt was still talking eagerly when the door swung open and Wessler strode into the room. His gaze, bewildered and tormented, found Lenz's.

"I know you say for me to stay outside. But I cannot. That this should happen after all there had been between us—that I cannot bear. I must make my brother know."

Ignoring Lenz's lifted hand, he crossed to Von Brandt's side and gripped his arms.

"Wolfgang, you cannot torture me so. We, the two of us, we have always loved each other, yes? We have been two brothers facing the world. You must your eyes open; you must see—see that I am your brother, Conrad."

Von Brandt made no effort to release himself from his brother's grip. The two of them stood close together, staring at each other: Wessler, wild urgent; Von Brandt cold as glass, with vague, distant eyes.

"*Wolfgang, hör'mich.*" Wessler shook his arms roughly. "*Ich bin dein Bruder—dein Bruder. Verstanden? Dein bruder . . . . Konrad.*"*

Neither Lenz nor I moved. It had become something out of our province, something that could only resolve itself in its own way. Wessler was still speaking, in quick imploring German; and Von Brandt was staring at him, remote, dimly curious.

Then, as Wessler's voice ran on, a subtle change came over Von Brandt's face. I hardly noticed it at first; then gradually I saw his eyelids flicker; saw that glassy indifference slide out of his

* "I am your brother, your brother. Do you understand? Your brother. . . ."

eyes; saw his lips drawn tight and then relax into an unsteady, twitching smile.

There was something horrible about that smile, something ominous like a growing crack in the foundation of an otherwise solid building. And it spread, spread over his face until every feature seemed part of that twisted, senseless smile.

His voice came hoarse and very soft. *"So ist es. So ist es. Konrad, du bist zurückgekommen. Du bist gekommen mein Stück zu entstehlen. Ich solt' 's gewüsst haben. . . . Ich . . ."**

The words drifted away into silence. For one second Von Brandt stood there gazing at his brother, his arms limp at his sides, the smile still flickering foolishly around his lips. Then he laughed, a high crazy laugh. His right arm lunged forward, clutching at Wessler's throat. He hurled himself after it, scratching and beating wildly with his other fist. In a flash the two brothers were rolling on the floor, locked together in a silent, meaningless struggle.

Almost instantly Lenz had two attendants there. They pinioned Von Brandt's arms behind him; dragged him from Wessler and out of the room. As they were pulling him toward the door, he was weeping and laughing and yelling like a madman.

Slowly Wessler got up from the floor. He wasn't injured, of course. He could have killed his brother with one hand tied behind him if he had wanted to. But I'd never seen a man so nakedly, tragically miserable.

He half stumbled to Lenz's desk. He leaned over it, whispering: "What is it? What then have I done? It is just that I want him to know me—his brother. What is it I have done?"

Dr. Lenz was watching him steadily. "When I saw how your brother reacted to you, I asked you not to come into this room."

"I know. I know. But I meant no harm. What is it I have done?"

"Frankly, I do not know yet. I did not expect things to turn out this way." Lenz's tone was sympathetic. There was the faintest

* "So that's it. Konrad, you have come back. You have come back to steal my part. I might have known it."

trace of a smile in his eyes. "But, at least, you have achieved my original purpose for me. Painful as it must have been to you, you have destroyed the delusion."

He rose from his chair, holding out his hand to Wessler.

"Whatever may happen in the future, Wolfgang von Brandt and Conrad Wessler are two distinct personalities again."

Chapter Twenty-six

LENZ WENT ON talking for a while, trying to cheer Wessler up. He wasn't successful. The Austrian was convinced that his brother had gone off the rails again and that he himself was entirely responsible.

Finally the two of us left, driving back to New York in dejected silence. I was worried as hell from the point of view of the play. Whatever psychotherapeutic good that wild scene might have done Von Brandt, it had set Wessler way back. There were only five more rehearsing days before my hypothetical opening night. Only five days! And I had Wessler in this condition and Mirabelle in danger of being poisoned. All that—not counting the police.

We had a miserable sort of snack together in an automat. Wessler said of course he was prepared to go to rehearsal as usual. After a brief visit to my office, I drove him down to the Dagonet.

Eddie was there, rehearsing odd scenes where Wessler didn't figure. I don't know how long it had been going, but no one was any too cheerful. On a property table, very conspicuous, stood a new bottle of brandy for Mirabelle. When I came on stage. Gerald Gwynne was standing over it, an almost too self-conscious guardian.

Theo crossed to us. I guessed she was going to ask about Von Brandt, but I managed to give her the high-sign in time.

Gloomily, I got the play started from the beginning.

Now, as I look back, I realize that one of the main reasons why I didn't abandon the production in despair was the fact that I never lost my enthusiasm for the play itself. Even that afternoon when, God knows, there was little enough to be hopeful about, I found myself getting a kick out of the rehearsal.

And, all things considered, it didn't go so badly. My only major concern was Mirabelle. At first, it was just the analyst's report on the brandy that worried me. Her performance seemed as smooth as ever. But, gradually, as the first act slid into the second act, it began to dawn on me that something was wrong again. She started missing her cues—a thing she'd never done before. She picked them up almost immediately but there was a queer, empty void between the last speech and hers, and I could see from her face that she was fighting desperately against an uncertain memory.

I didn't say anything. I just sat there, watching. It was about five minutes later she called for a glass of brandy. Gerald sprang to the table, poured a jigger and brought it to her. She gulped it down and went right on playing. It seemed to pick her up for a while.

But only for a while. Just toward the end of the second act, her voice cracked. She tried to say a line and couldn't. She tried it three times before she got it straight. I don't think the others had noticed anything wrong until that moment. But they noticed then. I saw Theo watching her curiously. Iris, too, kept shooting her quick, anxious glances.

I didn't know what to do. It was a pretty awful sensation, seeing her breaking up like that, thinking the things I was thinking, and not having any way of coping with the situation.

I decided to wait five more minutes and then make some excuse to stop the rehearsal. That seemed the only practical thing to do. Then, just before the five minutes had elapsed, Mirabelle broke off her speech with a little sob. She dashed across the stage to the brandy bottle. Her fingers shaking, she managed to pour some into the glass and gulp it down.

"Mirabelle," I called, "what's the matter?"

She stood there, staring out across the footlights, her cheeks the color of cigarette ash. Then she threw up her hands to cover her face. Gerald made a move toward her, but she pushed him aside. She started running zigzag like a blind man toward the swing-door.

We were all of us too shocked to follow. We just stood there watching, as her hand caught at the handle of the door and tugged it back.

In a second she was gone. There was nothing but the swing-door flapping monotonously back and forth.

Like a flash Gerald started after her. But I was even quicker. I was there at his side, gripping his arm.

I said fiercely: "It's the brandy. You were supposed to be taking care of it. You . . ."

"No, the brandy's all right." He swung back to me, his lips red and tight in his white face. "I tasted it. It's all right, I say."

I broke away from him, moving toward the table where the bottle was. He went there too. He got there before me, standing square between me and the bottle.

"Let me taste it," I said. "I don't believe you. Let me taste it."

"The brandy's all right."

I tried to knock him away but he twisted round. While my fingers were touching the bottle, he grabbed it. He stood there with it in his hand, glaring at me. Then suddenly, he lifted the bottle and sent it splintering against the boards.

That seemed to mean only one thing to me. I couldn't think of anyone but Gerald, standing there in front of me, his young face stubborn and defiant. I'd put him on to guard the brandy and he wouldn't let me taste it. He'd smashed the bottle before I could taste it.

I said: "You did it. I thought all along you did it. You . . ."

Then I broke off. Suddenly the whole stage seemed to be slipping away from beneath my feet. A voice had sounded behind me, a voice that wasn't Iris's or Theo's or Eddie's or Wessler's. It said:

"Seems like I came in at a dramatic moment. Is this part of the show? Or is it just—on the side?"

I spun round. There, smiling pleasantly up at me from the orchestra pit, stood Inspector Clarke.

He said: "You told me I could drop in on a rehearsal."

I stared stupidly at him until Gerald moved away, muttering: "Going to Mirabelle."

That spurred me into action. "You're not going to Mirabelle. You're staying here. I'm going," I said.

I forgot Clarke; I forgot the rest of the cast who were staring at me as if I were cuckoo. I shoved Gerald aside and ran to the swing-door.

I looked first in her dressing-room. She wasn't there. I went down to the doorman's room, asked Mac urgently whether Miss Rue had left. He said no, no-one had gone. I was up the stairs again in a flash. Without any deliberate plan, I swung up to the second floor dressing-rooms. Ahead of me loomed the door to the room where, that very first night, Theo had started the ball of mystery and danger rolling by her crazy experience with the mirror.

The door was shut. I went to it, swinging it open, glancing in. The room was in darkness. A faint smell of greasepaint floated out to me. No one was visible.

I shall never quite know what prompted me to switch on the lights. I suppose I was reacting instinctively to a situation which linked itself up in my mind with that other time when I had looked into that dressing-room.

My fingers moved to the switch and snapped it down, sending light to the little chain of bulbs around the mirror. My hand fell to my side. I stepped back, keeping myself from crying out.

At first I tried telling myself that I didn't believe it; that I couldn't possibly be seeing the thing reflected there in the mirror. The glass was on the side-wall at a slanting angle to the door. It threw back to me—not my own image, but a view of the curtained clothes closet and the corner of the room which the closet cut off from me.

Peering out from the mirror, behind the reflection of those curtains, was a face—the gray, agonized face of a woman.

There was a prickly sensation at the nape of my neck. The theater seemed suddenly void and desolate. Not a sound anywhere. Just that tingling at my neck and the reflection of that face in the mirror—that twisted, tormented face half shrouded by the curtains.

I crossed the threshold. The image slipped from the mirror. I couldn't see it now, but I was horribly conscious that something was there in the corner behind the closet. I walked forward. I reached the closet. I passed it—and stared into the corner beyond.

There, crouched on a chair, her head tilted backward, her hands clasped at her throat, was a woman—a woman whose face I did not recognize but whose eyes I knew, whose tumbled chestnut hair was as familiar to me as my own.

I dropped on my knees; I reached for her cold, stiff hands, clasping them in my own. I was half off my head with anxiety and fear.

"Mirabelle, darling," I said. "What is it? Tell me what's the matter? What's wrong with you?"

Chapter Twenty-seven

SHE DIDN'T SPEAK. She didn't move at first. Then, slowly, she pulled one of her hands from mine and raised it to cover the blank, twitching mask of her face. I stayed there on the floor, slipping my arms around her waist I didn't know what was the matter. I couldn't guess. I only hoped that somehow by being there I might be able to help her.

I don't know how long we stayed like that. But, gradually, the small body began to relax its tight, straining control. The fingers of her left hand, which had been clutching fiercely into the flesh of mine, eased their pressure. She gave a sob—so soft that I could scarcely hear it, and feel it only as a slight quivering in her spine.

"It's all right," she whispered. "It's—its passing off now."

The hand dropped slowly from her face. That ghastly mask of suffering was gone. Her cheeks were white, drawn, but they were Mirabelle's cheeks again. Her mouth tried to smile.

"Don't worry, Peter. I—I can take it."

I said: "I know what it is, Mirabelle. It's your brandy. They've been trying to poison you. I found out about it. It's—its my fault. I should have gone to the police."

She shook her head. "No, Peter, it isn't the brandy."

"But there was codeine in it. Someone . . ."

"Yes, there's codeine in it. But it's the codeine that's made it bearable. That's one of the things they gave me to help when—when the pain comes."

"The pain!"

"I tried not to have you know. I've been trying like hell to keep anyone from knowing. Only Gerald. He's been helping me; he's been wonderful to me. You saw my face just now in the mirror. You saw the way it made me look—hideous, like an old,

202

old hag, Peter. I couldn't bear any of you to know. It's been my nightmare that you might find out."

I still had her hand in mine. Slowly I could feel the warmth seeping back into her fingers. "But, Mirabelle, what is it—I don't understand."

Once again she tried to smile. "This is the way it hit me after—after the divorce and getting free from Roland. It came instead of a nervous breakdown. They say that's what causes it, your nerves being shot. They call it tic douloureux. It's a nerve in your face and it gets out of control. Suddenly it's there, twitching, distorting your face and you can't do anything about it. And it's hell, Peter. I never knew there was so much pain in the world. I couldn't have stood it all this time if it hadn't been for the codeine."

She added hesitantly: "I didn't want anyone to know there was something the matter with me. I didn't dare take pills. That's why I had the codeine made up in a brandy bottle with brandy flavoring and everything. I didn't mind people thinking I was a drunk. There's some sort of glamor even in being a drunk. But I couldn't have borne letting people know I had this—this damn, hideous thing. They'd have thought I was passée, breaking up. The brandy was just—just my idea of putting up a front."

For a moment I couldn't speak. I could only think how Mirabelle had been fighting this ghastly thing and yet playing brilliantly in my show, never letting anyone guess what she was enduring.

I said: "You poor darling! What you've been doing—I think it's the bravest thing I ever heard of."

"Not brave, darling. Just crazy. They told me at the hospital I was mad to start playing again. But you read me the script of *Troubled Waters*. I knew I had to play Cleonie. I wanted to more than anything in life. I was just damn well going to come and act for you. Nothing mattered but that."

She rose rather shakily and crossed to a chair in front of the dressing-table. "But I've been pretty mean and selfish. All along I could have explained so many of the things that were happening here. But I just let you take it on the chin because I was too vain to break down and tell you what was wrong."

"Why should you have told me?"

"Of course I should have. At least I can tell you now." She took a comb from her bag and started combing her disheveled hair. "While we were rehearsing at the Vandolan, it seemed to be all right. I took my dope to kill the pain. I got by. The first time it hit me when I wasn't ready for it was on the evening we moved here to the Dagonet. I'd just got to the iron grille. I was turning down into the alley when a messenger boy chased after me. He—he had that Siamese cat in his arms. He didn't say anything. He just thrust it at me and ran. I was astounded. I read the message on the label and I knew only one person could have thought that out. I knew Roland Gates must be back in New York."

She paused. "That was a shock, Peter. I was scared. I had the cat in my arms. I didn't know what to do. And then—then I felt an attack coming on. I couldn't go anywhere but inside the theater. I dashed past the doorman's room, hoping he wouldn't see me. I came up here where I thought I'd be alone until it was over. But I'd only been here a few minutes when I heard footsteps on the stairs. I couldn't bear to be seen in that state. I got into the closet. I had the cat. I still had it; it was sort of clawing its way up to my shoulder. I hardly noticed it because I was in so much pain. Then the footsteps stopped outside; suddenly the lights were switched on. I didn't realize about the closet being opposite the mirror. I found myself staring at Theo's reflection in the glass. I saw her face go all white with panic. Then she disappeared and I heard her running downstairs."

I didn't interrupt. I just stood at her side, listening to that quiet, incredible story.

"After Theo had gone, I didn't know what to do. I felt sure someone would come up to investigate. I couldn't really think straight. But I thought if—if only I turned out the lights again, it might be all right. I went to do that. That was when the cat got away; it clawed out of my arms and flashed through the door. You know the rest. You and Gerald came. Gerald had guessed. Somehow he managed to get you out of the room before you'd seen in the curtained closet. While you were upstairs, he smuggled me out into a back room. He told me to stay there until he gave me the sign. Then you found the cat, Gerald took it to the doorman and told him to go out and buy it milk. That's when I got out again. I just stayed in the alley till I saw the doorman come back. Then I made my second entrance. That was Gerald's idea so that you'd never guess it was me in the closet."

At least one of the Dagonet's mysteries was a mystery no longer. I knew now exactly who had been the woman with the light tan fur.

Mirabelle was saying: "Then we started the first rehearsal. I wasn't feeling too sure of myself. Those damn attacks take an awful lot out of you and all the time you people were worrying about the face in the mirror, I—I knew I was responsible and should have told you. And then, on top of it all, Kramer arrived. Gerald told you how he blackmailed me, didn't he?"

"Yes," I said, "Gerald said Kramer had some photographs."

She gave a dry little laugh. "You should have seen them. He knew what was the matter with me. He'd found it out at the hospital and somehow he'd taken a picture when—when the pain was at its worst. You can guess what that first rehearsal was like for me. And then, as a climax, Comstock staggered in and said that about the mirror and died. That shot me to hell. I knew I was responsible for the face Theo had seen. I—I couldn't imagine what had frightened Comstock. And yet I felt somehow it was my fault; that by not explaining to Theo, I'd got the old man so scared and superstitious that he'd frightened himself to death."

I said: "No, that hadn't anything to do with you, Mirabelle. That was deliberately staged. It was something quite different." I added quietly: "And you pretended your brandy was all gone because it wasn't brandy and you didn't want us to know?"

"Yes. And I knew, too, codeine wouldn't have been good for someone with a heart attack. That's why I lied. And that's why

I sent Gerald to get the bottle back from Wessler. I was frightened he'd find out. God, how I'd hate to have that man find out." She'd taken out a lipstick and was pushing it across her mouth. "After that, things were pretty tough. Kramer was always around; then he tried to force me into getting Roland into the play. Gerald told you. I was scared stiff of having to see Roland again. That day when I went to your office and tried to get Kramer out of the cast, I thought I'd reached the end, that I couldn't take it any more. That's why I broke down. Then Roland came in. It sounds queer but from then on, I knew I'd be all right. I had seen Roland; I'd spoken to him; and I discovered he couldn't hurt me any more. I had him right out of my system. He was just a cardboard villain in a puppet show, something you hissed and weren't really afraid of. That gave me courage with Kramer. I sent Gerald round to tell him to go to hell. Gerald didn't see him but he did find the photographs and destroy them. Then—then Kramer was killed."

She swung round on the thin, wooden chair, gazing at me earnestly. "Neither Gerald nor I know anything about that, Peter. We didn't kill him. We don't know who killed him."

It was amazing how she told that story, flatly, calmly, never for a moment stressing her own incredible courage.

"I might have been all right after that," she said, "after Kramer was out of the way and there didn't seem to be anything to be afraid of. But, last night at rehearsal, Wessler slapped me right there on the cheek, on the nerve. I—Gerald managed to get me away. He knew the wretched business would start up again. We were there in my dressing-room when you came with the brandy. I couldn't bear to have you see. But I was in hell, until Gerald gave me Theo's codeine pills. Somehow he'd managed to get her bag. I took half her codeine. I—I hoped it would last me through."

I should have guessed, of course. I should have guessed from Lenz's sign-off and Gerald's attitude that I was only making a fool of myself trying to get officious and prying over that stolen handbag.

"Last night," Mirabelle was saying, "late, after Gerald had gone and I was in bed I felt the attack coming on again. I searched for the codeine pills I had taken from Theo. That was all the dope I had in the house. I couldn't find them. The pain was so bad that I could think of only one thing to do—to call Dr. Lenz. I knew he'd be able to help me."

I remembered that hoarse, strangled voice on the wire. It was a vivid reminder of the torment Mirabelle must have been going through.

"But after I'd telephoned, Peter, I found the pills. I took them. They eased the pain so that I was all right again when you and Lenz came. Even so, I had planned to tell Lenz, but since you'd come along, I didn't have the nerve. I just pretended I hadn't called, that it was some practical joke."

"But Lenz guessed?" I said.

"Yes. He guessed something was wrong. He wrote me a little note. You knew that, didn't you?"

I nodded.

"It's Lenz's note that's going to save me, Peter," she said very quietly. "He told me he'd guessed I was ill. Next day I saw him and told him the truth. He told me of a new treatment. It's just been discovered. Some sort of alcohol injections. He says you can take them without giving up work and they stop the pain for always; they kill the nerve. I thought I'd begin them tomorrow." She got up, smiling ruefully. "With any luck, I'll stop being a problem for you soon. I'll be all right. I won't have to go through this senseless parade of subterfuge and—and misery any longer."

That was the only thing I gave a damn about just then. Lenz knew of something that would fix her up. Mirabelle was going to be all right.

She'd finished with her lipstick and compact. Somehow she had managed to look just the same as ever—the radiant, indomitable Mirabelle Rue.

"Well, Peter, that's over. I'm glad you know." She gave a little ironical smile. "When I joined the company I hoped I'd be able to do a bit toward helping you up to the top again. I've turned out to be pretty much of a hindrance, haven't I?"

I said: "I can't begin to say just how much of a help you've been and are going to be. You're swell, Mirabelle."

"Oh, no. Just an actress. We actresses have to do screwy things, otherwise we'd still be knocking around fourth road companies." She glanced at me oddly. "I think I better tell you the other crazy thing about me. Or have you guessed?"

"What?"

"About Gerald. Peter, you can't imagine how wonderful and loyal that boy's been. He's had his own problems. He fell heavily for Iris. You know that. He didn't have a prayer and at his age that seems so appallingly tragic. But, apart from that day when he wanted to quit for Hollywood, he's stuck by me one hundred percent."

"I'm glad," I said.

"And I'm very proud," said Mirabelle softly. "Not only because he's going to be a fine actor but because he's a thoroughly nice person too. A mother doesn't usually get it both ways."

I asked incredulously: "You mean Gerald's your son?"

She nodded. "Remember I told you the other day I'd been married before I came east to be an actress, before I met Roland? My husband was given sole custody of Gerald by the judges. I was supposed to be a scarlet woman. But Gerald came to me, Peter. And he didn't do it until he'd landed his first big part on Broadway. The theater's in his blood the way it's in mine. He's going to crash through." She paused, "I think I've done a pretty damn good job as a mother."

I thought of what I'd said to Iris about the Mirabelle-Gerald relationship. I was as far out on that as I had been on everything else.

Mirabelle said: "You won't let Gerald know I told you? He wants to stand on his own feet in the theater. He doesn't want to be Mirabelle Rue's son." She grinned. "And it'd be rather embarrassing for me to have to dazzle the world with a grown-up son when my official age is thirty-two."

"Of course I won't tell," I said.

Her eyes suddenly hardened. "Particularly you mustn't tell Wessler. He's so damn pompous and self-righteous. He has me down pat as the wicked woman who swills brandy and cradle-snatches. He just knows every damn thing about everything. I couldn't bear to have him find out the truth." She laughed harshly. "God, but it hits me as funny sometimes when he recoils from me as if I were the Seven Deadly Sins. Me—an upright American Mother fighting life squarely and cleanly with a bottle of pain-killer disguised as brandy." She laughed again. "Wouldn't he love me, though, if he knew the truth? Wouldn't I be the very prototype of the Heroic Hausfrau?"

I said: "You still feel that strongly about Wessler?"

"More and more strongly as the days go by." Her eyes clouded over, showing an oddly baffled anxiety. "Sometimes it scares me, Peter. It's as if I'm obsessed with him. I can't explain how I feel or why. It's something violent and primitive, something that makes me itch to bash his face in with my bare fists. I never hated Roland that way." She shook her head. "I guess it's nothing really. It's just that I'm neurotic and all mixed up emotionally with the play. Half the time I think he really is Kirchner and—and that I'm Cleonie."

I stared at her, saw the sudden tightening of her lips. "In the play," I said softly, "Cleonie feels that way about Kirchner because, in spite of it all, she's crazy about him. Maybe there's something in that."

"Me—crazy about Wessler!" Mirabelle tossed back her chestnut hair, she threw out her hands and gave a jarring laugh. "My God, don't be ridiculous, Peter. Hell, don't be ridiculous."

"Okay," I said. "I won't be ridiculous."

It didn't seem to matter much one way or the other. So many more important things about Mirabelle were straightening themselves out. As we started down the stairs to stage level, I felt almost cheerful.

It wasn't until we reached the swing-door that I remembered Inspector Clarke.

Chapter Twenty-eight

H E W A S S T I L L there, chatting amiably with a very glum, nervous company. He greeted Mirabelle and me as if there had been nothing at all unusual about our precipitous exits from the stage. He stayed while I got the rehearsal started again, sitting next to me in the house, his bland gaze fixed on the actors. He made me nervous as hell. As soon as was decently possible, I had the cast knock-off.

The inspector remained after the others had gone, standing in the aisle, watching me cryptically.

At length he said: "Remember Kramer, the guy that was asphyxiated in a coffin here, couple of days ago?"

"No," I said sourly, "I've forgotten all about him."

"I haven't." Clarke lit a cigarette. "I've been looking into his past. Seems he wasn't a very desirable character. Went in for a little blackmail on the side. Know that?"

"Did he?" I said.

"Yeah. Sort of a guy someone might easily want to get out of the way." Clarke's eyes were watching me over the burning cigarette. "Do you know what I've decided? I've decided that someone here at the Dagonet deliberately murdered George Kramer."

He couldn't know how ineffectual his shock tactics were. I smiled at him. "I suppose it's the bloodhound in you. All right, I'll stooge for you. Maybe I killed him in an absent-minded moment."

"No-oo. But you might admit that you and Lenz and probably the rest of 'em too know perfectly well what's been going on around here." He flicked ash onto the red plush carpet of the aisle. "I worked with you before, didn't I? You know you can trust me."

"Sure I trust you," I said. "But what has that got to do with the price of eggs?"

Clarke was still looking at me. "Of course I see your point. You're scared we'll close the show if we find out too much. Even so, are you sure you're being smart? You'd look pretty funny if you had a third accidental death around here, wouldn't you?"

He didn't give me a chance to crack back at that one. He strolled away from me toward the swing-door—and through it.

Sometime later that night, when I was in bed making a bad try at going to sleep, I made a good try at considering the mystery of the Dagonet, sifting what was explained from what still remained inexplicable. Mirabelle, with her story of suffering and courage, had accounted for so much. And, if my theory about Kramer and Gates had been correct, there was still an adequate explanation for the original attempt on Wessler, the plot which had killed Comstock. On the surface, it seemed as if each crazy incident had fitted itself into a logical pattern which had worked itself out and was now no longer a problem.

And yet, even if that were the ultimate solution, which I doubted, there was still something else which could not be thrust away into a conveniently air-tight cubicle. Someone had murdered George Kramer. I knew it and now Inspector Clarke knew it.

However sunny the future might appear, there was no getting around the fact that the Dagonet was still an arena for the most disruptive of all combats—a murderer versus the police.

That's how I was thinking when I fell asleep. And that's how I went on thinking the next morning and the next and the next. Although rehearsals were going encouragingly, although the business machine at my office ran smoothly, although advance bookings started piling up and the whole hectic process of getting ready for the opening got under way, I felt that constant sensation of uncertainty, something the way Damocles must have felt at that dinner party where the sword dangled above his scalp on one precarious horse-hair.

But nothing happened. During the last four rehearsing days, I could almost have believed that my production was just the same as any other guy's. I saw neither hide nor hair of Inspector Clarke. Mirabelle missed one rehearsal to go for her first treatment. But she was back on the job as sure and dependable as ever, drawing me aside and whispering that the doctor was confident he could cure her. There were no personality clashes and no exhibitions of temperament except an occasional show of testiness on Wessler's part. He got it into his head that the ending was false psychology and tried on several occasions to argue about it with Henry. But, since his arguments were always spluttered in German, to Henry's complete bewilderment, nothing ever came of it.

It was symptomatic, however, of Wessler's mood. As the opening night drew nearer, he became increasingly restless and irritable. This was the first time in his life he'd opened without Von Brandt constantly at his side, and I guess it was largely worry about his half-brother that kept him on edge.

Having come to that conclusion, I stayed cheerful. An anxious male lead seemed such a small item to put up with when I had expected so much that was worse.

Eddie was a marvel during those last days. He took all the practical problems off my hands. He had the stage set in record time. And the designer had done a job with the single Pennsylvania Dutch interior. Gradually, as the billboards were pasted over with announcements of *Troubled Waters* and the electric sign blazed Mirabelle's and Wessler's name across the Dagonet, I slid back into feeling carefree and exhilarated.

The night before opening, I had the first and last full dress-rehearsal. Things were chaotic and tense as they always are at dress-rehearsal time, but there was that indefinable atmosphere of gaiety which only comes when a cast know they have a smash hit on their hands. Mirabelle, looking magnificent in her Floradora gown, was swirling around, stepping over electric wires, skirting packing cases, kissing anyone in sight. Theo, completely transformed into the embittered farmwife of the play, chatted with a handsome, bewhiskered Gerald and a rather keyed-up Iris. I reacted to it all like a two-year-old hitting the stretch again. I was back in my element.

We had quite an audience in the house. Lenz was there with that Junoesque and almost mythical personage, Mrs. Lenz. In incongruous proximity sat Louise, my colored help, with one of the pantry boys from the Belmont. All the office force with friends and guinea pigs swelled the first balcony. There was, reassuringly, no sign of Inspector Clarke.

I was just handing out a last-minute word of good cheer on stage when Wessler hurried in late from his dressing-room. My Austrian star looked superb and exciting with his heroic body and his tattered farm clothes—like some pagan god fresh from battle. There was an intense, pent-up expression on his face.

I was giving the boys and girls a pep talk. As soon as I had delivered my spiel, he came up to me, putting a great hand on my arm and drawing me out into the wings.

"Mr. Duluth," he whispered eagerly, "for days now I have been thinking. It worries me because I am so near the truth, but I do not understand. Now at last I see it all. I am a fool not so long ago to have realized."

"Realized what?"

"About my brother, Wolfgang. Why he thinks he hates me— everything. It is so plain. I know." He threw a quick glance over his shoulder as some of the others strolled toward us. "You understand German, Mr. Duluth?"

"A little," I said. "If you keep it simple."

He leaned even closer, whispering in German. "After the rehearsal come please to my dressing-room. I wait for you there. I tell you just what is wrong—why these things have been happening at your theater. I know. And you are no more to worry because it will be all right."

I stared at him blankly. But the others were right up to us. Wessler just squeezed my arm and swung back onto the stage.

With that remarkable speech echoing in my ears, I picked up the jittery Henry and slipped down into the audience. I parked the author with my business manager and found a place away from everyone where I could watch the prologue to my come-back alone.

It was amazing how the Dagonet had been metamorphosed now that the heavy plush curtains were in place and an audience broke up the dreary monotony of the house. Until then, that theater had been for me just a gloomy setting for continuous disasters. But now it seemed to have shaken off its jinx and to have remembered its dignity as one of Broadway's oldest and most tradition-proud houses.

I shall never forget that dress-rehearsal. As soon as the curtain rose, I knew it was going to hit tops. There's nothing in this world harder to impress than that odd jumble of people who get roped in for a pre-view. But, within five minutes, I could tell we had them on tenterhooks—Dr. Lenz, Mrs. Lenz, Louise and all. Wessler had even more of a punch than I had anticipated. And from the moment of Mirabelle's entrance, the play flashed and flamed around the two of them. They made the surest-fire team I'd ever seen. It seemed incredible that this new incandescent Mirabelle was the same woman whom Broadway had known so long as the sleek sophisticate of the Rue-Gates drawing-room comedies. It seemed incredible too that such a dynamic relation-ship could be founded on nothing but extreme mutual antagonism.

As soon as the final curtain fell on Mirabelle and Wessler moving hand in hand toward the farmhouse door, I dashed back-stage. I didn't have to wait to hear what anyone had to say. And I was choking with hyperboles of my own.

I ran into Eddie, Iris and Gerald, all talking and laughing excitedly. I kissed Iris; then in a burst of enthusiasm, I kissed Eddie and Gerald too. I pushed past them to congratulate Theo who was standing behind in the wings, looking away from me onto the stage.

"Theo . . ." I began.

I broke off when I saw her face. It was very pale and pinched. Her eyes were fixed on something beyond us on stage. Curiously I moved to her side and looked over her shoulder.

I saw what she had been seeing; and I understood the tight constriction of her mouth. Standing at the back of the set, close to the rear door, were Mirabelle and Wessler. They were unconscious of everything except each other, as if still caught up in the spell of the play. Wessler's great, rough arms were around her waist, his lips were moving tenderly over her hair.

At any other time the sight of Mirabelle and Wessler in that rapturous pose would have seemed fantastic. Now it seemed perfectly natural, the inevitable climax to the tornado of emotion which had been let loose on the stage. I wasn't surprised. I just felt even gayer and more exhilarated. This added the last drop to my cup of happiness. The only outstanding problem in my production, the Wessler-Mirabelle feud, was petering out into moonlight and roses.

For a second I stood there next to Theo watching them, just as a few minutes before the audience had been watching them on stage. This scene had something of the same stature, the same theatrical magnificence of the play itself.

I heard Wessler's voice whispering: "So have we been blind. We have not known what was happening to us and we have been fighting and hating because we did not understand. Once you ask me if I have not seen you before. Now I may say yes, for I know. Always I have seen you. But it has been in my heart."

There was an odd little sound from Theo, something that wasn't quite a laugh. I knew just how tough this must be for her. Poor Theo, who had been ready to shoot Kramer for Wessler's sake, who had put all she had into her adoration for him—this was her only reward, this very swift kick in the pants.

I put my hand on her arm. I whispered: "Don't forget the red-haired waiter at the Waldorf, darling."

Then I left her, moving toward Wessler and Mirabelle. I touched Wessler's arm and the two of them started, breaking away from each other, staring at me. I took both their hands.

I said: "I never thought you'd spring this on me. But it's swell. You're both swell and the play's swell. And everything's very, very dandy."

Mirabelle was still looking at me. Then slowly her eyes moved to Wessler, scrutinizing his face with a sort of breathless astonishment.

"Peter," she said, "it's mad; it's crazy; it's absolutely cockeyed. But I'm in love with this man. Why the hell didn't I realize it before?"

Chapter Twenty-nine

I HAD NO time to be mellow and paternal over this eccentric romance. Suddenly the stage was besieged by excited, gesticulating people. Miss Pink, forgetting her role as the perfect secretary, clutched my hand and pumped it up and down. Mirabelle was swept away in an admiring throng headed by Louise and Mrs. Lenz. Henry Prince hovered at one elbow, saying: "It's going to go over, isn't it, Mr. Duluth?" Iris hovered at the other, saying: "Darling, this was nothing. We're going to wow them tomorrow night."

I tried to cope with them both at once.

Then Dr. Lenz appeared, quelled all conversation with a glance and invited the whole company to a supper of celebration at Sardot's. While I was still trying to disentangle myself from Miss Pink, Iris grabbed my arm and started pulling me down the stairs after the band-wagon. As we passed the doorman's room, Mirabelle sprang impulsively at Mac, kissed his wizened cheek and yanked him out to join the party too.

He brought Lillian with him. We must have made a pretty crazy procession, headed by Mirabelle and her bustle and flanked by a Siamese cat.

The party at Sardot's began on a very exuberant note. Gerald Gwynne, with charm full on, tried to persuade Mrs. Lenz, a one-time German prima donna, to give us Brunhild's war-cry. He had almost succeeded when Mirabelle swirled round the table and clutched my arm, her face rather anxious.

"Peter, where is he? I'm so happy, so indecently happy. I can't bear for him not to be here. And I'm worried. I'm sure he's had something on his mind, not just me, something else."

It took me some seconds to realize whom she meant. Then, as

I glanced around the table, from Eddie past Theo to Henry and Gerald, I understood.

Conrad Wessler was not with us.

Mirabelle was saying: "Darling, will you go back to the theater to look for him?"

"Sure," I drawled, "anything for love's young dream."

It was not until I had left the table and was strolling toward the door that I remembered the odd conversation I'd had with the Austrian just before the show started. Wessler had told me he had the mystery of the Dagonet all figured out. I had made a date with him in his dressing-room. Here I had been giddily celebrating a success which was still in the future instead of following up the one really vital development of the day.

With a queer feeling, half shame, half uneasiness, I dodged across Forty-fourth Street back to the Dagonet.

Since Mirabelle had kidnapped Mac for the party, there was no one on guard at the stage door. As I stepped into the bleak hall, with its faint aroma of stale grease-paint, the Dagonet seemed somehow to have slipped back into its old mood of passive hostility. It was completely silent, in violent contrast to the noisy jangle that had filled it a short time before. I climbed the stairs to stage level, losing most of my frivolity, feeling my irrational anxiety grow and spread inside me. I went down the passage to Wessler's dressing-room. The door was closed. When I knocked there was no reply. I tried the handle.

For a second it did not strike me as particularly odd that the door was locked. Wessler must have grown tired of waiting. He had locked the room and gone over to Sardot's to join the others. I shook the handle to make sure the door wasn't jammed. It was while I was doing this that I saw it.

I took a step backward, watching the keyhole in hypnotized fascination. Slowly, indolently, there curled out from it a gray trail of smoke.

As I stared, that spiral of smoke thickened; it seeped out with ever-increasing volume; smoke was coming from under the door, too, rippling upward like a horde of little serpents. I could smell its smell, the close, pungent smell of burning, and I could hear the faint, ominous crackle of invisible fire.

It's hard to describe what effect the sight of that smoke had on me. My mind really stopped working before there was time to take in anything but the bare, horrible fact that Wessler's dressing-room, behind that locked door, was on fire.

I never wondered in that first period of panic whether or not Wessler himself might be inside. Memories rushing back from the past, took complete control of me. Five years ago I had seen smoke, thin and insidious, just like this; smelt that acrid smell; heard the ominous crackling of flames which, before there could be any help, had burst into a raging, roaring bedlam. That had happened to me five years ago.

I had drunk myself into a nuthouse trying to forget it. Even now, it haunted my sleep, a brutal, seering nightmare. I had that back of me, burned deep into my subconscious. I was frightened of fire as crazily and unreasoningly as a wild animal.

And now I was faced with fire again. I was alone in that huge, bleak theater confronted with the monster of my dreams.

Every impulse in me screamed out for flight. I wanted nothing in the world except to rush away, to get into the street where there was fresh air, where I would be able to cleanse that stinging, coarse smell from my nostrils. And yet I didn't run away. Although there was no logical sequence to my thoughts, I knew that this had always had to happen to me sometime. That was the way things worked. Life built up some ghastly bogey-man for you and then it confronted you with it. When you least expected it, there it was. You had to fight yourself and win out—or you were sunk.

This was the acid test of Peter Duluth.

All those sensations had swept through me in a split second. I still had no definite thoughts or fears for Wessler. I just knew, although the knowledge slashed brutally across my most basic instincts, that I had to get into the room and stop that fire.

While the smoke wreathed its tentacles stiflingly around me, I threw myself at the door, bashing against it with my shoulder.

There was a groan of hinges, nothing more. Once, twice, three times I slung myself against the woodwork. At last the groan broadened into a splitting, screeching sound. A panel cracked inward. For one second the door teetered back and forth; then the lock went; smoke bellied out at me as the door lurched forward and down and I stumbled through into the dressing-room.

For the first few seconds I could not see; I could hardly breathe. There seemed nothing in the world but that choking fog of smoke and behind it the dull red glow that at any moment might blaze into riotous flames. Stray thoughts started registering at last. The fire was concentrated in the corner where the wardrobe stood. How could a fire have started there? How—unless it had not been accidental?

I hadn't thought of it that way before. Now, as I whipped out a handkerchief, pressing it against my nose, I saw one blinding, horrible explanation for it all. Wessler had the solution to the mystery. Wessler had stayed behind in his dressing-room to pass that news on to me. Now his dressing-room was on fire. And he, my star, the very foundation of my show, was missing.

Where was Wessler?

I stumbled forward, my eyes smarting, my breathing, behind the handkerchief, coarse and gasping. The room had lost all individuality. My groping hand struck wood, the back of a chair, the edge of a table. I veered right, away from the dull red glow in the corner. My foot tripped over something soft. I dropped to my knees, pushing my fingers forward.

They touched rough wool, the tweed of a jacket. They slid along it. They found a hand. My eyes, peering down, could just make out the dark figure of a man, sprawled across the carpet.

From then on I acted mechanically with the insane efficiency that comes in an emergency. I let the handkerchief drop from my mouth. With both hands I grabbed at that heavy, unresponsive body. Somehow I dragged it through the pall of smoke, toward the broken door and through it along the passage to the comparative safety of the stage.

I had guessed whose that body would be. There was only one

possible solution. But for a minute or two, as I stood there on the stage, panting and sweating, my powers of vision entirely deserted me. Even here, although the atmosphere was clear and a bright working light was burning, there seemed to be nothing but smoke, an impenetrable pall of it between me and the body on the boards.

Then, gradually, those imaginary mists dispersed. I fell to my knees by the body. I could see again, see with a sharp, hurting vividness. I saw the short blond beard, the huge shoulders thrusting out of the tattered farmer clothes.

Conrad Wessler had been locked in that windowless, smoke-saturated room.

Feverishly I worked over him, trying to do something and not knowing what to do. His eyes were closed, his face was waxy and stiff like a dummy's. Then, as I stared, I saw something else, something that jerked me up to the highest peak of panic.

Trickling from Wessler's matted hair, slowly dripping onto the boards of the stage, was a steady stream of blood.

The moments which came next are merged in my mind now in a blurred kaleidoscope. I suppose I must have rushed off the stage, down the stairs and along the alley to the street. But I have no recollection of doing so. All I remember is the cold night air on my forehead; the startled face of a complete stranger in a derby hat; and my own voice shouting:

"Over the way. Sardot's. Get there. Find Dr. Lenz. Dr. Lenz. Make him come here at once. Man with a beard. Big party. Bring him here at once. Make them call the fire department."

Then the stranger's face vanished from my ken forever. I was back in the theater again. In my hand was a scarlet fire extinguisher. I was in Wessler's dressing-room, back in the sickening geyser of smoke. At that stage, I wasn't just fighting fire. I was fighting ten thousand demons, exorcizing them with that extinguisher.

I have dim memories of the red glow in the corner paling, quivering and then fading into nothingness. I have even dimmer memories of staggering out into the passage and back along it to the stage, wrenching fresh air into my lungs, gazing down foolishly att he body of Wessler, thinking and not thinking, feeling triumph and despair at the same time, triumph because I had fought the fire and myself, despair because I knew with blank, heart-breaking certainty that Wessler was dead.

He had to be dead. From the very beginning *Troubled Waters* had been hounded by some superhuman, sadistic force. This was the only fitting climax, this savage finale, snatching everything from us on the very threshold of success.

Vaguely I heard hurrying footsteps somewhere behind me, offstage. I turned dizzily to face the door. It swung open at me; people started pouring through. I saw Lenz, Eddie, and behind them Mirabelle and Theo, together, with white faces and blank, staring eyes.

I remembered Mirabelle giving a stifled cry. I saw her dash toward Wessler; heard her tormented voice: "It can't be. Oh, God, it can't be now. Conrad . . ."

Theo's voice broke in quietly: "No, Mirabelle. Don't go to him. Please, stay with me. Let Dr. Lenz see him. Let Dr. Lenz have room."

She had put her arm around Mirabelle's waist, holding her back. Dr. Lenz had dropped to his knees. He was bending over Wessler. Eddie, his voice thick and low, was gripping my arm, pouring out questions. I suppose I answered them. I had my breath back then; I could talk; I could remember more than just the suffocating smoke.

But I wasn't listening to my own voice. I was just waiting, conserving all my faculties for what Dr. Lenz would say.

There was a long, throbbing silence. Eddie had slipped away to make sure the fire was extinguished. Only Mirabelle, Theo and I were there, waiting for Lenz to speak.

Mirabelle struggled to get away from Theo. She tried to get to Wessler. She said: "I can't bear it, Dr. Lenz. Seeing him there, not knowing—I can't bear it. You've got to tell me. Is he dead?"

Once again that taut, suspended silence. Then Lenz's voice.

"No, Miss Rue, he is not dead."

"Thank God. Thank God. But what is it—is it the smoke? Is he suffocated?"

"It is not only that, Miss Rue. There is a severe contusion on the back of his head. He has been struck by some heavy implement. I am afraid the skull is fractured. He is very, very seriously injured."

There was some talk about a hospital, calling an ambulance, calling the police. But suddenly I couldn't stand it any longer.

I thought: "So this is what I've worked for. This is what I've tried to rehabilitate myself for. Wessler's out. Tomorrow we open. We can't open without Wessler. We can't do anything. This time, we're through."

And I was through. I didn't give a damn about anything. For months I'd slaved, I'd hoped, I'd struggled against my desire for alcohol. I'd done that—just to have everything swept from under my feet.

It wasn't good enough. There was no damn sense in going on. I was through.

I slipped off the stage. I don't think the others noticed me. With one burning desire guiding me like a pillar of flame, I ran down the stairs. I was going to leave the Dagonet forever; I was going to get stinking, roaring tight.

I suppose I was somewhere near the stage door when I felt that small, cold hand on my arm. It meant nothing to me. I tried to shake it off. But it stuck.

Then I heard a voice. It said: "Peter, surely you're not in as great a hurry as all that?"

I paused. I shook myself. I looked at the man standing in front of me, watching me from flat, black eyes—eyes that had a derisive, surface smile.

"The doorman has told me the tragic news," said Roland Gates. "How very unfortunate for you all. But how fortunate that you took my advice and persuaded me to learn the part. There is nothing for you to worry about. I shall be more than ready to take over tomorrow night."

I hadn't said anything until then because I couldn't. There were no words inside me, nothing but an all-embracing, barbarous loathing of Roland Gates. He wasn't going to get in my show . . . not if ten thousand demons tortured me. I'd rather see it sink; rather go howling after it to hell.

"Yes, Peter," he murmured. "I think you'll find my interpretation of the part very stimulating. I . . ."

Maybe he said something else, but I didn't hear it. I lunged with my right fist, aiming straight at his jaw. I staggered forward after it. I didn't know whether or not I had made contact. I didn't know anything except that I was out again in the cool night air of the alley, hurrying forward.

I remember thinking: Then this is good-by to Iris, too. I'll never see her again. But that couldn't stop me. Iris was part of that flimsy dream I had thought I could snatch out of the clouds; she was something I wouldn't ever have been able to get, anyway.

Here was something I *could* get, now and forever—and I stumbled into the nearest bar.

Chapter Thirty

I SHOOK MYSELF. I screwed up my eyes, peering across the bar at a white, blurred disk that used to be a clock.

"What's the time?" I said.

"Two-thirty-two," said the barman. "Fifty seconds ago when you last asked, it was thirty-one minutes and fifty seconds past two. Looks like we're keeping up to schedule."

"Fine," I said, "nothing like keeping up to schedule." I swallowed my fifth? sixth? seventh? straight Scotch. "Pretty good clock, isn't it? Dependable."

"Sure," said the barman. "Why don't you wash some of that dirt off your face?"

"Good idea," I said. "Excellent."

Time elapsed. I could hear it ticking away back of the bar. But I was all right. I was clinging onto the rail. I wasn't going to tick away.

"So you're not going to wash the soot off your face?" said the barman. "Maybe you like it the way it is?"

"Certainly. I like my face the way it is."

"Well, I don't," said the barman.

That wasn't at all the thing one gentleman said to another. I knew it. I drew myself up. I said: "If you don't like my face, I have no desire to consort with you. Good evening to you, sir."

My fingers slid from the rail to my hat. My hat was on my head. A little trouble with a revolving door, but I was out again in the fresh air.

There were lights all around me. I knew what they were, lights on bars, movie houses, theaters—theaters. They couldn't fool me. I hadn't drunk hard liquor for over a year but I could still take it. Yes, sir. I was okay.

Somewhere, way, way down inside, a midget voice was

225

nagging: "Wessler's out. Your show's shot to hell. You're through." But I didn't pay any attention to it—not a damn sissy voice like that.

A bar with a brass rail; a bar with no rail; a bar with high seats, too high seats, you couldn't keep on them very well; another bar. What's the time? Three-thirty. What's the time? Four-fifteen. What's the time? Close on five o'clock, sir.

There was a hand on my arm. I turned. A girl was sitting next to me at the bar—damn attractive girl. She was smiling.

"Hello," she said.

"Hello," I said. "What'll you have?"

"Milk," said the girl.

"Make it two milks, barman," I said.

"Like to go places with me?" said the girl.

"Sure," I said. Then I was suspicious. I said to the barman: "Who the hell is this girl anyway?"

"If I was you I wouldn't give a damn," said the barman. "I'd take a brody."

I turned to the girl. "What's your name, kid?"

"Iris."

I said: "That's a nice name. I used to know a girl called Iris."

"What happened to her?" said Iris.

"She's out of my life," I said. "She's a damn nice girl."

Someone paid for the milk. I was out in the street with the girl. I was in a car. All the fixed stars of Broadway became comets, shooting past me to left and right. Hell of a lot of comets.

I started counting them. But what the heck? Why should I count any darn comets? I slid back against the seat. There was the girl at the wheel. Cute little silver slipper on the gas. I saw it; then it joggled out of focus; then it was gone.

Sometime later I was conscious again, conscious of speed, a tearing forward motion, a breeze blowing on my face. I was a disembodied spirit hurtling through the empyrean.

The girl was still there at my side, a girl in silver with dark hair floating backward.

226

"Don't tell me," I said. "Let me guess. We're dead. We're going to heaven."

"Right, darling," said Iris. Her eyes were fixed on the road. "And at the moment I'm trying like hell to avoid Philadelphia."

Then I smelt smoke. With a sudden stab of panic, I smelt smoke. It seemed to come from my clothes.

"I'm on fire," I said.

"No, darling. If you smell anything nasty, it's just Philadelphia. Don't worry."

So I worried . . . and began dimly to remember. I had been in a theater. There had been smoke—something ghastly had happened. I struggled with an elusive nightmare of memory. I pushed myself around to look at the girl with the silver slippers.

"You're Iris," I said.

"Yes, I'm Iris."

"Nice," I said. "Very nice."

The car rushed on.

I said slowly: "Something happened to Wessler, didn't it? He was burned, bashed over the head. He's dead."

"He isn't dead," said Iris. "He's in a hospital. They say he'll be all right."

"But he won't be able to act?"

"No—not for some months, I believe."

"Then it's all over. The play's through. No more *Troubled Waters*, no more work, nothing to worry about. Goody, goody. Whoopee."

"Whoopee," said Iris. "Don't talk any more, darling. You're getting me fussed and we'll end up in Philadelphia."

"Always end up in Philadelphia," I said. "Can't avoid it. Inevitable."

I didn't talk any more because Iris had told me not to. But we were there in the car. For hours and hours we seemed to be in the car. The darkness gradually went and a sort of dirty grayish light was everywhere—the dawn. Towns and things flashed past. Iris was driving very fast.

At last she got some place and slowed up. There was a boy at the side of the road. When we slowed up, he came to us, jumping on the running board. He had a pudgy white face with pimples and a sniff.

Iris said: "This is Elkton, isn't it?"

"Yes, ma'am."

"Could you please direct me to . . ."

The boy grinned, showing teeth and gaps. "You want a minister, eh? Sure, I'll fix you up. Best minister in town. J. B. Stott. Reasonable rates, smart service. Record number of splicings for the months of July, August and October 1938. Always accessible night and day. Never . . ."

Iris said: "That's a horrid little boy, Peter. Push him off the running board."

I looked at the boy. He had eyes like a pig. "On the contrary," I said, "he's an attractive little boy. Nice little boy. Interesting conversationalist."

The boy winked at Iris. "Tight, eh? Most of the husbands that turn out best are the guys you catch when they're cockeyed. Yes, ma'am."

Iris leaned over me suddenly. She pushed the boy. He fell sprawling back on the road. Iris started the car again.

I said: "You shouldn't have done that to the nice little boy. Heartless. So we're in Elkton?"

"Yes."

"And we're going to get married?"

"We are," said Iris, "but not by Mr. J. B. Stott."

That all seemed pretty swell to me, getting married and everything—romantic.

Iris drew up outside a building. There was a great black and white sign with a name on it. The name wasn't Stott—something else. We were inside the building. A man emerged; he seemed to know what we wanted; he brought a fat woman, his wife, and a girl with thick spectacles, an unattractive girl. They were witnesses, he said.

Iris and I stood there together. I had my hand in hers. The man started reading. All I had to do was pretty easy—just repeat

228

a couple of things after him. I knew what was happening. Iris and I were being married. We'd always wanted to be married anyway. Why the hell hadn't we done it before? The man who wasn't J. B. Stott was kissing Iris. For one moment of panic I thought the fat woman and the woman with glasses were going to kiss me. But they didn't.

We were all writing in a book. Iris was paying out money. Then the man was talking to me. He said how he raised chickens and how almost every bride and groom bought day-old chicks from him on the side. Would I care for some? I felt day-old chicks would be pretty damn useful. I ordered dozens. That's how you bought them, so much the dozen. He said he'd have them put in the car. I said fine.

Then Iris and I were alone in the car. We sat close together in the front seat. I looked at her. She was beautiful with those sloe-dark eyes and soft red mouth. As I watched, her lips trembled. She tried to keep them from trembling but she couldn't. Suddenly she was in my arms, crying like a baby.

"What is it, darling?" I said. "What's the matter?"

She said: "Oh, Peter, what a lousy way to get married."

"It isn't lousy, darling. Don't cry. Please don't cry. It's fun; it's gay."

For a while she stayed there against my shoulder, sobbing. "It isn't gay. It's horrible. I've tried not to let down, Peter. But you don't know what it's like. Ever since I was a kid, I dreamed about shimmering white satin and bouquets and all my most unattractive friends as bridesmaids so there wouldn't be any competition." She looked up. The tears were still gleaming on her cheeks. "But I've got you, darling. Even if I did have to take six dozen day-old chicks as well, I've got you."

"I'm not much to have," I said.

"You are, Peter. You're a hell of a lot. I wouldn't have put in so much spade work if I didn't think that." She drew herself away. She started the car, looking efficient and executive again.

"Where are we going?" I said.

"On our honeymoon," said Iris. "In Elkton's grandest hotel."

Some time later I was in a hotel room with Iris. I wasn't tight any more—at least not so tight that I didn't know what it was all about.

"Happy, darling?" she whispered.

"Happy as hell," I said. Then I heard something which wasn't at all a normal sound to hear. I added: "But I think there's a little stranger under the bed."

"There is," said Iris. "Six dozen of them, chicks."

Chapter Thirty-one

A T S O M E L A T E R, indeterminate time, I stirred on the bed. I opened my eyes onto a blur which gradually resolved itself into an unfamiliar bedroom. My head was splitting; red hot pins were being stuck in my eyeballs. I wanted to die.

I shut my eyes again. That didn't help. Then a door opened. I made myself look. Iris was coming in, cool and calm in a silver evening gown. That gown made me remember last night or this morning or whatever it was. I felt a bit better.

"Hello, wife," I said.

She sat down on the edge of the bed. She took one of my hands "Thank God you remember. I couldn't have borne it—not if I'd married you when you were completely unconscious."

"Sure I remember," I said. "This is the grandest hotel in Elkton. Where are the chickens?"

"They've gone. We've got to go too, darling. I want you to dress. How do you feel?"

"Terrible." I tried to move. It was difficult. With a sudden sense of sin, I added: "Iris, I've—I've got the original hangover."

She said: "Darling, never mind that. Here are your pants."

With her help, I dressed. I was very groggy on my feet, but I managed a fairly straight line following her downstairs and out to the car. I was very obedient. I didn't ask any questions. I didn't even want to ask any.

As the car started forward, I lapsed into a sort of post-alcoholic coma. I had the dim sensation of its being latish in the day. The light, when I did open my eyes, grew more and more opaque. Somewhere on the journey, Iris switched on the headlights.

Once I asked: "Where are we going?"

"New York," said Iris. "Home."

I left it at that. And we did drive home—back to my apartment. Iris was very quiet, also dominating. She persuaded me into
a tuxedo, spent a few minutes in the bathroom and came out
looking even more beautiful than before. Then we went downstairs again in a car, driving crosstown. I was getting my bearings
vaguely. I saw the Wrigley goldfish; then we were parking. We
got out of the car and headed toward something that was blazing
with lights. Dozens of other people seemed to be going there too.
We were jostled by other tuxedos and expensive fur wraps.

"We're going to the theater, aren't we?" I asked meekly.

"Yes," said Iris. She guided me into a crowded foyer, up some
stairs and down a passage to a door. She opened the door. She
kissed me and whispered: "Cross your heart for me, darling."
She pushed me gently forward through the door. I heard her
say: "He's here. Everything's all right." Then she was gone.

For a second I hated being without her. Then I switched my
slender quota of intelligence onto trying to figure out my sur-
roundings. Somewhere an orchestra was grinding through the
"Merry Widow Waltz." I was in a small darkened room. There
were people close to me and ahead of me. Beyond them was
cavernous darkness and the "Merry Widow." Unquestionably I
was in a theater box. I saw an empty chair in front of me. I knew
how to behave with dignity in a box. I moved forward, somehow
reached the chair and sat down.

I could now see the orchestra responsible for the "Merry
Widow." It gleamed below me in a lighted pit. Above them,
tall, red, opulent curtains covered the high proscenium arch.
Behind them stretched the house. It was a large house; it was
packed with people, rustling programs, buzzing at each other
like innumerable wasps. I saw dazzling white fronts, gleaming
dinner gowns. I was probably at an opening, a very dressed-up
opening.

I flicked my aching eyes sideways to the figure on my right.
The light, coming up from the orchestra pit, played on his face.
It was a familiar face, round and tense, with horn-rimmed
spectacles and straggling black hair. Henry Prince. To the far

side of him, I saw another face I knew, an alert young face with gray eyes. Inspector Clarke.

I was on a theater party with Henry Prince and Inspector Clarke.

"Hello, Henry," I said.

"Hello," he said.

I suppose all told I'd only been in that box about ten seconds. That was why I did not notice the imposing presence on my left until a hand touched my arm and a magnificent, bearded face smiled close to mine.

"I am indeed glad that you arrived in time, Mr. Duluth," said Dr. Lenz "I understand from a telephone call that you are to be congratulated on your marriage."

"Yes," I said. "Just on my marriage—not on anything else."

"And how are you feeling yourself, Mr. Duluth?"

I said: "Terrible. Godawful." I was ashamed but I knew I had to tell him. "Last night I got tight—stinking, hellish tight. Still don't know whether I'm coming or going. That's the sort of patient I am. Better give me up. I'm through."

The orchestra was now playing Whosit, the witch of the wood. I hated being in a theater. I didn't want to be there at all. I only wished I could get my brain to work lucidly.

Vaguely I heard Lenz's voice: "On the contrary, Mr. Duluth, I have no fault to find with you as a patient. Under the circumstances, I myself would have prescribed liquor for you last night."

"What?" I said.

Lenz repeated that amazing sentence. He added: "You had been through more than any man can endure without some sort of false stimulant. Now that you have the more abiding stimulant of marriage I see no chance of your returning to the liquor habit."

That struck me as amusing. I giggled. I said: "Aren't we having more fun? Where are we, by the way? I don't want to be inquisitive. But one does like to know these things."

I could see a pucker of surprise crease Lenz's forehead. He said: "Surely you know where you are, Mr. Duluth. We are at the Dagonet Theater. This is the opening night of your production, *Troubled Waters*."

I sat up. I looked down again into the crowded auditorium. it did look like the Dagonet—very like.

"Don't say it if you don't mean it," I said. "Don't say it."

"But naturally I mean it, Mr. Duluth. Your business manager reports what I believe is called a sell-out at the box office. He . . ."

"But how?" I was getting in control of myself now. Things were coming back straight. Everything that had happened last night was clear and sharp. I could understand the whole works except for this. This was incredible. "It can't be possible. It's crazy. Wessler—you don't mean he's all right, after all?"

"I'm afraid I do not, Mr. Duluth. Had it not been for your heroism last night in saving him and extinguishing that fire, he would undoubtedly have succumbed to the very brutal attack made upon him by the murderer of George Kramer. As it is, the severe contusion on the back of his head, where he was struck, necessitates a minor brain operation which will incapacitate him for some time. Although there is not the slightest doubt of his ultimate recovery, I am afraid you will not be able to count on him for the run of this particular show."

I wished the orchestra would stop playing so that I could hear better. "Then we're opening without Wessler," I said. "You're trying to tell me that. It's not possible. It's—" I stopped the sentence, swinging round to Lenz, gripping his arm fiercely. "You can't have done this to me. I'd rather die than have it happen. Stop the show, make them stop the show. I'm not going to have that little pimp, Roland Gates . . ."

"No, Mr. Duluth, Mr. Roland Gates does not figure in tonight's production." Lenz gave a low chuckle. "I'm afraid he is in no condition to play in any production for some time to come."

I remembered then how I had swung at him last night when I staggered out of the theater. In my exuberance, I forgot everything else. "Then I did hit him. I did lay him out."

"Once again, no, Mr. Duluth. Last night, I regret to say,

your aim was not at its surest. You may have hit at Mr. Gates, but you missed him. The actual striking was performed by Mr. Gates himself. It appears that the doorman stepped between you, attempting to avert a struggle. It so happened, in the melee, that Mr. Gates struck him, rendering him unconscious and dislodging two teeth. Inspector Clarke arrived at the theater almost simultaneously with the blow. When I informed him of Gates' general behavior, I persuaded him to arrest Mr. Gates for disturbing the peace. He is to be shut up for an indefinite period."

That was funny; riotously funny. It seemed as if, after all, there was some type of poetic justice somewhere. Then I banished Gates from my mind and gave it a chance to grapple with the vital problem.

"But who," I said, "who in God's name is playing the Wessler role?"

At that moment the lights in the orchestra pit flickered; a buzzer sounded offstage; the "Merry Widow" faded into a rustling which, in its turn, slipped into taut, expectant silence.

Dr. Lenz's lifted hand indicated his unwillingness to speak at this most crucial of all moments. Slowly the curtain slid upward, brilliant lights played on the Pennsylvania Dutch interior. I clung to my chair, feeling dizzy and tormented with apprehension.

Troubled Waters had begun, the play on which I had pinned my existence, the play which I had deserted, the play which, miraculously, had outlived my captaincy of it and was opening here in the Dagonet before a crowded audience on the scheduled night.

Chapter Thirty-two

I T W A S A M A Z I N G for me, watching that play begin, when so long ago I had resigned myself to its complete and utter disintegration. There on the stage, crouching over a brick fireplace, was a girl in a gray, gingham dress. I knew, of course, that the girl was Iris. That was the way the act started, with Iris there alone. But I couldn't believe it. It was something out of a dream. I thought of all the things that had happened to Iris in the last twenty-four hours. She had rescued me, God knows when, in God knows what bar; she had driven me to Elkton; she had married me; she had got me into some sort of shape; she had brought me back to the theater and to life. She'd done all that and here she was on the stage, starting the ball rolling, acting her part as if nothing had happened. Iris, who had never seen the stage until a few months before, was facing the biggest ordeal in an actress's career.

Iris Duluth was an honest-to-God trouper.

I sat forward in my seat, clutching the rail of the box. In two seconds Kirchner would appear—the role by which the play stood or fell, the role which was going to be played neither by Conrad Wessler nor by Roland Gates. I had a moment of excruciating agony while Iris left the fireplace and crossed to the window. That was the cue. Kirchner had to enter then.

And he did. A man came in from the side door. He paused there, saying Kirchner's first line of dialogue; then he moved across the stage to Iris. He was a tall man, not so tall as Wessler but of the same build, a man with dark hair and a straight, insolent carriage.

For a second, as the truth dawned on me, I could not speak. Then I whispered hoarsely: "Von Brandt."

"Yes, Mr. Duluth." Lenz's voice just registered on my eardrums. "Since neither he nor his brother is known to American audiences, Mr. Prince and I did not feel it necessary to make any official announcement of a cast change."

I swung round on him. "But it's not possible. You can't have done it; it's crazy. You're giving the play over to Von Brandt. It's all got to rest on him. You can't do that. He's—he's insane; he's mad."

"Do not be alarmed, Mr. Duluth. There is a certain amount of risk, I admit. But it is very slight. You know yourself that Herr Wessler managed to break through the insane delusion that day when he made his brother recognize him. Since then, there has been a great change in Wolfgang von Brandt. He is almost well—I say almost, because I can only hope for a complete recovery after tonight. Your play has been struck by a tornado, Mr. Duluth, but it is one which bears out the truth of the proverb about the ill-wind. Herr Von Brandt needed just one thing to restore him to a normal state of mind. He needed to fulfill his suppressed ambition; he needed to appear on a stage before an audience. The tragic accident to Herr Wessler has given his brother the one chance to find himself again. I am hoping that he will be able not only to save the play but to save himself."

That was just words to me, fantastic words from a textbook psychiatrist. Less than a week ago I had seen Wolfgang von Brandt spring on his brother in a fit of violent maniacal rage; I had seen him carried screaming away by trained attendants. That's all I knew about Wolfgang von Brandt. Now he was here acting in my production before a crowded house. I, Peter Duluth, was responsible for whatever was going to happen.

I didn't dare look at the stage. As I sat there, looking down at the dusty floor of the box, the dialogue of the play droned through my ears. It had no meaning to me. I could distinguish the various voices—Iris's, Theo's, Gerald's. Then, dominating them all, that strange voice, a slow, vibrant voice with a German accent, the voice of Wolfgang von Brandt.

I don't know how long that horrible suspension of existence

237

lasted. But gradually it began to seep through to me that the play was progressing without a hitch; no one muffed his lines. Nothing was going wrong.

I looked up. I stared straight at the brilliantly lit stage. I remember that first impression—the four people grouped in a striking tableau, Iris, Theo, Gerald, Von Brandt. They were staring at the door, listening to the faint cry that heralded Mirabelle offstage.

It was right. It was exactly the way I had directed that scene. The tension was there; it held just the correct length of time before Gerald and Von Brandt exited. Then they were back again and with them, vivid, electric, magnificent, was Mirabelle Rue.

With Mirabelle's entrance, that awful wound-up sensation slipped away. From then on, I knew that by some miracle the play was all right. For the first time I began to feel the audience around me; I began to drop into their mood, see the show through their eyes and realize with tingling excitement that they were carried right out of themselves.

And it wasn't only Mirabelle. Although I knew the tumult of anxiety and fear for Conrad Wessler that must be penned up inside her, she was dazzlingly good. But she didn't have to put the play across single-handed. Iris and Gerald and Theo were immense. And there was Wolfgang von Brandt.

By that time I could look at him impartially, judging him as an actor, forgetting the crazy circumstances of his presence on stage. His technique was quite different from Wessler's; it was less violent, subtler, with a quiet, devastating strength. But it was beautiful; it made a sensational foil for Mirabelle. And he was completely on top of the situation. He was Hans Kirchner of the play; he was living and breathing that imaginary character.

I sat there between Henry Prince and Dr. Lenz but I had no sensation of being near either of them. I was soaring in some shadowy world of elation and triumph. The act went on and then it came to an end. The curtain dropped on it and instantly, like a dammed-up wave, applause roared from the house.

I wanted to stand on my head. I slapped Henry on the back. I shouted congratulations to him over the din of clapping. I turned to Lenz, saying: "How did you do it? Tell me how did you do it? He's colossal. He's as good as Wessler. And he knows the play backwards, every line, every bit of business; it's as if he'd been rehearsing with us for months. How did you do it?"

The lights had snapped on. Still applauding, the audience below us was breaking up into individuals, streaming out for cigarettes and drinks.

Dr. Lenz was smiling, a grave, satisfied smile. "Herr Von Brandt's performance does not surprise me. You know the way his mind has been working all through these years. He himself has explained it to me. Always, in Vienna, it was his overwhelming ambition to act. He wrote several plays, excellent plays, with a big male part. Each time he hoped to be able to act that part himself. Each time, the managers, the directors and Herr Wessler himself insisted that his half-brother should play them. Von Brandt's normal ambition became an abnormal dream. At last, tonight, he has attained his goal. He has studied this role; he has loved it; it is for him now not the work of another but his own play. He is his own creation. This is his heaven on earth."

I had no time to ask any more questions. The door to the box had opened on a swarm of people, rushing in with congratulations. The play was only one act gone but everyone took it for granted that we had a smash hit. They overwhelmed me with compliments; I was dizzy from shaking hands and saying "Thank you," and keeping people from guessing that I was only half an hour out of the worst hangover in history.

The second act got under way. I'd always been sure of the second act. It was dynamite from the opening line to the curtain. I knew we'd get by with that. And we did. It was exhilarating to feel that tense mass reaction to it. When the curtain fell for the second time, I soared upward on the crest of the enthusiastic applause.

I didn't wait for Lenz or Henry or Clarke to say anything. I

239

got up, slipped out of the box and dashed around backstage. I ran onto the set. I didn't care whether they'd finished the curtain calls or not.

Everyone was there. They were all milling around me. I kissed Iris. I said: "Darling, it's a knock-out. You're a knock-out. God, I love you. You're wonderful. And I'll never drink again—never, never again."

I was shaking Gerald by the hand. Mirabelle was swirling around me, saying: "Darling, it's good, isn't it? It's getting them. Hell with everything, it's getting them." Her eyes for one second showed the suffering behind them. "I thought I couldn't make it, Peter. Not at first. Now I've heard the news from the hospital. It's all right. Wessler's going to come through. I guess it's sort of for the best. When he's well again, I'll be through with my damn treatments too. We'll both be hygienic and eupeptic together. God, isn't it exciting? What a house! What a house!"

I kissed her too. I pushed past them to Wolfgang von Brandt. I took both his hands. He was smiling, a queer, half incredulous, half triumphant smile.

"It goes well, Mr. Duluth?"

"It goes splendidly."

The smile spread over his face. "But I am so happy. Always I know it is to be this way. It is my part. It has always been my part."

It had. I told him so. I told everyone everything. Then Theo Ffoulkes clutched my arm and dragged me away.

"Darling," I said, "oh, darling, darling, darling."

She said: "Peter, my boy, we're coming through." She grinned, that frank, sardonic grin of hers. "Isn't Von Brandt marvelous? It's sheer genius; it's incredible; he's better than Wessler. And he's so gorgeous to look at. I never thought . . ."

I knew then she was going to say. "You never thought you could do it again, darling," I said. "First the red-headed waiter, then Conrad Wessler, now Von Brandt. More power to you."

She said: "Peter, you're still a louse."

Eddie came up then, beaming from ear to ear. He dragged Theo away and threw me off the stage. They were ready for the last act. I went back to the box.

Lenz and Henry and Inspector Clarke were alone again, sitting side by side, making as incongruous a trio as I'd ever seen. It seems incredible to me now, but not for one moment that crazy evening had I stopped to consider just why Inspector Clarke was in our stage box.

While the audience hustled back to their seats beneath us, I turned exuberantly to Lenz and said: "It's a riot. I can never thank you enough. It's not only Von Brandt; it's everything. There couldn't have been any play if it hadn't been for you."

Dr. Lenz looked at me quizzically. He said: "You are thanking the wrong person, Mr. Duluth. It was completely beyond my power to have enabled the play to open. You owe the success of this evening entirely to Inspector Clarke."

I said, suddenly uneasy: "Just what do you mean?"

"Surely you have not forgotten the disturbances which have taken place at the Dagonet during the past weeks, Mr. Duluth." Lenz's thumb stroked his imperial. "You must also remember that last night a murderous attack was made upon Herr Wessler. Someone waited in his dressing-room; struck him on the back of the head; set fire to the wardrobe and then locked the door. That was a deliberate homicidal attempt. That alone would have been sufficient to have the play closed—under normal circumstances."

It was true, of course, I just hadn't thought of it, that's all.

"And," Lenz was continuing, pausing a moment to bow to some other impressive beard in the house, "Inspector Clarke is fully cognizant of the fact that Mr. Kramer was murdered and that Mr. Comstock died from a shock which was criminally administered. If Inspector Clarke had chosen to make an immediate report to the Commissioner, *Troubled Waters* would not have had the slightest chance of opening tonight, if at all."

I was completely sobered by then. The lights had dimmed; the curtain had gone up. But I hardly noticed. With a dull sensation of anxiety, I realized just how airy a bubble this success actually was. Here had I been deliriously whooping it up with one murder, one murder-attempt and one homicide all hanging like mill-stones around my neck.

"However," Lenz was continuing softly, "Inspector Clarke has been unusually generous. At the risk of his own reputation, he is holding back official police investigation until tomorrow."

Clarke leaned toward me over Henry, smiling wryly. "It's just that I didn't want to miss the show," he said. "I figured out from the rehearsals I was going to like it."

"It's swell of you," I said doubtfully. "At least, I guess it is. But what about tomorrow? Tomorrow you'll be tearing us limb from limb. We'll have opened just to get a bunch of favorable reviews. Tomorrow we'll fold up again like the Arabs' tents."

"I do not think so," put in Lenz. "You see, after tonight there should be little or no investigation at the Dagonet itself."

"What?" I said. "Little or no investigation when there's so damn much to investigate?"

Lenz smiled. I could just tell it from the movement of his beard in the darkness. "On the contrary, Mr. Duluth, there is little or nothing to investigate. You see, during your absence, Inspector Clarke and I stumbled upon the solution of the Dagonet's mystery."

I stared at him, my mouth open.

"Dr. Lenz is being modest," cut in Inspector Clarke. "I didn't have anything to do with it. He figured the whole thing out himself."

Vaguely I was conscious of my company down there on the stage below, of the vivid flame of Mirabelle's dress, of Iris, and on the far side of the footlights the serried ranks of faces that were the audience.

"Yeah," Inspector Clarke's voice was casual, offhand. "Lenz has it all figured out. He's given me the facts on a silver platter. All I have to do when your show's over is to take a certain warrant out of my pocket and arrest the party who killed Comstock, murdered Kramer and tried to do away with Conrad Wessler. . . ."

Chapter Thirty-three

THAT WAS A stunner. I said weakly: "But who—who're you going to arrest? What was it all about? How did you find out?"

Both Inspector Clarke and Dr. Lenz leaned forward, putting their elbows on the rail of the box. Henry and I were sandwiched anxiously in between.

Lenz said, pitching his voice low enough to avoid angry shushes from below: "As soon as I learned how Miss Rue figured in the case, I realized what a simple problem we have been up against, Mr. Duluth. I told you once that there was more than a single thread of mystery at the Dagonet. That, of course, was the trouble. It was impossible to fit everything into one pattern. But now, with the elimination of extraneous matter, the motives behind the disturbances at the Dagonet seem as logical as they were ruthless."

They didn't seem that way to me. It was a queer sensation, listening to Lenz with one ear, desperately keen to know what he had to say, and yet, all the time, being conscious of the play going on below me, gauging every line of dialogue that was spoken, checking every second of action against the yardstick of perfection in my mind.

"For a while," continued Lenz, "you felt, Mr. Duluth, that the trick in the dressing-room had been engineered by Mr. Kramer and Mr. Gates with the object of frightening Herr Wessler from the cast and substituting Mr. Gates in his place. I was ready to accept that theory until I realized how untenable it was. Even assuming that they had been successful in forcing Herr Wessler to resign, how would that help Mr. Gates's cause? He must have known there were other actors besides himself in New York. Failing Herr Wessler, you would have chosen one of a dozen candidates before you chose Gates."

"You're right," I said. I was thinking, "Mirabelle's a fraction too much upstage. Theo didn't get that inflection across. But no one's going to realize it."

"Having come to that conclusion," Lenz went on, "I decided there was only one logical approach to the problem, an approach based on the assumption that the three major crimes, the frightening of Comstock, the murder of Kramer and the attempt on Herr Wessler were all the work of one person, motivated by one all-important impulse. With that hypothesis in mind, it was not difficult to work out the reason behind the murderer's behavior."

Henry dropped a program. Someone coughed. The sound echoed hollowly around the silent, absorbed house.

"I feel you should hear the solution now, Mr. Duluth, so that you will be prepared when Clarke serves his warrant. I will pass it on to you just as it came to me." Lenz glanced at me, gauging just how much of my interest was on him and how much on the play. "It was clear that someone in your company had a reason for wishing to remove Herr Wessler from the cast. At first I do not think he wanted to kill him. He merely wanted to sever his connection with the production because Herr Wessler was a menace to his own security." He paused. "Just how real a menace he was, no one except the murderer knew—not even Herr Wessler himself."

Inspector Clarke was whistling very softly through his teeth. On the stage Gerald and Mirabelle were doing a lovely job with a tricky calf-love scene.

"This individual," said Lenz, "was living in constant danger of exposure by Herr Wessler. His only hope for self-preservation was to drive Herr Wessler from the cast. His opportunity came at the Dagonet; he knew of Herr Wessler's fear of mirrors; he had learned the Lillian Reed legend. By the merest chance, Miss Ffoulkes failure to recognize Miss Rue's image in the glass and Mr. Comstock's hysterical outburst gave him the ideal opening to take the first step in a proposed campaign for terrorizing Herr Wessler. In the manner already discerned by us, he arranged that

244

grisly effect with the false mirror. The wrong person fell into the trap. Mr. Comstock was killed. From then on, this individual's position was even more precarious. He had failed to drive Herr Wessler from the cast; and, in addition, he had a semi-accidental homicide on his hands. That first rehearsal at the Dagonet was trying for you, Mr. Duluth; it was far more distracting for the man who was later to murder George Kramer."

I said: "Then Kramer wasn't murdered just because he was a blackmailer? . . ."

"On the contrary, Mr. Duluth, he was murdered because he was a blackmailer. But he wasn't killed for any of the relatively minor reasons which have already come out. Such as Mr. Prince's domestic problems or Miss Rue's photographs. George Kramer tried, as they vulgarly express it, to bite off more than he could chew. He endeavored to blackmail a person desperate enough to be really dangerous. George Kramer found out why this member of your company was afraid of Herr Wessler. We cannot at the present time tell exactly what steps he took. Perhaps he threatened exposure; more probably he attempted to extort money in exchange for his silence. In any case, he became even more dangerous to this individual than Herr Wessler himself."

My excitement about the play was taking second place now. More and more, Dr. Lenz was annexing my entire interest.

"So he killed Kramer?" I asked.

"Exactly. Inspector Clarke agrees with me that the scheme which resulted in Kramer's death was as diabolically cunning as any he has ever come across. Were it not for the suspicions aroused by what had gone before and the chance discovery that the rat-traps had been tampered with, we might never have guessed the truth. As it is, one can appreciate how simple it would have been for this person, having instigated the fumigation, to have purchased some form of cyanide and slipped it into the coffin just before rehearsal time. Mr. Kramer was killed. Ostensibly Clarke was satisfied with the accident theory. For a while it must have seemed to the murderer that he had nothing more to worry about."

"Except Wessler?" I asked.

"Except Wessler. I have said that at the time of the first attempt upon him Herr Wessler was completely unaware of the vital knowledge he had in his possession. But, after Kramer's death, something happened to give him the clue. As the days moved on toward tonight, he started to think and gradually he arrived at the truth. He saw how all along the solution had been within his grasp. He came to you before the dress-rehearsal; he told you that he knew what was behind the disturbances at the Dagonet. The murderer of George Kramer overheard that conversation. He realized there was only one hope for him! Not only did Wessler know of this thing in his past he had been trying so desperately to hide; Wessler also knew that he had murdered Kramer. Wessler could have sent him to the electric chair. That is why, at the last minute, he made that crude, hurried attempt upon Wessler's life."

I didn't understand. Still I hadn't the faintest notion about the identity of this shadowy criminal.

"It was the very desperation of that final act which gave him away." Lenz's voice moved softly on, with the actor's voices on stage making a dim obbligato. "As you may have noticed, Mr. Duluth, everything which happened before, bizarre and outlandish as it may have seemed, was brilliantly camouflaged as an accident. Even if we had wanted to, we could hardly have been able to present the police with enough evidence for them to suspect foul play. For a while it puzzled me that this person should have been so abnormally careful. Then I realized the truth." He paused, his eyes for one absorbed second focusing on the stage. "All along, Mr. Duluth, you have been justifiably worried that the disturbances at the Dagonet would result in the closing of your play. Perhaps you never realized that there was someone else even more desperately anxious than you for *Troubled Waters* to open. That person was the instigator of the disturbances."

Henry was pushing a package of cigarettes at me. I took one and started to smoke it furiously. I was thinking how probably there had never been anything crazier than this—an author, a psychiatrist, a theatrical producer and a policeman, sitting together in a box, bristling with tuxedos, watching a play which by all the laws of logic should never have opened, and discussing an unknown member of its company as a murderer.

I said: "It's getting a bit straighter in my mind. But not much. Who is this person? And what did Wessler have against him?"

"Those two questions, of course, complement each other," said Lenz. "Perhaps if I tell you in what way Herr Wessler constituted a menace, you will be able to realize who it is that had reason to fear him. Herr Wessler, as you know, has an extraordinarily retentive memory for faces. That is the key to it all. In the past, Herr Wessler saw this person once; he saw him in a certain situation which, if it came to light, would have destroyed everything this person had worked to gain. That is why, at first, Herr Wessler was only a potential menace. He had it in his power to remember this person's face. That is why, at the end, he became a very real, immediate menace. For suddenly it dawned on him when and where he had seen this person before."

Lenz was smiling. "Both Inspector Clarke and Mr. Prince were able to guess my little conundrum at this juncture, Mr. Duluth. Cannot you do likewise?"

"No," I said emphatically. "I haven't a dog's chance of doing likewise. I don't . . ."

The play was working up to its climax now, and for some minutes I had been the battle ground for two conflicting and equally strong desires. It was vital for me to hear the end of Lenz's story. I should have been ready to banish all other considerations from my mind. But I couldn't.

I guess it was only human of me. It mattered like hell, of course, which member of my company was responsible for the murderous outrages committed at the Dagonet. But the play mattered, too. In spite of all the crazy qualifications, this night was the high-spot of my career. I'd been through hell struggling toward the goal. Here was I, Peter Duluth, one-time drunk, one-time has-been, sitting at the first night of my come-back production. I'd just been married; there was the tingling excitement of Iris. There was the shattering excitement of what was happening on stage. These minutes were making history in my life. They would never, never come again. I had to enjoy them. For these last moments of the last act I had to turn my back on murder and murderers. I had to snatch my little moment of triumph.

That's why I didn't even finish the sentence I had started to Lenz. All my attention was riveted on the stage, where now the play was riding inexorably to its close. The audience, undisturbed by the problems in our box, were caught up in the spell from beyond the footlights. It was almost terrifying—the intensity of interest which the play had aroused.

I started feeling uneasy again. I had always been troubled by the actual end. It lacked the ringing authenticity of the rest of the play. It went over the edge into hokum. Maybe Mirabelle and Von Brandt couldn't pull it off. Maybe, never having rehearsed together before, they wouldn't be able to carry their miracle through to the final curtain.

I watched them, the pulses in my wrists throbbing. Never throughout the evening had they dropped one inch from the incredibly high standard of their opening scene. They were alone together now. Theo, Gerald, Iris had all slipped out of the picture. They were both completely sure of themselves and of their audience. It was incredible that those two people who never before tonight had set eyes on each other could fuse into so perfect a team.

With the house tensely silent, Mirabelle went into her final speech of triumphant passion where she challenged Kirchner's hatred of her, taunted him with the fact that in his heart he lusted after her and recklessly dared him to give up everything and follow her anywhere—nowhere. It clicked. She got it superbly. It rang true.

But it was Kirchner's answering speech which had always worried me; his sudden crumbling from the man of iron into the shoddy sensualist; his hysterical renunciation of reality; his final departure with the girl into the slowly sinking waters of the flood.

In rehearsal I had always hoped it would get by. Now, as I thought of it, it seemed screamingly wrong, a violent wrench out of character. I waited in miserable suspense to see how Von Brandt would carry it off.

Mirabelle had finished now. My eyes were glued on that tall, dark figure, the man who had been crazy and who was destined to be the rage of New York. I knew his dialogue by heart. For one interminable second I waited for the words to come.

They didn't. There was still absolute silence on stage. Von Brandt and Mirabelle were still close together staring at each other.

My heart sank like a plummet. Now, at the very last minute, Von Brandt had let us down. His memory had failed him. He had forgotten his final speech. The audience hadn't realized anything was wrong. But in a second it would.

Very slowly, however, Von Brandt pulled himself away from Mirabelle. With a gesture of infinite contempt, he turned his back on her. He moved away from her toward the old grandfather clock. He took the audience with him every step across the stage.

Only gradually did I realize what was happening, realize with a flutter of excitement and panic that Von Brandt was changing the end. He wasn't going to have Kirchner succumb to the tinsel lure of Sex. He was keeping him in character. It was a crazy thing for an actor to do, to swerve away from the script at the very climax of the play.

He didn't say a word. His back studiedly ignoring Mirabelle, he lifted one arm to the dial, unhooked the key and slowly, ritualistically started to wind the clock.

It was simple, but it was brilliant. With that one little domestic gesture he showed more forcibly than any words could have done his complete victory over what was shoddy in himself. But the agonized tension inside me did not let up. This was the perfect resolution of the Kirchner character, but how the hell was the play to end? What was Mirabelle going to do? Now it was up to her.

For one split second I could tell she was at sea. This violent alteration of mood coming now after the steady emotional flow of the play was a frightful ordeal for any actress. I might have guessed, however, that Mirabelle Rue could take it. Without letting the tension slacken one iota, Mirabelle saw and did the only thing to carry the final curtain.

Like Von Brandt, she said nothing. With a slight, defiant shrug of her shoulders, she crossed to the actor as he stood there, stolidly winding the clock. For one instant she posed in front of him, head tossed back, hands on hips. Then, suddenly, derisively, she spat on the floor.

In the shocked silence that followed, she started toward the door of the farmhouse, her whole body revealing her bored contempt of this male who had failed to come up to scratch. She threw open the door, hesitated a moment, gazing out at the expanse of water beyond. Then, abruptly, she stepped out and disappeared back into the flood from which she had emerged. From nowhere.

Mirabelle had gotten away with it.

The curtain was falling now. It came as a signal for feverish applause from the house. The whole world seemed to be drumming with the hollow echo of palm on palm. Beside myself with excitement, I grabbed Lenz's arm and dragged him out of the box. I wanted to have a basket of flowers so that I could strew them giddily in my wake. Everything was swell; everything had excelled my wildest dreams.

There was bedlam going on backstage. I was seized by my publicity agent. He was moaning hysterically: "I've talked to Brooks Atkinson. I've talked to Brooks Atkinson. He's giving us a rave. He's crazy about us. Everyone's crazy about us. Pulitzer Prize, Pulitzer Prize, Pulitzer Prize . . ."

Iris was flinging herself at me, weeping and sobbing: "Hell, Peter, hell, hell, hell, I'm so happy." Mirabelle floated around me, caroling: "God what an end! God, Peter, what an end." I went up to Von Brandt. I shook him by the hand. I tried to say something but I couldn't. He was smiling dazedly. He said: "Please excuse for the change of end, Mr. Duluth. Always I have been bothered by the end. Never until tonight did I realize..."

"It's dandy," I said. "It's colossal. I..."

Eddie appeared from nowhere; he shouted for order and yanked all the company back on stage for a curtain call. I saw them obliquely from the wings; saw them lined up in the brilliant light, bowing to blackness beyond—blackness and applause.

Then the curtain dropped on the audience's undiminished enthusiasm and the cast were swarming around me again. Someone kissed me. Theo stumbled over the coffin and fell. Eddie was at her side in a flash, dropping to his knees and rubbing her left ankle.

"Lucky I took up massage at the hospital, Miss Ffoulkes. Little bit of everything comes in handy for a stage-manager."

I had crossed to them, planning to find out if any damage was done, when Lenz laid his hand on my arm. There was a slow twinkle in his eyes.

"Aren't you interested to hear which member of your company is going to be arrested, Mr. Duluth?"

That pulled me up with a jerk. I stared at Eddie and Theo and then at Lenz.

"W-why, of course," I said. "Someone whom Wessler had seen somewhere he shouldn't have been, wasn't it? Someone whose face Wessler gradually remembered?"

Theo and Eddie were gazing at us as if we were nuts. Then they went away for the third curtain call. Lenz and I were alone in the wings. I tried to get my breath, it seemed to have gone off in so many different directions.

Lenz said: "You remember that first morning when Mr. Kramer told us the story of Herr Wessler's breaking the mirror in the Thespian Hospital, Mr. Duluth?"

"Yes," I said. "Yes."

"As you may also remember, he told us he had learnt the story from a male nurse who had taken care of Wessler while he was blind and had been switched to Von Brandt after he had found

Wessler breaking the mirror. Wessler had refused to have anything more to do with him?"

"Sure," I said. "I remember."

The audience wouldn't let the cast leave the stage. Mirabelle was bowing and then Von Brandt. The applause was still deafening.

"Herr Wessler had therefore only seen this man's face once; he had never heard him speak any language but German. No other person in the world would have recognized that person when he saw him again. Because of his astonishing memory. Wessler did eventually recognize him."

"Then it was that attendant at the Thespian Hospital?" I asked. "You mean he's here in the company?"

"He is."

"But what had he done to Wessler? What was he afraid would come out?"

"He had done nothing to Herr Wessler himself, Mr. Duluth. What he did, he did to Herr Von Brandt. As you know, before his psychosis developed, Von Brandt had a few days of sanity. At that time, this man was taking care of him. Von Brandt guessed there was a chance of his losing his reason permanently. Therefore he entrusted to this person his most cherished possession, something no one, not even Wessler, knew he possessed. He entrusted it to this man, making him promise to keep it safe for him. This man went back on his promise; thinking Herr Von Brandt would never recover, knowing that no one but himself knew what had happened, he kept that thing for himself, exploited it as his own."

At last the curtain had fallen. The actors on stage relaxed but they didn't come out in the wings. They knew by now that they'd have to give one, two, three, four, five more calls. Eddie was hovering behind us, watching the stage with the conscious pride of a father.

"The only danger," Lenz was continuing, "lay with Herr Wessler. If he happened to remember that he had seen this man

252

at the Thespian Hospital, it was possible for him, by putting two and two together, to arrive at the truth. That is why he was attacked. That is why Mr. Kramer, who knew him well, who had guessed this precious secret, had also to be killed. Surely you see now, Mr. Duluth. What could a man have stolen from Herr Von Brandt in a sanitorium? What could it have been that Von Brandt, who was passionately devoted to his brother, would have held too precious even to pass on to Herr Wessler?"

"I . . ." I began.

Vaguely I heard voices now from the other side of the curtain, voices rising above the applause. They were shouting:

"Director!"

That sent the blood zipping through my veins. Mirabelle was dashing toward me. I tried to hold back; I didn't really mean it, but I tried. She pulled me forward, however. Eddie signaled for the curtain to be raised. And I was there, in the middle of the cast, holding Mirabelle's hand on my right and Theo's on my left. Everyone was clapping; someone was cheering. I bowed. I kissed Mirabelle. I kissed Theo. The curtain stayed up.

Peter Duluth had his come-back all right. Oh boy, he had his come-back.

The curtain dropped. I returned to Lenz. He was still standing in the wings with Eddie, Inspector Clarke and Henry at his side.

Lenz said: "Well, Mr. Duluth, have you not guessed my little riddle?"

"No," I said. "No, I haven't. God, I'm so happy. Hell, I'm so happy."

Lenz said: "Think, Mr. Duluth. What was Herr Von Brandt's one ambition in life? What caused his temporary loss of reason because it was denied to him? Think."

I tried to think. I swear I tried to think. But they were still clapping and stamping outside in the house. Once again they were shouting. At first I couldn't get the words. Then, gradually, they became distinct.

"Author! We want the author. We want the author."

I swung round to Henry. I gripped him by the shoulder. I was glad as hell he could get his break too.

"Come on, Henry, my boy," I said. "Come on. Your public wants you."

I started to drag him forward. Clarke and Lenz came with me. I was about to step up onto the stage when, suddenly, I froze in my steps.

They were still wildly calling for the author. The curtain was zooming up. Mirabelle, Gerald and Theo had all scuttled out into the far wings. One person was there on the stage alone. One man, in tattered denim, bowing to the audience.

They clapped; they clapped him like hell. But still some of them kept shouting for the author. Von Brandt raised his hand. Instantly the place was silent as a grave.

"Ladies and gentlemen," he said, "in the name of all the company I wish to thank you for your so very kind appreciation. For myself, I cannot speak the happiness which is in me. That you should have taken me so to your hearts when before you know so little of me—how can I say but to let you know that after times which have been tragic and terrible I can now say that life is good for me again. That is all I wish."

I still had my hand on Henry's shoulder, ready to push him forward. But I was carried away by the little, halting speech. It meant so much, so horribly much more to me than it could ever have meant to the audience.

"There is one thing more," said Von Brandt. "I offer you great thanks that you should like this play. In Austria I wrote many plays which have had a little success; but this play, she has never been acted in Vienna. She is something, I hope, so much finer than these others which always were to me an apprenticeship. I am proud indeed to have my best play first performed to you people here in the United States. I thank you—as an actor and as an author, I thank you."

For a second I couldn't move. I couldn't really think. The whole universe seemed to have gone nuts.

"What the hell . . .?" I began.

Lenz's voice broke in quietly. "You have heard the solution to the conundrum now, Mr. Duluth. This is what was stolen from Herr Von Brandt. He wanted to act in this play so badly that he did not even let his brother know he had written it. He was afraid that what had happened before would happen again, that once the world saw the script, Herr Wessler would inevitably play the leading role. Von Brandt kept the play secret from everyone until he feared he was going mad. Then he entrusted it to the only person he had at hand—the attendant at the hospital who took care of him, who spoke English but who understood German, the man who translated it, adapted it to a Pennsylvania Dutch setting and sold it as his own."

The curtain had fallen for the last time. The applause was fading into a slight throb in the distance. Wolfgang von Brandt was crossing the stage toward us, his face radiant.

"It is clear surely why Mr. Prince was so frightened of Herr Wessler. Should Wessler have identified him with his brother's attendant at the hospital, it would not be difficult for him to guess the actual origin of this play which had so much in it that must inevitably have been reminiscent of Von Brandt's other works."

"But," I faltered, "but, but, but . . ."

Stupidly I turned to Henry Prince. His skin was the color of chalk. His lips were twisted in a thin, fatuous smile.

But I saw all that only vaguely. For I was actually looking at his right wrist. It was attached to that of Inspector Clarke by a pair of gleaming steel handcuffs.

"Yes," Lenz was saying: "It was clever of Mr. Prince to put you off the trail by that plausible story of Kramer's blackmailing him because of his father. It was clever of him to keep away from rehearsal as much as possible so that Wessler would have less chance of recognizing him. It . . ."

"Peter!" Iris suddenly descended upon us. She was looking wild and disheveled. She hurled herself into my arms. "It's all over, Peter. At last it's all over. And it's a success. There's

255

nothing to stop us now. Right away, we'll get into a car; we'll drive South; we'll go to Elkton and get married."

I kissed some indeterminate part of her ear. I said, "Darling, you made an honest man of me exactly nineteen hours ago. Remember?"

She broke away from me, staring from very wide, dark eyes.

"My God," she said, "so we have. And I forgot . . ."